TRACKER220

Jamie Krakover

Tracker220
Copyright © 2020 Jamie Krakover
Interior Format: Dorothy Dreyer

Published by Snowy Wings Publishing
PO Box 1035, Turner, OR 97392

ISBN Hardcover: 978-1-948661-91-1
ISBN Paperback: 978-1-948661-90-4
ISBN eBook: 978-1-948661-92-8

In loving memory of Tom Krakover,
who introduced me to science fiction and made sure it always filled
the house.

One

"**C**ome on, Kaya. You know you want to." The black box in Troy Ackerman's hand flirted with me like a bad boy. Half thrill ride, half arrest warrant.

We were going to get caught. No question about it.

Masking your tracker signal got you a date with the authorities at best, and at worst... I didn't want to think about it. I wasn't lucky enough to stay out of trouble. I was never that lucky.

Troy held the radio wave generator between his thumb and index finger as if he were expecting me to take it at any moment. While his bulky torso was slightly intimidating, his height wasn't.

The buzz from falling off the tracker grid—pure silence and vision devoid of popups and apps—wasn't worth the risk of losing control, losing the connection and security of the network. If the authorities showed up, brain probing us to check for tracker glitches would be the least of our problems.

Troy waved the box in my face. "You sure? It's such a rush!"

I shivered despite the bonfire blazing in front of us. "I'm good. I don't need a record."

"Wasn't it just Yom Kippur or something? You should be good on the sin front for a while." He thrust his hips toward the box and my best friend Lydia let out a quick giggle, batting her long lashes at him.

Ugh! Of all the boys why did she have to be into him? "You know that's not how it works."

That little box was trouble. Worse than Pandora's. My muscles tensed at the thought of all the chaos about to be unleashed. At least if I refused to disrupt my tracker signal, I wouldn't have to lie about breaking the law.

Trekking into the woods to watch everyone attempt to beat the record for longest signal disruption was insanity. Why couldn't we hang out at the fly-in theater instead? Anything other than pursuing a one-way ticket to tracker juvie.

But the guys loved the thrill of tempting fate—the ultimate game of chicken. At best, they had about five minutes of interrupted tracker signals before the network alerted the authorities.

I leaned into my boyfriend, and he put his arm around me wafting the comforting sea breeze scent of his aftershave in my direction. Harlow would never ditch me. But most of his friends wouldn't hesitate to use me as authority bait if the agents showed up. Not if—*when*.

"Looks like your girlfriend's afraid of getting caught." Troy should have known by now his taunts wouldn't work.

And yet, my insides warred. I twisted my hair back into a stubby ponytail wishing I hadn't recently chopped off ten inches. By the time I let my hair go, the rule-follower piece of me prevailed like always. "I'll watch for now."

"Maybe after you see how it's done?" Harlow squeezed my shoulder, making my muscles tense more. Their stunts were dangerous enough without him dragging me into it. Last time, we'd spent an hour trying to evade the authorities and nearly missed curfew.

I shook my head.

"She's a wuss."

"Stuff it, Troy. If you want to scramble your brains, fine. I'm out." It shouldn't be a fight to do the right thing.

"It's just a little signal interruption. But if you want to be a wimp about it…"

A blinking chat bubble appeared in the lower left-hand corner of my vision with the initials *H.G.* for "Harlow Green." I thought about the message and blinked twice in rapid succession to open it.

H.G.: You don't have to if you don't want to.

There wasn't a chance Troy could talk me into it. But Harlow's support gave me extra confidence, even if it only came through private chat. He cared too much about his image to say anything in front of the guys.

As I minimized the message to save it for later, a second icon appeared to the left of Harlow's message, with the initials *T.A.*

I closed my eyes, took a deep breath, then let the message enter my mind. As the message opened in my line of sight, an image of a chicken emerged. It flapped its wings and ran in circles.

Instead of collapsing and disappearing like normal, the image of a bomb exploded, obliterating the circling chicken. When the fake dust cleared, the picture was nowhere to be seen.

Laughter drew my attention to the crowd.

Great. That wasn't so private.

Harlow punched Troy in his well-defined biceps. "Let it go, man."

Troy was lucky that was all he'd gotten. If I hadn't promised Lydia I'd be on my best behavior, I wouldn't have had to clamp my mouth shut. If it weren't for her, I'd have sent out a chat bomb of my own that would transform Troy's ego into a limp balloon. Harlow had sent me pictures and messages, the kind that Troy wouldn't want to go public. And once you put something on the tracker network, it never fully went away. I could bury him if it weren't for Lydia.

I'd do anything for my best friend, but I wasn't sure her crush on Troy was worth getting arrested over.

Troy pulled the box away and turned to Lydia. "How about you?"

Her cheeks pinked as she twirled her long, black hair around her finger. "Why don't you show me?" she asked with a giggle. She was laying it on extra thick. I didn't like who she was around him, but I wasn't sure how to tell her.

"Sure." Troy pulled the radio wave generator apart at the center then flipped the switch on. A red light blinked on each half of the unmarked box as it hummed softly. "Who's got my time?"

"Me." Wes stood up from an adjacent log, his thin frame towering over everyone. He blinked twice in quick succession, opening a timer program from the tracker network. "Ready?"

"I'm going to crush this."

"Okay, go." Wes blinked twice again. The timer was running.

4

Troy placed each half of the device on his temples. Lydia nudged Troy with her elbow—any excuse to touch him. "So what's the record?"

"Who cares?" I asked. "The only thing getting broken is us if the authorities show up." The woods sat far enough from town that minor issues weren't worth the authorities' time. But it was close enough that if anyone messaged, we could make it home in a parentally acceptable amount of time.

Lydia shot me her knock-it-off face before returning an innocent smile at Troy. I gave her a sorry-please-forgive-me-look. Silently, I prayed they'd get bored and give up. Then I wouldn't have to risk disappointing her.

"The record is five minutes and three seconds held by yours truly." Harlow flexed his biceps. I rolled my eyes at his standard macho routine but secretly enjoyed the show. His muscles were fantastic, even if the display required zero intelligent thought.

"Not for long. Your record is about to be shattered." Troy paced like his adrenaline was bottling inside and taking up the remaining space his brain cells used to occupy.

"One minute," Wes called.

Harlow nudged Troy as he paced between him and the fire. "Want to quit yet?"

"Not a chance. I have five hundred bucks riding on this."

"Oh, big spenders," I said. "Get a hobby."

"We've got one," Troy said. "If you don't like it, leave."

Lydia kicked the heel of her calf hugging boots at the toe of my sneakers with enough force to tell me she was going to kill me if I didn't stop immediately. I took a deep breath to calm my nerves. I wanted to support her, but the rumors of what happened to people who got caught ghosting their trackers were enough for me. The fact that we were teenagers wouldn't matter to the authorities. They wouldn't hesitate to haul us off to lockup in Global Tracking Systems and leave needles in our brains for the night—or so the rumors said.

I blinked and pulled up the Mystery Gems app and allowed it to fill half my vision as I played the mindless game. Anything to distract me from the insanity.

"Does it hurt?" Lydia asked Troy, pulling my attention from the game and causing me to lose my last life.

Dang it.

Now I needed a new distraction, as it would be an hour before I regenerated another life. This inane game of theirs would be long over an hour from now. Hopefully.

Troy didn't remove the device from his temples but stopped pacing in front of the log we were sitting on.

"Nah, it's mo… mo… morrrrr…" Troy started to shake, slowly at first. But it quickly morphed into full-on convulsions. His eyes rolled back as he collapsed next to the fire with a long moan.

Lydia shrieked. My mouth dropped open as my heart threatened to pound out of my chest. I placed my fingers on Troy's neck to check for a pulse. Nothing. I shifted my fingers around in a frantic attempt to see if I could find one but failed to remember the right spot. If he hadn't been so hellbent on disrupting his tracker, it would have already signaled for an ambulance.

"I'm—" I swallowed the lump in my throat that was preventing me from speaking. "I'm calling for help!"

Troy burst into a fit of laughter. He sat up and shook his dark, curly hair while still holding the boxes in place. "Gotcha!"

I wanted to knock that smug look off his face, but my body was too stunned to react.

"You should have seen your face."

I kicked his calf, wishing I had daggers on the end of my shoes. "Why are you such an ass?" My face pinched into a scowl before I could stop myself. Why was I the only one not laughing?

Even Lydia giggled and kissed Troy on the cheek. "I'm glad you're okay."

"Four and a half minutes," Wes said between laughs.

And my nightmare continued.

Harlow rose from the log and stalked over to Troy. Inches from Troy's face, he asked, "Scared yet?"

"No. I'm going to destroy your record." The shape of Troy's upturned lips cemented his determination.

Harlow's hands balled into fists.

He better not start a fight.

"Five minutes," Wes called, then he counted out the seconds.

At six, Troy dropped his arms.

"And we have a new record!" Wes raised Troy's arm into the air like the winning boxer in a championship match. "With an outstanding time of five minutes and six seconds, our new victor, Troy Ackerman."

The guys took turns chest bumping Troy. There was so much testosterone flowing between them I was afraid all the stupid would rub off on me.

A message with TA popped up in the corner of my vision. Against my better judgment, I opened it and found an image of Troy with a crown on his head, twirling scepter in his hands. The word WINNER flashed above his dancing figure.

"I'll take my five hundred bucks now." Troy held his palm

out to Harlow in anticipation of his payment.

"I'll hold on to my money. I'm just going to shatter the record again anyway."

"*If* you beat it." Troy's grin morphed into something downright demonic. "In the meantime, enjoy this payment hack app I found."

"What the hell, man?" Harlow blinked twice before stomping to the edge of the clearing and punching an oak tree.

Those apps were annoying as hell. They clogged your vision until you took care of the money you owed. Landlords used the app to force tenants to pay. Since Troy's dad owned several high-rises, he had inside access to such an app.

Harlow clenched his fists, more hurt than his face let on.

"Harlow, what are you thinking?" I was sick of the hothead routine. It was not a good side of him, and lately, it was making a frequent appearance. I clasped his hand in mine and ran my fingers around the edges of his wound. He'd split several of his knuckles open. "Lydia, get my purse."

I grabbed it from her and dug out some tissues to clean the dirt out of his wound. "What's wrong with you?" But I already knew the answer—he hated to lose.

He placed his fingers under my chin, lifting my head until our gazes met. "I'm sorry. I wasn't thinking." Leaning in, he kissed me on the cheek, spreading warmth across my face. After eight months, he still managed to make my knees go weak with a single kiss. As much as I hated these games, I was glad Harlow was there. He'd never let anything bad happen to me. Then again, he was responsible for putting me in a messy situation in the first place.

"You have to get over this sore loser crap."

Based on the mixture of disappointment and frustration on his face, I had a small window to calm him down.

I kissed his split knuckles, hoping it would soften his mood. "All better."

"Thanks," he said, letting the word hang in the air with regret.

I brushed his long, dirty blond bangs to the edge of his forehead, then stood on my tiptoes so I could kiss him. He pulled me in and slipped his arms underneath the back of my jacket, grazing the skin that peeked out between my tank top and jeans. His soft lips caressed mine, causing me to shiver. He pissed me off sometimes, but the guy could kiss.

"All right, lover boy, time to show us what you're made of."

I shot Troy a death stare for interrupting our moment. Pulling away from Harlow, I stood between them.

"Unless you're too chicken to try and beat *my* new record," Troy said.

With a single taunt, Troy managed to reel Harlow back in like an addictive drug. If I allowed Harlow to seethe any longer, he'd start foaming at the mouth.

"You don't have to do this. The agents will be swarming if you try to break that record." Despite my best puppy dog face, his eyebrows narrowed—the same tenacity he got on the soccer field right before he was about to score. "A few seconds is one thing, but you know the authorities don't mess around with the five-minute rule."

I had a feeling it wouldn't matter what I said. There was no convincing his stubborn ass.

"No, it's cool. I've got this." He strode inside the ring of logs around the fire and swiped the radio wave generator off the ground.

"Harlow, wait." I called after him, unable to give up on a fight I knew I'd already lost. When Harlow decided he wanted to do something, he never wavered. Although his expression appeared even, I could see the fire building inside him. He hungered for the challenge.

Sometimes I hated that I cared so much about all the trouble he got himself into.

Ignoring me, he turned to Wes. "Time me."

Wes blinked twice and pointed to Harlow, who pressed the boxes to his temples. Things were spiraling out of control faster than I could process.

I thought about a timer and quickly blinked twice. An image of a clock appeared in my line of sight. I focused on the ticking numbers, then moved my eyes to the lower right. The box followed, and I blinked again to lock it into place. The timer wouldn't be exact, but at least I'd have a better idea of how deep Harlow was diving in.

Everyone grew silent. Wood crackled and popped inside the fire. Birds screeched from the branches above us. A cool wind whipped up, rustling the leaves. I drew my jacket around me and zipped it.

Each ticking second on the timer app blurred into the next. When I couldn't take the silence anymore, I said, "Harlow, please stop this. You don't have to prove yourself to anyone." I wrapped my arms around his waist and gazed up at him. He was half a foot taller than me, but until recently, I could stare him down even when he was putting on his macho routine for the guys. "Come on. This is stupid."

"Four minutes and forty-five seconds," Wes called.

My clock hit four minutes thirty seconds. Great, I was fifteen seconds behind. That was an eternity in tracker time.

"I can't stop now." Harlow grunted, almost as if what he said was an automated response.

"Yes, you can," I said in a firm tone.

"Five minutes." Wes called out again, then he counted out the seconds.

"Okay, you proved your point."

Harlow gritted his teeth and pivoted from me, his lame attempt to keep me from swaying him away from the madness. "No, I'm going to show Troy how you really shatter a record."

Any minute the authorities would overrun our tiny wooded refuge. I hoped trekking beyond the edge of the city was too much effort for the authorities. If only I could track them like they could track us.

I thought about the First Responder app, then blinked. A moment later, the app appeared in my vision. It was meant for emergencies, part of the tracker alert install, but it should do the trick. Besides, the situation kind of was an emergency. Tiny red circles spotted the map. They were at least a mile away. But one dot rounded a corner and doubled back in our direction. Maybe it was a coincidence. But when a second circled the block and headed toward the outskirts of town, my stomach sank. Of course the authorities had nothing better to do.

"Twenty-eight, twenty-nine, thirty, thirty-one." Wes's counting dragged my attention from the map. I blinked twice to minimize the app.

I grabbed Harlow's arm and yanked with all my weight, trying to pull his hand away from his temple, but he didn't budge. *Damn his muscles.* I never thought I could hate them so much.

"Six minutes!" Wes yelled.

The silence persisted well beyond the point of uncomfortable. When I could no longer take it, I said, "*Please*. I don't want you to get caught."

His muscles twitched with fury, an indication there was no stopping him.

"Six minutes, twenty-two seconds," Wes called.

I maximized the first responder app again. The dots had closed the gap between us and them by half.

I tried one last plea. "Enough is enough! The agents are on their way."

Harlow blinked, like he was trying to understand what I'd said, then lowered his hands.

I let out a long breath in relief.

"And *that* is how you break a record." Harlow laughed like a mental patient. "What was my final time?"

"Six minutes and thirty-three seconds," Wes said.

Harlow dropped the device at Troy's feet. "Beat that." He spun on his heel and paraded around the circle, waving his arms in triumph. A chat with *HG* appeared at the bottom of my sight. I opened it and a rain of money flooded my vision with an image of a proud Harlow standing among it. Behind him, Troy's head had been pasted on top of a snorting pig.

I had to hand it to Harlow. He certainly had a flare for getting even.

Some of the guys patted him on the back, but a few stood silent. I remained next to Lydia, unsure what to say to Harlow. She'd be there for me not matter what. I couldn't believe he'd taken the stupid bet so far. Thankfully, it was over and nothing bad had happened, other than Harlow dancing like a monkey and rubbing Troy's nose in it. Everything would be fine as long as the red dots turned around. They usually gave up when trackers popped back online.

But they didn't.

Harlow abruptly stopped parading around. No, not just stopped, he froze completely. As unmoving as a boulder. *What's he doing?* As the question crossed my mind, dread swirled inside. They'd gotten to his tracker, controlling his movement. He wouldn't be able to go anywhere if he wanted to. In a matter of minutes, the woods would be crawling with authorities. My stomach dropped. *Why did I have to be right?*

On cue, the beating sound of the unicopters swooshed in my ears, growing louder by the second. The small crafts' blades blew leaves up from the forest floor. Within moments, a spotlight beamed from above.

"Stay where you are," boomed a voice through the speakers hanging from the unicopter's composite frame.

Everyone scattered. Troy scooped up the device from the ground. Grabbing Lydia's hand, he dragged her away from the clearing.

"Come on, Kaya." She held her hand out to me as she ran past.

My mind screamed *run*, but my heart said *stay*. "I can't leave him."

I hated myself for following the rules to the letter. Part of me wanted to bolt, be the rebel like my friends. e worse than facing tracker diagnostics was a lecture from my dad about morality. Brain probe or not, he'd make me apologize to the authorities for wasting their time, which was infinitely more humiliating if they had to chase me. It was pretty sick if you asked me. Not like they'd apologize to me for the drive-by lobotomy.

My friends disappeared deeper into the woods, where they'd stashed their flying crotchrockets. My breath caught in my throat. I should have run.

I hated that Harlow made me do stupid things. I hated my moral compass more. I was too smart for illegal activity, and yet there were the authorities circling above like vultures.

Five unicopters landed around Harlow. Four uniformed agents stood up from their seats in the small, open-aired vehicles. In one fluid movement, they ducked under the upper part of the frame, briefly balancing on the running board before their combat boots hit the ground with a thud. They marched toward Harlow, leaving the unicopter blades running on low. The fifth approached me, flipping up the visor on his black helmet. The rest of his body was covered by the black authority uniform, complete with black gloves. The glint of the silver bands on his belt was the only hint of color.

"Miss, what happened here?"

"I… I…" A huge lump in my throat prevented me from speaking, which was good because I wasn't sure I wanted to tell them anything.

"This one's in shock. Get the kit." The agent reached out for my arm.

I blinked and snapped to, yanking my arm away from him. "I'm fine," I said. "Is he going to be okay? I don't know what happened." Playing dumb when it came to the authorities was usually the best tactic. Which was convenient because after this stunt, enough dumb had rubbed off on me.

"Seems like a tracker malfunction. But we need to take him

in for some diagnostic tests."

I nodded, sweat beading on my forehead. The authorities made my skin crawl. You couldn't argue with them. They always made you feel like you'd done something wrong, even when you hadn't.

"Miss, you best head home. It's getting late."

I forced a quiet "okay" in response. Heaven forbid they actually offered me a ride home. But they didn't care about anyone's wellbeing unless it involved a malfunctioning tracker or a bribe.

He flipped down the visor on his helmet and jogged to his vehicle.

An agent cuffed Harlow with the silver bands. When they clicked in place, a red light flashed three times before a loud beep rang out. Harlow swallowed as his shoulders relaxed. He clenched his fists a couple times, but his feet remained planted in place.

Two agents hauled Harlow to one of the unicopters and slammed him into the rear-facing seat before securing the arm and leg straps into the clip at his chest. An agent jumped into the remaining seat in the front. He pulled back on the stick, and the vehicle rose toward the sky. As quickly as they'd swarmed in, they were gone—leaving me alone in the woods.

TWO

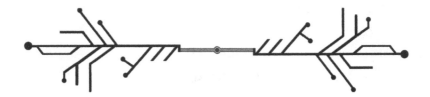

At school the next day, I sat in History of Science and Technology waiting for Harlow to arrive. Mr. Jennings droned on about our current unit—desktop computers—while the class shifted in their seats pretending to pay attention to the lecture forced onto our trackers. Images of old tech and server rooms showed up in my vision in an attempt to prove how massive computers used to be.

Despite the lecture screens taking up large portions of our vision, most of us opened other network windows and chat apps to pass the time. It was what everyone did when they got bored. I was constantly pinging Harlow about last night and yet no answer.

I blinked and opened yet another chat window.

K.W.: Any word?

I blinked again and thought of Lydia, sending the message on its way.

An instant later a chat bubble appeared with *LY.* I opened it.

L.Y.: Nope. But think I can use it as an excuse to message Troy?

I rolled my eyes and minimized the window without responding. She wasn't going to give that up.

Mr. Jennings rubbed his bald head with an exasperated look on his face. He knew what was going on throughout the classroom, but he couldn't prove the lack of attention, beyond the random blinking and quiet snorts. Too bad for teachers the weekday ban on tracker surfing for students didn't pass the popular vote. Despite all the distractions, I found desktop computers intriguing.

But class had started thirty minutes ago, and Harlow's absence tugged at my mind and refused to let go. It was third period already. Where the hell was he?

My lack of focus was making my tracker screens on the right side of my vision minimize at random. *I hope the authorities aren't still holding him.* A message from Harlow would have been nice.

Wes's hand shot into the air, drawing me from the agony of my unanswered chats.

"Yes, Wes?" Mr. Jennings asked.

"Why would anyone want a big machine they couldn't take with them? Who wants a whole room of computers that takes hours to respond? I can message and access the network in a split second just by thinking about it."

The class groaned. Wes always asked an insane amount of questions that annoyed everyone. Normally, I'd continue to tune out, tracing doodles on my palm with my finger or outlining projects in the tracker's drawing app. Art had ended two hours ago, and I was already itching to get my hands on more paper. Drawing on the tracker network didn't have the same rush as moving a pencil in my hand. Not to mention it was impossible with Mr. Jennings' lecture occupying valuable real estate in my field of vision.

But I straightened in my chair, his question piquing my interest. The satellite link to our trackers let us access information by thinking of a topic. So why didn't the desktop computer have something similar?

"Technology develops and changes over time," Mr. Jennings said. "The ability to keep a personal computer in the home changed the world." The images in my sight shifted from racks that stretched floor to ceiling to monitors that could sit on a table to even smaller handheld devices with screens. "As the internet developed, information became more readily available, but not in the way we access it today."

I raised my hand. Not something I usually did in class, but a question nagged me.

"Kaya?"

A low murmuring erupted around the room. *Is everyone staring at me?* I shrugged it off. "So how did we go from inconvenient machines like the computer to what we have today? I mean, why didn't someone just think of the tracker to begin with? We could have skipped over all this other stuff."

"Excellent question." Mr. Jennings smiled, like I'd given him the perfect transition. "We have to start somewhere. Sometimes bigger is easier. Computers used to take up whole rooms. When they moved to desktops, it allowed for more advanced technologies. Society always wants something faster, smaller, and more accessible. Rufus Scurry took advantage of that when he invented Tracker220. What each of you carries inside your head is one million times more powerful than a desktop computer in a fraction of the size."

"So desire for something better drove technology?" I asked.

"Exactly."

The door swung open. Harlow strutted up the third row of chairs toward the vacant one on my left. A breath caught in my throat as I inspected him. He appeared unharmed, wearing his number forty soccer jersey and comfortable jeans with the tear in the right knee. I let out a sigh of relief.

"Mr. Green, nice of you to finally join us." Mr. Jennings said.

The class snickered.

"You should have a note, check your inbox." Harlow replied, as his attention caught mine. He smiled as he stretched his legs underneath the chair in front of him as if last night didn't register in his memory. God, he was hot. There was something about that jersey.

"Hey, babe." He blew a kiss to me, and I melted like a hot chocolate chip cookie. My lips started to curl upward as he reached across the aisle and squeezed my knee.

Since he confirmed that he was back to normal, I could focus on other issues. Like how I'd had to walk home alone last night and barely squeaked in before curfew because of his stupid stunt. And if it weren't for tracker maps, I would have gotten lost in the woods more than once.

I checked the front of the room to ensure Mr. Jennings was busy teaching and no longer paying attention us. "You get arrested last night and all I get is 'Hey, babe'?" I crossed my arms over my chest and turned sideways in my chair so I could full-on glare at him.

He flashed his perfect white teeth. When I said nothing, he shifted in his seat. "What did you want me to do? I didn't think they were going to haul me off. It was a stupid game."

"I warned you." I faced the front of the room, pretending to pay attention to the lesson.

"Don't give me that. You have no idea what I've been through." His shoulders slumped. I hated it when he pouted, and he knew it.

Be strong, Kaya.

A blinking chat bubble with *HG* appeared in the lower left-hand corner of my vision.

His message better be an apology.

But I knew that it wasn't. Against my better judgment, I thought about the message. It expanded in a tall, thin column next to Mr. Jennings' lecture.

H.G.: I still feel the stabs of the needles.

I crossed my arms. He would not win.

H.G.: It went on for hours.

Oh great. He'd loaded a stream-of-consciousness app.

H.G.: I lost count of how many needles…
pierced my skull.

I clenched my teeth. It sounded horrific, but he'd done it to himself. I'd warned him. He should have listened. Then he wouldn't have been in trouble.

H.G.: The only thing that got me through it was knowing you were safe.

I flinched because he hadn't known that. Something could have happened to me on that very long walk home. He was lucky nothing had. I could have tripped and twisted my ankle in the woods. Explaining to my parents why I needed an ER visit after a night out with friends would have gotten me grounded for an eternity.

H.G.: Knowing I'd see you again soon.

I crossed my legs and angled my head so I couldn't see him out of the corner of my eye. I couldn't let him think it was okay. As bad as it was, it could have been so much worse for everyone. He could have dragged me down with him.

When he let out a long breath, turned toward Mr. Jennings, and blinked twice, my heart sank. He was actually paying attention and taking notes. He never took notes. I always sent him mine. Maybe I was being too hard on him.

I leaned across the aisle and put my hand on his shoulder. "I'm sorry."

He blinked twice again to close out the program and turned to me. But I didn't get the usual warmth from him. His faraway expression haunted me. "There were so many."

I didn't need him to finish the sentence to know he was talking about the needles again. I'd never experienced tracker diagnostic tests, but I'd heard horror stories about Global Tracking Systems. Hours of scans, poking, and prodding. He must have been terrified having to go through that by himself. I grabbed his hand.

"Afterward, they called my dad to pick me up. By the time I got home, it was four A.M., so my dad let me sleep in."

That explained the lack of messages. Harlow could sleep through a bomb going off.

"Well, that was nice of him." I rubbed my thumb over the scab on his knuckle. His father normally wouldn't have allowed Harlow to miss any school. The tests must have been pretty bad.

A red light flashed three times in my sight, signaling the end of class. The lecture window closed, and I let out a breath, relieved to have my full vision back under my control.

"Read Chapter Five for tomorrow," Mr. Jennings called as I grabbed my purse. A homework notice appeared in the corner of my vision and would remain there until I completed it. So much for having my vision back.

Harlow took my hand, and we followed Wes into hallway. The hallway grew silent as a million people zeroed in on us. A flurry of whispers erupted. Most kept their distance as if they might get in trouble by association. But Troy strutted toward with Lydia a half-step behind him. I guessed she was still looking for that window to talk to him.

"Hey, Har, how was tracker juvie?" Troy didn't bother to stifle the laugh that erupted which was rich from the guy who'd provoked Harlow.

Harlow squeezed my hand tighter.

Oh God! It was way worse than I thought. "Leave him alone. He went through hell last night. No thanks to you."

Harlow slung his arm around my shoulder. "Totally worth it, just to see your face when I obliterated your record."

"This guy is a legend. It's all anyone's talking about." Wes high-fived Harlow to further prove how awesome the stunt had been.

Troy's face twisted in a poor attempt to hide the scowl on his face. "Whatever. It shouldn't count if you get arrested. He didn't prove anything except how to get caught."

Lydia giggled and whispered something into his ear. I guessed Lydia didn't need an excuse to talk to Troy anymore.

"Oh, bull. You're just pissed I had the balls to obliterate your three-second record." Harlow shot back faster than a message on the tracker network.

"The balls? Ha! As far as I'm concerned, I beat you. Your consolation prize was a date with the authorities and a probe."

A chat bomb exploded in my vision and a picture of Harlow sitting in a chair surrounded by large needles appeared when the virtual dust cleared.

The whole hallway snickered, and Harlow tensed. I wondered how long the thought of needles would get to him.

Troy inched closer to Harlow, but he didn't budge. Harlow pulled his arm from around me and shoved Troy against the wall. Troy swung his fist, but Harlow ducked and Troy lost his balance, falling to the ground.

Seriously? "Knock it off. You guys are supposed to be friends." First the arrest and now the fighting—I was about to collapse into a puddle of nerves on the floor. With my luck, I'd get an in-school suspension for trying to break up a fight.

"Friends recognize each other's accomplishments." Harlow leaned over Troy as he stumbled to his feet.

"Fat chance." Troy lunged, fists in the air. Wes caught him

around the midsection and pushed him across the hall against the opposite wall.

"Dude, let it go," Wes said.

When Troy relaxed, Wes released his hold.

"Come on, Lydia. Let's go to lunch." Troy pressed his hand to her waist, guiding her toward the cafeteria.

I grabbed Harlow's face and turned it toward me. "Why do you egg him on?"

"He started it with the animated chat bomb. A record is a record. He needs to recognize it."

"How about we keep the records to the soccer field? I can't handle any more fighting. I don't want you hurt or arrested. Again." Fighting led to challenges and challenges led to episodes like last night in the woods. I couldn't handle another run-in with the authorities. Last night had been enough for one lifetime. I wrapped my arms around Harlow, hoping he'd reciprocate and calm my nerves.

"Okay, fine." He bent down and kissed me. Even though the quick peck sent electric chills through me, it lacked the luster of his normal kisses.

"How about some lunch?"

"Yes, I'm starving." His lips quirked upward briefly in place of his usual smile.

I tried to laugh it off, but it didn't sound the least bit genuine. "You're always hungry." I laced my fingers through his and we headed to the cafeteria. If I couldn't keep everyone from fighting and pulling stupid stunts, it was only a matter of time before we'd all have field trips to tracker diagnostics.

Luckily, hunger was easy to fix. Getting him to admit tracker diagnostics had scared him more than he'd let on might not be.

Three

When our tracker displays turned red for five seconds, signaling the end the school day, I met Lydia by the girls' bathroom so we could walk home together. Life would be a lot easier if our parents would let us drive flying crotchrockets like practically everyone else at school. Too bad my dad said flying motorcycles were too much for a new sixteen-year-old driver. I'd kill for a bike. Even though the walks home restricted us to the decaying sidewalks, at least Lydia and I had plenty of time to talk alone.

"Sorry I ran off with Troy. I didn't know Harlow was going to get arrested." Lydia nudged me with her elbow, a quick gesture to let me know she cared.

"Neither did I or I might have run with you. It was a long walk home."

"That's awful. I'm glad you're safe. I wanted Troy to go back for you, but he said you'd probably gotten arrested with Harlow, and it wouldn't do any good for us all to get hauled off." And that was why she was my best friend. When it mattered most, she at least tried to make things right.

"So, what's going on with you and Troy?" I asked, desperate to change the subject.

Her cheeks pinked. "I really like him."

"Yeah, I know. What happened between you two last night?" I kicked a rock and it skidded across the concrete into a pile of trash. People really needed to stop tossing stuff out of their flying cars. Just because most people didn't spend much time on the sidewalks didn't mean *no one* did.

"After we ran from the authorities, Troy drove me home on his bike."

We rounded the corner heading toward the residential high-rises. A few cars whipped by overhead, but the sky was relatively clear for the start of rush-hour traffic. "Do your parents know?"

"Of course not. They'd kill me if they found out I got on a bike. It's bad enough I snuck in after curfew."

After her brother's accident, Lydia's parents would ground her for an eternity if they found out she'd gotten on a bike. They were even stricter than my parents, who frequently reminded my brother and me that getting caught on a flying motorbike would be the least of our concerns. But if my brother was in a coma my parents probably would be that strict too.

That hadn't stopped Jake or Lydia's brother from sneaking out on flying crotchrockets anyway.

Thinking of my brother stung. He'd been a real jerk since he'd left for college. After the accident, Jake and I had become nearly inseparable. But since he'd left home, he'd completely stopped responding to my messages. I didn't understand what had happened. It wasn't like we'd had some massive fight.

26

"You broke curfew?" I asked to distract myself from the hurt feelings that swelled when I thought about Jake.

"Yeah, but it was totally worth it. Even if I would have gotten caught, which I didn't. If they ask, I was studying at your place last night. We were finishing up an assignment, which was why I was a little late."

"Right." I had no problem covering. She'd covered for me a couple times when I'd lost track of time making out with Harlow on the roof of his high-rise. Nudging her in the arm, I asked, "But what were you really doing?" Troy might have been a jerk sometimes, but weren't all guys? Lydia was crazy about him. She deserved to find someone.

"Getting a ride home from Troy."

Could she be any more cryptic? The high-rises towered over us, as if they were concealing her secrets. The shadows cast from the dark siding threatened to swallow the information into oblivion. I wished she had an endless wall of windows into her thoughts like the buildings around us. She was going to make me drag it out of her. "You told me. Anything else? Come on. A girl's gotta know."

A laugh escaped her lips. "Making out with Troy on the roof."

"I knew it. So are you guys a couple now?"

She shrugged. "I don't know. We're just having fun."

"Uh-huh."

I pulled open the front door to our hundred-story apartment building. We crossed the cream-colored tile and scuffed our feet over the ugly red-and-purple rug in the middle of the lobby. At least the black leather couches next to the doorman's vacant desk weren't so hideous. As we stepped into the elevator, a small app with a building map opened and *DESTINATION* flashed in my sight.

Home.

And with a single thought, the button illuminated for the thirty-fifth floor. In seconds, the doors closed. The lift hummed softly. "So are you going to make it official with Troy?"

"I dunno, maybe. He told me to call him tonight."

"Tonight it is then." I laughed as the elevator doors opened on our floor. "I want to hear all about it tomorrow. And I want every detail!"

"Fine." She waved to me and went to the right, toward her place. "Remember we have movie night this weekend. I want to hear all about your new artwork."

"Sure. Avoid the issue. Just remember, you can't hide. I know where you sleep." I waved back, reassured I could always track her down and force it out of her if I had to—the perks of being neighbors for the last ten years. And there wasn't a day I wasn't thankful Lydia's dad had gotten transferred to St. Louis. With Jake ignoring me, I'd be lost without her.

As I approached my front door, I didn't hear the familiar click of the lock. I pushed against the door, but it didn't budge.

"Damn this thing," I muttered as I thought about the backup unlocking program. But before I could blink to open it, my tracking chip activated the lock, and the door swung open.

Both my parents were in the living room with the news blaring. They glanced over the back of the couch with worried looks. I tensed. What was Dad doing home so early? And Mom always greeted me with a smile, but there was no evidence of one now.

I dropped my purse on the floor by the coatrack. "What's up?" I flopped onto the recliner on the opposite side of the coffee table, unable to ignore my mom's horror-stricken face.

"It's all over the news," Mom said.

"What is?"

Dad wore a blank expression. His kippah sat lopsided on his full head of dark brown hair. Sometimes I wondered if he wore it more to cover his tracker incision scar than for his faith. But looking at his drooping eyelids, I got the sense he was just tired. Tired of being forced to pretend to be something he wasn't.

Trackers trumped faith. It hurt him more than it hurt me. He remembered what it was like to unplug completely. I would never understand that. And as much as I wanted to connect to Dad on a spiritual level, I wasn't sure I wanted the space and quiet.

Observing Judaism came with sacrifices I self-imposed. Having a tracker came with sacrifices I had no control over.

"I got a national tracker message. It requested all nonessential personnel return home immediately," Dad said.

News. I blinked twice and headlines scrolled across my vision. Words like *"Armed Robbery"* and *"Critically Injured"* caught my attention and images of red skulls filled the sides of the search. I couldn't focus on one story through the jumbled mess.

Blood pulsed in my ears. If what I caught on the newsfeed was any indication, things were serious. Combine that with Dad's nationwide tracker message, and we were talking something massively wrong.

Once I turned eighteen, the government would add me to the distribution list. I'd too know the joy of security alerts. Until then, I was stuck with my own limited personal searches and whatever was on the news. "What happened?"

Both my parents shook their heads and pointed at the news screen. Most families had gotten rid of theirs in favor of individual streaming on the network. Mom and Dad insisted we still do things together, which included watching the news and movies. Dad said it didn't count as interaction if we all sat mindlessly in the same room watching different things on the network. I didn't mind most the time, except when we all couldn't agree on what to watch on the only screen in the house.

Messages scrolled across the bottom of the news screen. A computer-generated image of a man took up half the screen with the word SUSPECT below it in big, bold letters. The man, around my parents' age, had fair skin with brown, curly hair and a scruffy, graying beard. His piercing green eyes seemed to accuse *me* of the crime instead of implicating him.

The announcer spoke: "If anyone has seen the man depicted in the composite, please contact the authorities immediately. I repeat, do not attempt to engage this man. He is considered armed and dangerous. We now return to Janis Covington, live at Brentwood Square, where the incident took place."

"What's going on? They can always find people. I thought that was the point of the trackers."

"Kai, quiet please. We are trying to figure that out." Dad's attention remained glued to the screen.

Missing person. I blinked twice and five-year-old images of missing kids popped up on the edges of my line of sight. Kids of all backgrounds, but one of a young girl with long, mousy brown hair caught my attention. Her blue eyes refused to release their hold on me. "Damn wrong search," I muttered, quickly clearing everything out of my line of sight.

"Would you stop surfing the network and pay attention to the news? You'll never get the full story if you're multitasking."

"I was trying to—"

Mom's hazel eyes focused on me without a word. A sure sign that if I didn't knock it off, there would be consequences.

"Never mind." I blinked twice while thinking about the *minimize* function. All the apps disappeared from my vision except the essential operations on my tracker, which blinked in the lower right-hand side of my vision. Once everything was as close to off as the system would allow, I faced the news screen. I don't know how Dad knew when I had a million functions open, but Jake always joked that Dad had installed extra security on our chips to keep track of everything we did. He used to report directly to Rufus Scurry, the head of Global Tracking Systems, so it was best not to risk it.

A blonde female reporter with freckles on her nose appeared on the screen. Her concerned expression said everything.

"Thanks, Don. Right now, we know the suspect entered the building around 2:00 P.M. When the store owner refused to sell him a large quantity of lead wiring due to shortage laws, the man pulled a gun. The pair exchanged heated words, and the suspect fired on the shop owner, running away with the merchandise. The shop owner died on the way to the hospital."

"I don't get it." I shook my head. "There hasn't been a crime in over five years."

"I know, Kaya. Let's hear the rest." Mom's voice was soft but stern, meaning the situation was more serious than I'd originally realized.

"Mystery still surrounds this incident. The authorities are unable to track the man. They suspect he was acting with the Ghost movement."

A red skull symbol replaced the composite sketch of the man.

"The Ghosts, an extremist group known for fighting the

Tracker220 technology, threatened to make a reappearance just before going into hiding twelve years ago. Many are speculating this is the start of their return. Vandals have marked many businesses that support Global Tracking Systems with the red skull, a symbol adopted by the Ghost movement. Even more troubling, Rufus Scurry, the creator of Tracker220, was unavailable for comment on how this man bypassed the system. Live for KSDK, this is Janis Covington."

"How could they let this happen?" I asked.

Dad switched off the news screen. "We've all put a lot of faith in the tracker technology, but it's not perfect."

"But the Ghosts? Why didn't they hunt them down ages ago?"

"They rounded up a lot of suspects, but many evaded capture."

"How can anyone hide with a tracker? It's not like you can just go offline or shut it down." My friends' shenanigans in the woods aside, none of the story made sense. It went against everything I knew about tracker technology, which admittedly wasn't a whole lot beyond apps and day-to-day usage.

"Simple," Dad said. "You don't draw attention to yourself. The crime today was strategic. Someone wanted the Ghosts to get blamed for what happened. They've got everyone in a panic. They like to create mass hysteria."

"Why would they do that?"

"Most likely so they can divert attention away from what they're really up to. Their reappearance brings with it the fear that the attacks will start again."

"Attacks? What attacks?"

"Something I hoped I'd never have to explain," Dad said with a furrowed brow. "When you were a baby, Global Tracking Systems started distributing the tracker technology on a large scale. The Ghosts spoke out against the technology, claiming it was an invasion of privacy. But their claims were dismissed because the tech it replaced had the same concerns."

I knew about the tracker monitoring, but who cared if I searched for silly pictures on the network and chatted with my friends? "Why would the Ghosts care? Did they have something to hide from the authorities?"

"Some people think so. But most of the world agreed the benefits of instant access to infinite knowledge and the health monitoring capabilities far outweighed the few opposing voices. When it became clear that everyone would receive a tracker, the Ghosts waged attacks on Global Tracking Systems and other government buildings. That's why they sent me home early today."

Dad worked in a tech division for the government that monitored tracker diagnostics. He had a unique understanding of the situation since he was part of the team that finalized the tracker technology. He always knew how to explain things in a way I could understand.

"So why isn't this part of our history lessons?"

Mom sat on the arm of the recliner. She twisted blond hair into a knot like I did before I cut mine, then put her hand on my knee. "People don't want to remember that horrible part of our history. And the government thought it was too brutal to discuss with children. It was a dark time. We didn't leave the house much. Anyone who worked for Global Tracking Systems was a target."

A pounding at the front door interrupted our conversation.

Dad walked to the door and opened it.

"Who's here?" I asked, peering over the back of the couch.

Four uniformed authorities stood in our doorway, dressed in full combat gear.

Four

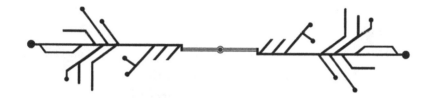

The head officer pulled off his helmet. "There's a tracker offline at your location." His three agents fanned out in the room with their rectangular monitoring devices. One agent loomed over each of us. "Our records indicate there should be three trackers at this location. We better not catch any stowaways."

I flinched. Did this have something to do with the robbery? The thought of some criminal camping out in our apartment made my insides crawl.

Dad loomed over the head authority. He always said it was best to establish who had the real authority upfront, but I always clammed up whenever they showed up. "No, it's just the three of us. My son is away at college."

I didn't know why Dad had bothered to mention Jake. The authorities knew where he was if they wanted to find him. They had records and advanced programs for that stuff.

The agent nearest me grabbed my arm and dug his gloved

fingers into my skin. *Ouch.* Stinging red marks appeared, but I struggled to keep my face neutral. The less I spoke, the faster they'd be gone. He moved the monitoring device over the back of my skull. He pulled it away, tapped the screen, and scanned the device over my head again.

Across the room, the agent next to Mom said, "She's functional."

"Him as well," said the agent with Dad.

Mom let out a long breath, but Dad didn't react.

Maybe it was all a big mistake. The agent hovering above me still had a vise-like grip on my arm. "It's this one."

My stomach churned.

"That's impossible," Dad said. "Check again."

"I did, sir. Multiple times," the agent said.

I blinked twice, trying to generate a search, but nothing came up in my vision.

He yanked me toward the door, but Dad long strides allowed him to beat the agent to the door and block his path.

"Where are you taking her?" he demanded.

"To headquarters for diagnostic tests."

My body froze. *What if they know about last night? What if something happened to my tracker when Harlow and Troy were playing around?* I hadn't noticed anything unusual until now. Maybe I'd missed a warning sign. Fear tore through me. I didn't want to go through tracker tests.

"Hold on a minute. You're not taking my daughter anywhere. I know you have tests you can run here."

"Sir, it's best if we do these tests at the lab."

"You can do the tests here." Dad crossed his arms and firmly planted himself in the doorway even though his thin frame didn't

36

block much of it.

"We can do them here but—"

"Then do it," Dad said.

"Sir, it's not recommended."

"I don't care. She's my daughter, not yours. Get out your kit and do it." Dad waited silently while the guard shifted his weight. I knew from experience if it came to a battle of wills, Dad could outlast anyone. "Unless you want me to report you for protocol violation."

"Fine," huffed the head agent. "Take her into the kitchen." He disappeared out the front door, muttering something about government employees.

"Dad?"

"Just do what they say, and they'll be out of here quickly," Dad whispered in my ear as he followed me into the kitchen.

Thank goodness for Dad's knowledge of tracker diagnostics. If my tracker had gone offline last night, I would have been screwed. The agent grasping my arm shoved me into a wooden chair at our kitchen table. My parents stood flanked by the remaining two agents, their faces etched with worry lines.

What are we waiting for? The anticipation clawed at me. The temperature in the room slowly rose with each passing tick from the clock mounted on the kitchen wall. Maybe I didn't want to know what was coming.

Five minutes later, the head agent strode into the kitchen with a black kit. He unzipped it on the table. Five syringes with colored liquids and several other ominous silver and black instruments gleamed up at me. My lunch threatened to make a reappearance.

The head authority paced the kitchen. "When did you notice

your tracker wasn't functioning?"

I shrugged. "I didn't." I tried to remain neutral on the outside, but my insides were freaking out. I blinked twice again, trying another search, but nothing appeared in my vision. While having all the apps minimized was usually relaxing, it was now the source of my nightmare. If my tracker never came back online, would they have to perform brain surgery to replace it?

"How could you not realize your tracker was offline? Hasn't your head felt a little empty?"

"No. I was on the network a little bit ago but shut off most the major functions to watch the news." Maybe the agent was right. Maybe all the minimalist function stuff Dad always babbled about had made me miss something. But Dad had taught me that just because I had a tracker didn't mean I should use it all the time. He always told me it wasn't wise to solely depend on one thing. "What if one day it's not there?" he'd asked which made no sense. He helped build the tech it's not like it was going anywhere.

But I knew the truth. It was his way of grasping on to the quiet Shabbats he'd had as a kid. Ever since he'd had the tracker installed, he'd lost the ability to totally unplug. The blinking lights and minimized critical functions never fully went away. It was impossible to turn off a tracker. I'd never experienced a tech-free Shabbat. And I wasn't sure I wanted to, either.

I respected his new way of observance, reducing his tracker to the least possible function allowed. Even though using trackers in any capacity on Shabbat was a complete violation of his faith in Judaism. At least that was what he believed. There was a big disagreement in the Jewish community about trackers and how to properly observe Shabbat with them.

The agent's suspicious expression told me he saw right through my weak lie, even though I wasn't lying. Most teens treated their trackers like another limb—always multitasking. I was an anomaly. And telling him I was Jewish would only further complicate things. Jewish beliefs didn't mix well with trackers, and anything that challenged the tech was a threat.

"These things don't just happen. Were you tampering with your tracker?"

I shook my head as last night's antics replayed in my mind. To stave off his concern, I quickly added, "It rebooted a few times, but it didn't seem strange." We got software updates all the time.

"Messing with your tracker is a Class A felony. Don't you think you should have told someone it was malfunctioning?"

I opened my mouth to answer but stopped when the agent next to me raised a large syringe with blue liquid.

"How many times does she have to tell you she didn't tamper with it? And if she didn't, no one did. She's not a criminal." Dad was a few minutes shy of going nuclear on the guy.

The agent side-eyed Dad and his unreadable expression, then tapped out the bubbles on the syringe and grabbed my wrist. I yanked away, but the agent slammed my arm against the table, pinning it down.

My body shook as the agent plunged the needle into my forearm. The liquid burned up into my shoulder then through my chest until my entire body exploded with the heat of an inferno. "What are you doing?" I asked through clenched teeth. "What is that stuff?"

The agent ignored me and jammed another needle in my arm before I had time to flinch. A low whine slipped out of me as the fire burning inside me blazed even hotter. Mom lunged toward me, but the closest agent caught her arms and held her back. Her expression silently said, "I'm sorry."

When the burning sensation dulled to a tired ache, the agent grabbed a small black box from the kit. It resembled the device Travis and Harlow had used the night before, but I knew it couldn't be the same. He placed the device on the back of my head. The agent in charge gestured for him to continue

A moment later, a stabbing pain thrust into my head like a sharpening knife carving into a drawing pencil, tearing away the exterior and revealing the raw material beneath. As the probe punctured the back of my head, a horrifying scream started inside my mind and worked its way toward my mouth until I could no longer contain it. Tears streamed down my face, blurring my vision. The pain cycled between stabbing and throbbing.

I slumped down in the chair. My drooping eyelids made it impossible for me to blink. With each breath, my lungs fought to expand. I didn't have the energy to panic about my lack of air supply. I could no longer express the terror building. It bottled inside me with no exit, the weight excruciating.

I could no longer see the world through my vision. I was viewing Dad through a filter—like I was watching *through* myself instead of actually being there. And somehow in that room full of people, I'd fallen into a lonely oblivion.

"I'm so sorry." Dad sounded like he was in a tunnel. "Kai, it's almost over."

The sound of his voice saying my nickname returned me to reality. I dug my fingernails into the sides of my chair to keep from falling out of it and pulled myself upright.

"What are you doing to me?" I tried to yell at them, but it

came out as a hoarse whisper.

"Jumpstarting your tracker." The agent pulled out a third syringe with red liquid and thrust it into my upper arm. The brief sting was a pinprick in comparison to the pain I'd already endured. My father gave me a weak, apologetic smile. His expression told me the tracker restart could be a long process.

My head vibrated as the box activated. The charred taste invading my mouth made me want to vomit. The agent read his monitoring device. I silently pleaded with the agent that he end my nightmare. He didn't notice. Instead, he kept tapping the screen and checking the device latched on to my head. He pulled out a fourth syringe with yellow liquid and lifted it behind my head. "Don't move."

I sucked in a breath but felt nothing. My head was numb from the initial sting. "Is it…" My vision went white. "Uh, I can't see anything."

I wobbled in the chair but quickly found the armrests.

"That will pass. Your tracker is rebooting after a hard reset," said a voice from behind me.

"How long will it take?"

"A couple of minutes."

If my stomach was any indication, I didn't have a couple of minutes. I coughed and choked down my bile then tried to slow my breathing.

After the longest "couple of minutes" of my life, my vision slowly came into focus. I blinked several times, each flutter of my eyelids releasing some of the weight holding them down. "That's better." I paused to make sure that really was the case. "Is that all?"

"No." The word snapped out of his mouth. "We need to

41

check your functionality. Open a mental pad."

Not wanting to cause trouble, I blinked twice. A blank form opened in the upper right-hand corner of my vision.

"Did it work?"

Afraid to speak, I nodded instead.

"Good, now compose a message."

The best I could come up with was

K.W.: Hi.

The letters appeared on the pad, followed by

K.W.: It's Kaya.

"Okay, now what?"

"Send the message."

Blinking twice, I thought of Dad. The message collapsed out of my view.

Dad blinked twice. "I have her message."

The agent checked his device then motioned to continue. "Fine, one more test. Do a search."

The first thought that flitted across my mind was *asshole*. I hoped a picture of the agent would pop up, but I quickly amended my thought to *vacation* in case the agent was monitoring my search. I pushed the thought out onto my link to the network. Instantaneously, images of beaches and airfare deals floated across the corner of my vision. I blinked twice to clear my field of vision.

"I think you've put her through more than enough today. It's time for you to leave." Dad's tone was firm.

The head agent opened his mouth then closed it. He waved his agents out. The two by my parents walked into the hall. The one behind me removed the device. I shivered as the object slid out of my head. The crushing pressure in my skull eased. I ran my fingers over the raw area, catching them in the damp spot where the device had latched on moments before.

"Keep an eye on that tracker. Be certain it doesn't happen again."

"Okay," was all I could manage to get out. As if I had any control over it. Of course, the authorities would put the blame on me rather than admit their tech was faulty.

The head agent dipped his head. "Thank you for your time, sir. Contact us if you have any more difficulties."

Ha! Not likely. I was sure they'd be more than happy to beat down our door again should any issues arise. They clearly had no issue invading our home to violate my personal space.

Dad walked them out. When the front door slammed, I slouched in the chair.

Mom raced toward me and wrapped me in a tight hug. I tensed to stave off the emotional break, but the tighter I squeezed my muscles, the more painful everything became. When I lost the ability to hold everything together, I collapsed in her arms, quaking.

"It's okay. It's all over." Mom rubbed her hand down my back, but her touch only made me shake more.

Tracker diagnostics was the furthest thing from okay, but I appreciated Mom trying.

Dad leaned against the doorway to the kitchen. Mom pulled away and started needlessly opening cabinets as if searching for something that wasn't where it was supposed to be.

"How could you let them do that to her?" she asked, slamming another drawer closed.

"You know I didn't have a choice," Dad said. "This was the least invasive option."

They were talking about me like I wasn't in the room, but I didn't care. A thick fog flooded my head, making their words slur together.

And before I knew it, Mom was in my face.

"Can I get you anything? A blanket? Want me to adjust your tracker settings to combat the pain?"

I gave her an "I'm fine" expression, but she didn't seem to notice.

"How about I make spaghetti for dinner? I know it's your favorite."

"Thanks, Mom, but I've lost my appetite. I'm going to lie down." I couldn't imagine what the authorities would have done if they had hauled me off like Harlow. But their invasive probing had been more than enough.

Standing up from the table, I wobbled, gave Dad a weak shrug, and stumbled down the hall past all the smiling photos of our family. Despite Jake laughing in most of them, there was nothing to laugh about now. Funny, because it was usually his laugh that could bring me out of any funk. If only I could hear it now.

Too bad the authorities couldn't do something useful like arrest Jake for refusing to answer tracker messages. It was brutal. Jake had gone away to school and it was like he was dead instead of one state over. College might be awesome, but there was no excuse for the three-word message he'd sent me months ago.

J.W.: Miss you, Kai,

was all it said.

Thanks, Captain Obvious, for the lame attempt at endearment. Jake had never said so little in his entire life, especially not to me. And he'd never ignored me this long, either. My parents weren't the least bit bothered by his lack of interest, some parental babble about growing up and needing his space. I didn't buy it, but I didn't have a way to beat down his door and make him talk to me or answer my millions of messages.

I stepped past my room and turned the knob to his bedroom door. As boring as the day he'd left it, right down to the wastebasket full of crumpled-up paper that he never let anyone throw out for him. Only Jake was allowed to decide when he was truly done with a writing project. I kicked the can, and it crashed to the ground, spilling the wadded-up paper balls onto the floor.

He wasted more paper than me trying to perfect his stories and poetry. He never quit until it was just right. And rather than erase or store his musings on the tracker network, he insisted on having a pen in his hand and a clean sheet of paper to mess up. Jake loved to create, turn something into nothing and connect dots with words. He also didn't trust that someone wouldn't screw with his work on the network, so his most prized projects stayed in hard copy.

I bent to the floor and picked up a crumpled wad. If his most important work was on paper, then maybe there was something here to soothe me. I unwrinkled the first ball—nothing super enlightening, just the start of a poem about water and submerging in it. I wadded it up and chucked it into the trashcan. The next paper was more discarded poetry, about a cave and the darkness within. It had much better cadence to it than the previous one. I folded it and shoved it in my pocket. If I couldn't have him, at least I had a piece of his writing.

I grabbed another paper ball and unfurled it. It was short, a few sentences, but surprisingly addressed to me.

Kai,

I've tried to write this so many times. I'm not sure how to say it. I don't know if I can, so I'm leaving you this note instead. I—

My heart raced. I what? I flipped over the paper, but it was blank. What had he been trying to say to me that he couldn't? I flopped onto his bed and held the note to my chest. I inhaled deep, slow breaths, hoping they would stave off the sadness.

I knew he couldn't have left without a real goodbye and no further communications. We couldn't last one hour at school without talking. His lack of contact from college was suspicious at best. And here in my hands was the start of an answer. But why had he never finished it? The hole in my heart that was usually filled by his laughter felt like a crater.

My head throbbed and swirled with thoughts. The mystery wasn't solved, but I had one puzzle piece. And then there was the whole separate puzzle around why my tracker malfunctioned and the authorities busted down our door.

Everything in my life was falling apart and multiple puzzles were mixed in the same box. And the one person who could always help me sort through the mess wasn't here when I needed him most. Jake would have had fifty different explanations for why my tracker had malfunctioned.

Of course I could always ask Dad, but that meant sitting

through hours of technical mumbo jumbo just to answer a simple question. It was never worth it.

Instead, I was left in the darkness wondering if the crazy tech in the woods had anything to do with the surprise brain probing. And if Jake's half-written note told me anything, I was on my own to solve the mystery, which was harder to swallow than all the wasted paper on the floor.

Five

I raced through the halls before school searching for Troy. I'd prefer to talk to Harlow, but he never made it to school early and was ignoring my messages. Again.

He was getting as bad as Jake, and I needed answers about Troy's little toy. Murmurs of the robbery filled the halls rather than the usual buzz about the big game and Harlow's epic display of defiance. I'd completely forgotten about the crime until I'd stepped into school that morning. After the visit from the agents, the news sat on the bottom of my list of priorities.

I rounded the corner toward the student lounge and crashed into some freshman. My purse fell to the ground. Pencils, pastels, Kleenex, and lip gloss scattered across the floor. Glaring at the freshman, I collected my belongings.

When I rose to my feet, I found myself face to face with the wall Jake had painted his senior project on. It was a short piece of poetry about the importance of found family over blood. Most people thought it was about some secret girl he'd been dating.

But I knew the truth. Jake had important people in his life, and a secret girlfriend hadn't been one of them. If there'd been a girl, I'd have known about her.

He never had to tell me the poem centered around his best friend, Denny, Lydia's brother. It hinted at how Jake and I had chosen to be friends in addition to our sibling bond after the accident. I'd refused to let Jake's worst moments keep him down, helping him find his laugh again. In return, he'd shielded me from trouble and pain, making sure I found the right solutions to every problem I faced. Now the world played a cruel trick on me with the constant reminders that our once-indestructible bond was broken—possibly beyond repair.

I flipped my bangs out of my face and turned away from the poem before it gutted me. At the far end of the hall, Troy barreled past three upperclassmen headed in my direction. I rushed to intercept him, channeling my pent-up emotion into the impending encounter.

I reached for his wrist, but it slipped between my fingers.

"Troy!"

He spun in the direction of his name, never missing an opportunity to bolster his popularity. But the minute he saw me, his face sank as if saying, *Oh, it's just you.*

"Hear me out. I've got a question for you." I knew misleading him to think it was about Lydia was the only way to get his attention.

"Sure. I've got half a second."

"Not out here. Somewhere more private." I motioned to the janitor's closet.

He puffed out his chest and followed me into the closet. The stench of wet mops overwhelmed me.

"A dark closet. Wow, Kaya, I never knew you felt this way about me." Half his mouth curled into a twisted smile that contained a hint of deviousness mixed with flirtation. But not the kind that made me giddy.

"Seriously? This is not the best way to win over my best friend."

"Oh, have a little fun. You don't always have to have a stick up your butt."

I didn't have time for his games. I grabbed his face and whipped it directly in front of mine.

"Damn, Kaya," he said. "You don't have to be so rough."

I instantly dropped my grip. I was in way over my head and Troy knew it. "Answer a couple questions for me and I'll help you out with Lydia." Bargaining with him appeared to be my only option.

"Who says I need your help?"

"Who says you don't?" I knew he didn't, but if I could put a shred of doubt in his mind, he might answer my questions.

"Fine, but I want some premium intel."

"Deal." It was too easy.

"Intel first. I want to make sure it's good."

Okay, maybe not so easy. "One now and one after."

"I can live with that."

"Lydia loves symphony music and is a sucker for cheesecake." Lydia had once told me a concert followed by cheesecake for dessert was her idea of a perfect date. If that didn't seal the deal, I don't know what would.

"What am I supposed to do with that?"

He really was that dense. "Ask her out. Take her to—"

"Right, I got it. Now what's your question. I don't have all morning."

"Tell me about that radio wave generator you guys were messing with the other night."

"What do you mean?" A blank expression crossed his face.

"Don't play dumb. Where'd you get it?"

He rolled his eyes, as if I'd asked the most moronic question ever. "My cousin."

"Where'd *he* get it?"

"Why does that matter?" He stepped toward the door, an indication I was running out of time.

"It all matters." I paused, unsure if I wanted to tell him. Taking a deep breath, I said, "Four authorities showed up at my door last night."

"So? Who cares? It's not like they don't do random checks."

I gritted my teeth to avoid losing it. "This wasn't a random check. My tracker went offline. They wanted to run diagnostics."

"You get hauled off by the authorities and you think I had something to do with it? That's thick, Kaya, even for you." He reached for the door but paused before opening it. Whatever came next, he didn't want the whole world to hear it. "I know you hate me, but I had nothing to do with this."

"It has to have something to do with your device. The authorities had one just like it. How do you explain that? And I never said I hated you." Hate? No. *Strong dislike* was more accurate. I only tolerated him because of Lydia's crush.

"You don't have to say it. It's obvious." He turned to the door. "Just because you had a little visit from the authorities doesn't mean my device had anything to do with it. You're the only one who had authorities at your door last night, so get over yourself." He stormed off before I could respond.

My tracker blinked in the lower left-hand corner with the initials *TA*. Maybe he did have answers. I maximized the note.

T.A.: Question me again and I'll turn Lydia against you.

What an ass!

Not the answers I was hoping for. He was such a waste of skin.

The red light flashed three times. Class was starting. I bolted out of the janitor's closet toward art class. My worthless encounter with Troy had made me late. One more thing to resent him for. I'd have to find a redeeming quality if I was going to be supportive of Lydia's crush.

As I rushed through the halls, a blue light blinked in the corner of my vision. I opened the pending message.

LOW BLOOD SUGAR. YOU SKIPPED TWO MEALS.

Great. I was so worried about getting answers, I'd rushed out of the house without eating. I minimized the message, but the blue light kept blinking. That would be an annoyance until lunch. At least it wouldn't be as bad as Yom Kippur fasting. Just about twenty-four hours of blinking. I could have stopped for snacks, but I'd lost my appetite with everything going on. And I refused to miss any more of art class.

Because of Tracker220, painting and drawing were dying forms of expression. Despite all the wisdom and connectedness of my tracker, I'd grown to cherish art class. Drawing let me express myself without people judging me. For one hour, I didn't have to worry about breaking rules because there weren't any.

I plopped onto a stool across the table from Harlow, who was flicking paint from his brush at the back of Wes's head.

"Why do you take this class if you don't enjoy it?" I asked.

Harlow shrugged. "It's an easy A. It'll help me get sports scholarships. Plus, Mr. Marcus doesn't care if we *actually* do anything." He nodded to the corner of the room, where Mr. Marcus had his cowboy boots propped up on his desk and quietly dozed with a Cardinals baseball cap pulled low. He was only good for two things—playing yenta, which was how Harlow and I had gotten together, and supporting my love of art with an endless amount of supplies. If Mr. Marcus wanted to sleep on the job, I wasn't going to turn him in.

"Well, if you aren't going to do anything, at least stop wasting precious resources. Art supplies are an expensive commodity."

He spun on his stool. "What's bugging you?"

Busted. Harlow knew as well as I did that my mood wasn't about the art supplies, but I wasn't ready to talk about it with him. At least not yet.

I reached for a clean sheet of paper and the colored pencils sitting across the table and began to draw. The strokes calmed my frazzled nerves, but the drawing was far from perfect. I reached for an eraser and scrubbed out some of the lines I didn't like and tried again. The image still wasn't right.

Woods. I blinked twice and several images popped into my view. I scrolled through and found one with a clearing that matched what I was envisioning. After making my selection, I closed the other images. I did the same for an image of a bonfire then superimposed it onto the picture of the woods already on

53

the right side of my vision. There. That was what I wanted. I positioned the picture in my line of sight so it sat next to my piece of paper.

I tried again, but for some reason my hand wasn't doing what my brain wanted it to. I huffed and positioned the image from my tracker over the paper and resized it to match. Normally, I would never trace lines from an image, but I was sick of messing up. And the blinking blue light wasn't helping, either. Maybe I should have gone for snacks.

As I fixed the lines, I caught Harlow staring at me out of the corner of my eye. He was waiting for an answer.

Without looking up from the paper, I blurted out, "The authorities showed up at my door last night."

"What? Why?"

I took a few more deep breaths. "My tracker…" I said. "This stuff is so messed up."

"What is?" His tone was even. I admired his ability to keep calm despite the crazy nonsense spilling out of my mouth.

"They can just burst into your house and probe your brain like that?" My body trembled. My breathing grew ragged. "It's not right."

A message with *HG* blinked. I opened it and my vision filled with cute baby animals and little hearts. There was a baby panda and a tiny giraffe with its tongue out. Normally, I'd laugh, but no amount of cyber goof would fix what had happened.

Harlow stroked the top of my left hand. At his touch, my shoulders clenched before relaxing. My right hand kept rhythmically swooping across the paper as I continued drawing.

In time with the scratching of the pencil, I recounted every horrifying detail of what the authorities had done. By the end, my mouth was so dry, I could only whisper. We sat in silence, Harlow squeezing my hand.

"I'm so sorry."

I dropped the pencil in an attempt to focus on Harlow. He scanned the room, but most the class was sleeping or zoning out on the tracker network.

"I never meant for anything bad to happen to you," he said.

I slid off my chair and rounded the table. I leaned into him, resting my head on his chest. Even sitting on the stool, he was taller than me. He wrapped me in a hug.

"I don't blame you for this. It's not your fault."

"I know, but…"

I cut him off, pressing my finger to his lips. "I don't blame you," I repeated in a firm tone before giving him a peck on the lips. "I just wish I knew more about Troy's device."

"You think his radio wave generator had something to do with this?"

"It's the only explanation I can think of."

"But you didn't even use it."

"I know, but when I tried to stop you—" I shook my head, trying to clear my thoughts. "I don't know what happened. None of this makes sense."

"The technology isn't perfect."

"I know, but the chance of malfunction is so rare. I just thought…" I stopped as three red lights flashed. *Damn, class is over.* I reached across the table and stacked up the art supplies. "I have to go, or I'll be late. You know how Mrs. Perkins is about tardies." I picked up my purse and my drawing.

Harlow grabbed my hand as I spun away from the table. "Wait, you're coming to the game tonight, aren't you? I need my good luck charm. It's going to be brutal."

"Of course." My hand slipped from his. Before I hurried off to English, I said, "I wouldn't miss it." After everything, I could use a distraction.

Six

"Uh, Earth to Kaya? Hello. Anyone home?" Lydia's voice ripped me from my haze.

The soccer game, if you could call it that, was in full swing on the field below. Huge freestanding lights illuminated the massacre in progress. Our team was down four goals, and two guys nursed injuries on the bench.

Even the roar of the crowd didn't disrupt my train of thought. I'd been carefully constructing a series of searches on how trackers functioned. I hoped to find clues, but half the time, I hit blocked searches. I was quickly nearing my flagged searches limit for the day. Any more and I'd ensure another date with the authorities.

I blinked to close the search boxes. "Sorry. What were you saying?"

"Are you sure you're okay? You're a little pale."

"It's this whole tracker thing. It's really bothering me." I'd told Lydia all about my terrible night on our way home from school. Between Lydia, Harlow, Troy, and my searches, I kept coming up empty. I'd even sent a message to Jake earlier, but he'd ignored it like the previous twenty billion before it. I'd kill for that three-word message now. But what if there was more to that note I'd found? I hoped he was over trying to prove how cool he was to his ΑΕΠ frat brothers by ignoring me.

Jake was my last hope.

Without his help, I'd have to question Dad when I got home. That was a conversation I was hoping to avoid. I didn't want him to worry about me anymore than he already was.

"Are you sure Troy didn't mention anything about the radio wave generator to you?"

"Kaya, I think it's just a fluke. I wouldn't worry so much." She twisted me toward the field and pointed. "Watch the game. They're putting Harlow in."

I minimized all my tracker functions to avoid temptation then turned my attention to the game. Even from the last row of the bleachers, I could make out his sweaty hair and muscles as he ran onto the field. He high-fived Wes and Troy. The whistle blew. At the sideline, Wes threw the ball into play. Harlow took possession and started down the field with Troy keeping pace. "They do look good out there. Don't they?"

Lydia let out a laugh. "Damn good."

Harlow outmaneuvered a defender and passed the ball to Troy, who spun around a second approaching player. Troy kicked to Harlow, who shot it into the high right corner of the goal. It sailed over the goalie's hands into the net.

I blinked twice as I thought about compliments. A big flashing WAY TO GO image popped up. I thought of love and Harlow and sent it on its way. Harlow pivoted toward the stands and waved at me then ran at Troy. They chest-bumped midair.

"Why can't they get along like that off the field?" I asked.

"It's all about teamwork on the field. But off the field, there's that competitive edge. They have to show off for their women."

"They all have ego-itis."

Lydia raised her eyebrows.

"You know they love to play mine's bigger than yours."

"Oh, come on. You can't tell me you don't find it hot when they show off."

"Actually, I don't." I started to say more, but I didn't want to start an argument I knew I couldn't win. I'd let her have this one.

Harlow wasted no time stealing the ball from the opposing team. As he headed toward the goal, the crowd cheered. The sound of unicopters in the distance caught my attention. *Please don't be coming here.*

Harlow drove at the goal, weaving in and out of players. As he lined up for a shot, the roar of the unicopters grew louder as they appeared over the treeline—at least a dozen followed by a large, black semicopter. The silver authority shield adorned the side of the rectangular shipping container, which attached to the back of the unicopter on a flatbed. *Shit! They're here.*

Spotlights focused on the game as the vehicles descended onto center field.

The two sets of overhead blades on the semicopter slowed as the rectangular container crashed to the ground with a *bang.*

The players stopped the game and headed toward their benches, anticipating what came next.

A voice boomed from the speaker. "Nobody move. There's a tracker malfunction at this location." Whispers erupted in the crowd, but everyone obeyed. They stood in place, scanning the sea of people for the culprit.

Please don't be me. I blinked twice, frantically trying to open a mental pad.

Nothing.

Damnit!

After the vehicles landed mid-field, twelve agents from the unicopters fanned across the field. A couple more released the door on the semicopter to create a ramp and dozens more agents poured out. They formed a line stretching the length of the soccer field and marched as one toward the bleachers.

I tried my tracker again hoping it reset on its own.

Still nothing.

Why is this happening to me again?

The line of agents had reached the base of the bleachers. I couldn't let them haul me off. I wouldn't give them another chance to jam needles into my arms and carve into my skull.

I searched the field for a quick exit, but I was trapped, nowhere to run. I leaned over the back of the bleachers. It was my only chance.

I turned to Lydia. "It's me. I have to go." I gave her my best "I'm sorry" expression.

"Kaya, wait!" she yelled, but I had already launched myself over the top of the bleachers and climbed halfway down. The height didn't bother me. When I was ten, I'd figured out how to climb out my bedroom window and across the ledge on the side of our building. The quick climb took me right to Lydia's bedroom window. The height of thirty-five stories never fazed me. The descent was like stepping off a sidewalk in comparison.

When I reached the grass below, I ran toward the woods behind the school. It was only fifty yards away. I could make it, but then what? If my tracker restarted, they'd find me instantaneously because of the jump from one location to the next while being offline.

My heavy breaths echoed inside my head as my feet slid on the wet grass. The woods grew closer, and I pushed on harder. With each frantic breath, I caught a whiff of pine. The scent grew with my anticipation of escape. I was almost there, but I needed a plan.

My vision went white. Unable to see, I skidded to a halt. *Great! Now my tracker is rebooting?* If it fixed itself, then maybe I was off the hook. I strained to listen for footsteps, but the blood pulsing through my ears drowned out all other sound. Holding my arms out, I inched forward, each step in time with the blood pumping through my veins.

"Kaya Weiss," a deep voice yelled from far behind me.

I whipped my head in the direction of the voice. My vision slowly blurred into focus. Agents marched toward me. *They know it's me.* The agents were closing in from the woods as well cutting off my escape route. *How did they catch up so quickly?* The giant lump forming in my throat made it difficult to breathe.

A buzzing like wind in my ears rang through my head. My mind screamed to flee, but I stood frozen as the swaying trees taunted me with their effortless movement. The authorities had a lock on my tracker. I wasn't going anywhere.

A blue light blinked.

ALERT.
INCREASED HEART RATE.
BREATHE DEEPLY.

Great. Just what I needed. More crazy messages clouding my

vision.

The buzzing in my ears grew more and more intense, consuming my every thought. I ached to clutch my head, but none of my muscles responded. My knees and legs wobbled involuntarily. I wanted to collapse into a ball, to shrink into oblivion, but I couldn't. My eyes dried as they fought to blink, forcing me to watch the agents draw toward me like robots.

As they closed in, a crotchrocket roared from above. I fought a screaming headache to see skyward. I didn't recognize the descending bike with a four-leaf clover painted on the front. The rider's black leather pants, jacket with red insets, and full helmet with opaque visor dared someone to challenge them. Definitely not one of my friends, but maybe it was my good luck charm.

Revving the engine, the figure spun the bike in a large circle, forcing the agents away from me. With each inch of space between us, my lungs filled with additional air. Each engine rumble removed a layer of haze from my mind. Each circle around me unwound the imaginary rope holding me in place. I pushed against the invisible barrier and forced the buzzing in my ears to a dull hum. My legs and arms tingled, and my toes wiggled. Somehow, I was fighting the tracker control. I clung to the tiny piece of hope, wondering if I still had a chance to escape.

A scream erupted between my lips like a battle cry. Thoughts raced through my head so quickly, I had trouble keeping up. I shoved them onto the network to clear my head, but different screens rapidly opened in my field of vision. The faster my thoughts came, the quicker the boxes flew. I released every hateful and pained emotion onto the network. Unable to track the expanding boxes overwhelming my vision, I shut my eyes for a moment of peace.

When I opened them, everything had vanished. I blinked twice, trying to open a mental pad. No response. My tracker was offline again. Only I thought I shut it off on purpose.

Was that even possible?

Between the circle of agents and the gathering crowd, I was surrounded with no way out.

"If you're looking for a way out, this is it," the rider called to me, their voice distorted behind the helmet.

I counted agents, eyeing the kits on their belts. A shiver crawled through me and wrapped around my neck, threatening to suffocate me. My breaths grew short as mortifying thoughts of what they'd put me through flooded my thoughts. They'd drag me to Global Tracking Systems for sure. But I wasn't going let them hurt me again. For the first time in my life, I wanted to break the rules. I wanted to find a place where the authorities couldn't torture me, and I hoped that such a place existed.

I scanned the crowd for Harlow.

"Kaya, don't. Let them help you." Harlow pleaded with me from behind a couple of agents who inched closer to me. "I promise I won't let them hurt you."

An empty promise. He couldn't protect me. I wasn't sure he ever really had, not like Jake, and especially not when it came to the authorities.

They already had hurt me in ways words couldn't begin to explain.

I studied Harlow's facial features, committing his brown eyes to memory as my feet edged away from the crowd. My legs prickled with each tiny step. Almost as if they had minds of their own. Without another thought, I whipped around and bolted toward the mysterious rider.

As I climbed on the bike and wrapped my arms around the rider's waist, I noticed a red skull emblem on the back of the helmet, the symbol I'd seen on the news, the symbol of the Ghost movement.

Seven

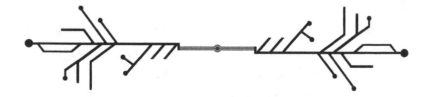

Before I had time to change my mind, the roar of the engine drowned out my racing thoughts. Wind thundered past, and we were airborne. The authorities scattered, running for their unicopters. My stomach lurched as we banked hard. I tightened my grip on the rider to avoid sliding off.

On the field, the unicopter engines whirred to life and headed skyward in pursuit.

We twisted through sickening turns and crossed over our path multiple times. The lights marking the sanctioned skyways blurred as we crisscrossed them, darting around traffic flying in the opposite direction. The driver yanked the handlebars, and we shot away from the traffic, off the skyway, and into open airspace.

Whizzing under metal bridges and whipping around glass buildings, we made our way to midtown. I barely caught my breath as we threaded between the hotels and office buildings. Midtown disappeared in a haze. The even taller buildings of downtown grew in scale as we zoomed onward.

As the traffic increased, we continued to weave around buildings in a snake-like pattern—the turns tighter and tighter the more densely populated the buildings became. But no matter what the rider tried, the unicopters gained on us. Despite the cluster of large buildings, there was nowhere to hide from the authorities.

If they caught up, an arrest for flying outside the sanctioned skyways would be the least of the driver's concerns. As for me, I was an accomplice. The punishment for keeping company with a Ghost was a million times worse than tracker diagnostics. I tried to focus on the horror I'd avoided, but one question kept creeping in. Had I escaped one nightmare and landed in another?

My stomach wrenched as the mysterious rider swooped in low, then banked, narrowly avoiding a skyrise. The unicopters whooshed above, afraid to brave the tight spaces between the buildings. They kept a high beam on us, tracking our progress. After weaving around another large building, the steel of the Arch burst into sight, lit up in the night sky. I gasped for air in an attempt to keep calm on the roller coaster ride from hell.

As more of downtown came into focus, the unicopters spread out behind us, and the skyscrapers gave way to shorter buildings. Nothing blocked the path between us and them. The engine revved beneath me. We sped toward the Arch. Flying underneath it was illegal—earning you a life sentence—yet we headed straight for it. The steel structure grew steadily larger, tempting us as we approached.

"Are you nuts?" I screamed over the engine. The rider gunned the bike again, and the rumble vibrated through me.

Two unicopters flew in close, flanking us. The agent on our right spoke through the loudspeaker. "Land your vehicle immediately."

The rider leaned forward on the handlebars and twisted the motorbike, swiping the rear wheel on the steel of the Arch as we passed under it. The unicopter on our right peeled away. The other veered left, but the rotor blade caught on the Arch leg, tearing a gaping hole in it with a sickening crash of metal grinding against metal. The blades lodged in the opening and ripped from the body of the unicopter. It spiraled toward the ground, leaving a trail of smoke in its wake. A fireball erupted on impact. The heat from the blast radiated off my face while we swerved around the smoke plume. We were one wrong turn from becoming a fireball.

"One down, eleven to go." The rider laughed, the sound distorted through the helmet, then angled the bike at the river. We dove down, my gut doing somersaults. I tightened my grip on the rider as we leveled above the water. Behind us, two unicopters braved the drop. The first flattened its course in time to glide above the water and continue to trail us. The second skidded off the surface. A geyser of water sprayed me, but I didn't have time to shiver because the fallen vehicle erupted into smoke and flames, heating me like a hunk of meat over an open flame. With no helmet and no seatbelt, I'd be in the fire if I couldn't maintain my grip. If the rider didn't kill me, the authorities would.

We followed the river south, flying close to the surface, stuck in limbo—between two states, between two fates. If I wanted to, I could have reached out my foot and touched the Mississippi River. The thought made my insides knot. I squeezed my eyes shut to avoid seeing the terrain whip by, but the rushing wind made me want to hurl.

I focused on the rider, trying to calm my nerves. "There's no way we can outrun them. They'll send reinforcemen—"

The bike veered toward the Missouri side of the river. Bile burned up my chest and invaded the back of my throat, gagging me. The height didn't bother me, but the erratic driving could end me at any moment. My hands were numb from clutching so tightly.

We shot higher at a steep angle and sped toward a huge forested area illuminated by the chasing unicopter's light.

"Ground your vehicle immediately," boomed the speaker on the unicopter. "Failure to comply will result in hostile measures."

The rider let out a sadistic laugh. The bike lurched, pushing on faster. I twisted my head to see the unicopters in pursuit. One maneuvered directly behind us at a distance. A wave of dread washed through my body. There was nothing between us and the dart missile hanging off the frame of the unicopter. I was along for the ride on a deathcycle. I refused to let missiles firing in my direction be the last thing that ever happened to me.

A giant flash erupted from the front of the unicopter and zoomed toward us. The rider twisted to peer behind, then yanked the bike left, narrowly avoiding the dart missile that whizzed past. It crashed into the field below, exploding on impact. I risked another glance at the unicopter. A second fireball burst from the front of the vehicle.

"Incoming!" I yelled.

The rider angled slightly toward the ground. The engine quieted to a hum then fell silent. We coasted for a brief moment before careening toward the forest below. My heart flew into my throat. Branches slapped my face and tore my clothes, scratching my skin. I bit the inside of my cheek to avoid crying out in pain.

A dozen feet from the forest floor, the rider kickstarted the engine and flipped off the headlights. We glided to the ground, continuing to hurtle and whip around giant oak and maple trees. The thick canopy cast dark shadows on us.

"You're going to get us killed!" I shouted.

No reaction.

The rider shut off the engine a second time, and the bike rolled through the woods toward a rundown barn. The unicopters thundered above, drawing my attention to their searchlights, which couldn't pierce the forest ceiling. How did we lose them so quickly?

"They'll thermal scan these woods. The authorities will find us."

The rider snorted through the helmet. "No, they won't." Despite the muffled sound, the voice carried a hint of knowing they were right.

The barn doors swung open. We slid through them, stopping between two other bikes. Old rusted pitchforks and farm machinery from the previous century lined the walls of the barn. A moldy stench invaded my nose.

I climbed off the bike, my wobbly legs threatening to betray me. The room spun around, making me more nauseous. I stumbled toward the barn doors, seeking a breath of fresh air, but they swung closed in front of me.

Turning, I choked out, "Open the door." I glared at the dark visor on the helmet, wishing I could see inside. With a shake of the head, the rider walked to the far corner of the barn and twisted a hanging pitchfork to the side. They motioned me over as a wooden floorboard creaked and slid along a series of ropes opening a hole in the floor. I hesitated, searching for another exit, but when I saw the trap door was the only way out, I inched toward it.

I peered into the hole and down the wooden steps. If the decaying stairs didn't kill me, whatever was stinking up that hole might.

The rider pointed down the stairs. "After you."

Eight

I sucked in a breath before braving the rotting wood. Each stair groaned beneath my feet, expressing a feeling I didn't dare show on my face. I jumped as the trap door banged closed. The rider latched it behind us, making the cellar appear more prison-like by the second. My throat tightened.

At the bottom of the stairs, the rider led me through a concrete corridor lit by hanging overhead lights. I trailed behind, each step heavier than the one before it. The impending doom ticked twice as fast as my feet dragged across the concrete.

We emerged into a wide-open room filled with equipment and monitors I'd only seen in pictures on the network and in old movies. Hundreds of personal computers showed everything from maps to weird charts and graphs. A few dozen people looked up from their monitors at us.

No, not at us.

At *me*.

I turned to the rider, who stood among the glowing

machines. After pulling off the gloves, the rider removed the helmet, allowing long, wavy brown hair to fall out. My jaw dropped.

"You're a... you're a g...g..." I stammered, trying to get the word out.

The girl, around my age, glared at me with piercing green eyes like I was an appetizer to a very large meal. I shouldn't have been surprised by her, but before I could apologize, a tall guy, also around my age, with wild, curly brown hair stormed at us.

"Peyton, you stole my bike again."

"If you'd let me fix mine instead of allowing those bozos at it, I wouldn't have to steal yours."

He scowled at her for a moment longer before facing me. "Hi, I'm Bailen." He extended his hand. "You must be Kaya. I was wondering when we'd be seeing you here."

I stared at his hand as if it were poison. "Where is *here* exactly? And how do you know my name?"

He dropped his hand, but his face remained calm. "Welcome to the Hive."

"The Hive?" I circled around, taking in the room. There weren't just old computers, but projection screens, tall racks with flashing lights and miles of wiring strung together like Christmas lights. Stuff was crammed everywhere, stacked on the tables, and shoved against every inch of wall space.

Even with all the equipment, the enormity of the room couldn't be ignored. But as more people stared in my direction, the room collapsed in on me. I crossed my arms and ran my hand from my elbow to shoulder.

"Impressive, isn't it?" Bailen asked with a smile that I assume was supposed to be welcoming. But it didn't help.

"I... I don't know." If I were being honest, I would have agreed with him, but I didn't know these people or what they wanted from me. I'd jumped on the bike to escape the authorities. Maybe it had been a giant mistake, but it was too late now. I'd made a decision, and I'd have to see where it took me. The uncertainty made my insides crawl, but I couldn't let the Ghosts see any fear. "What is this stuff?"

His smile faded slightly. "The computer equipment? It's here to help us. Even you," he said. "Especially you."

"Help me do what?" For all I knew, he was going to lobotomize me for my tracker. The Ghosts weren't exactly helping humanity. Their goal was to challenge authority and instill terror in the public. Were they really any better than the authorities?

"Your situation is...unique."

"You don't know a thing about me or my *situation*."

"We've been watching you."

I stepped away from the creep. "Stalker much?"

"Bailen, stop it. You're scaring her," Peyton said.

"Am not," he protested, giving her a half-grin and a raised eyebrow. An expression I assumed was supposed to be charming. Others around the room laughed quietly at their banter.

"You are." She shook her head. "I can't watch you try to woo people any longer. You might have an IQ over a hundred and fifty, but you have the social IQ of negative five. I have a bike to fix." Peyton stalked off with her helmet tucked under her arm.

"What?" he called after her before returning his attention to me. "We've been waiting for you."

"For me? Why?" I felt like a thousand satellites were monitoring me, which was ironic because for the first time in my life, none actually were. I was free, but I'd never been more trapped with fewer options.

"Your tracker. What you can do. Simply amazing. I can't even—"

"You did this." I raised my finger and inched toward him. "The Ghosts broke my tracker. Why are you doing this to me? Fix it and take me home. *Now!*" I hadn't even realized I was yelling until I'd finished.

Bailen leaned against a desk littered with wires and large monitors. "You don't understand."

"No, I understand perfectly." Before I could finish my tirade, two dark, brawny arms grabbed me from behind and carried me to the far wall like I was a plastic bag instead of a person.

"Let go of me!" I flailed, trying to break free, but whoever had me wasn't budging.

"Put her down. She isn't going to hurt me," Bailen said.

Easy for him to say. He didn't understand that my entire life had been ruined. I was in the middle of nowhere, far from my family, held hostage by the terrorist group that had broken my tracker. If the Ghosts were the ones who'd screwed me over, I was out of options. The pile I'd landed in was so far over my head, I couldn't make out the top.

The guy holding me loosened his grip and lowered me to the ground. I lunged in an attempt to put some space between me and the big guy, but he caught me, dragging me by the collar. I choked against the constricting neckline.

"Careful, she's feisty," said the deep voice from the muscle behind me.

Not feisty, just scared and searching for an exit.

"Fine. We hoped you'd cooperate so we could give you some

freedom around here. But considering your actions, I don't think that's possible."

"Why should I trust you people?"

"Because we had nothing to do with your tracker malfunction. You did that all on your own. We were just waiting for you to figure it out. It was only a matter of time."

"I don't believe you."

"You think we could do that with all this old equipment? Global Tracking Systems is high tech and tightly controlled. There's no way we could shut off a single tracker on the network. How would we even begin to single out one person?"

He had a point, but I wasn't going to give in that easily. If they were my only option, then I needed to make sure it was a good one.

He turned to his monitor and typed a few things into the computer. A graph with two lines, one red and one blue, popped up. "This is a normal tracker." He pointed to the red line. "And this blue line is yours. See how it's higher than the regular line?"

I nodded, unsure what else to say.

"Your tracker is the only one that operates at this frequency."

"So you could single me out if you wanted to."

His expression jerked like I'd just slapped him in the face. But before I could push further, he said, "Your frequency is so infinitesimally different that you would have to know what you were looking for to see it."

"And the Ghosts do?"

"We do. We knew of an anomaly out there, someone whose tracker would act differently. And you're that someone."

"Lucky me."

The corner of his mouth curved upward. "I wish I had half

75

your luck."

"You can have all of it. As soon as I figure out how to get this thing out of my head. Then maybe everyone will leave me alone."

"It's not that simple."

"No?" But even as I said it, I knew he was right, at least about the simplicity of the situation. "How did this happen?"

"I'm not entirely sure, but it's clear that someone altered your signal to allow for loopholes. Your tracker has a function no other trackers have."

"Like what?"

"You can mask your normal tracker functions. And you've figured out how to control it."

"I accidentally shut it off a couple times. That's hardly controlling it." *Great.* He thought I was some savior, but really, I was just some stupid kid trying to do the one thing my dad had taught me.

"No, I don't think that's what happened. Your tracker is still on, but that slightly different frequency is keeping it hidden from the authorities."

"How do I know that image is real?" He was sounding crazier by the minute, and I wouldn't let him drag me down that rabbit hole so easily.

"No amount of scanning on my end is going to convince you, so believe what you like." He turned back to his computer. "But I have better things to do than forge a tracker signal."

"So no matter how accidental, I did this?" When he nodded, chills raced through my body, and my head spun with confusion. Unless he was a world-renowned poker player, he was dead serious. There was no faking that face. And yet despite pieces ringing true, I was still missing part of the bigger picture. "But how? I didn't even know I did it the first time."

"That's what we hope to learn. There's a weakness in the tracker network, and you're going to help us find it." He leaned against the desk, crossed his arms over his chest, and tossed his hair out of his eyes with a flick of his head.

"Hold on a sec." I jabbed my finger into the air, wishing it were Bailen's chest I was prodding. Now he was toying with me. The truth churned like a muddy watercolor. "You want to use me in your war against the tracker network?"

"Well, to put it bluntly, yes."

"You're insane. You know they'll find me when my tracker resets." I didn't want another run-in with the authorities, but he didn't know that.

"Your tracker isn't going to reset. It's operating on a whole new level. A level we hope to exploit."

"I don't believe you." I blinked, trying to open a mental pad. Nothing happened. I pushed thought after thought after thought onto the network, but it didn't respond. Bailen tilted his head to the side with a slight smile as I repeatedly tried to access my tracker. Without it, the authorities would never find me. There were definite advantages to that, but it also meant no one else could find me, either. Thoughts of my family and friends swirled through my head. Dad would love it. I wished he were here—any of my family or friends, really. But I knew deep down whom I needed most. I collapsed into the hold of the muscular guy. He loosened his grip, and I fell to my knees.

"I'll fix it." The phrase came out as a hoarse whisper. It was the least accurate thing I'd said all week. I had no idea how to fix my tracker. I wasn't sure anyone did.

"Even if you could figure out how to override the new

frequency, which I wouldn't recommend, your tracker's main functions may not work as originally intended. We have no idea what toying with that glitch might do to your head."

"You're just trying to scare me."

"You're scary enough on your own with all that crazy blinking and twitching."

I stopped and attempted not to blink like I'd entered into an eternal staring contest. Maybe the safety of the overbearing authorities was better than joining a room full of outdated, techy terrorists, most of whom were around my age. Were these really my only options?

I let out a long breath. "Why should I help you?" I didn't really want to know the answer to that question, but maybe if I played along, I'd find a better way out than becoming a Ghost lab rat.

Bailen knelt by me so he was eye level. His brilliant green eyes softened, and his gaze lingered a second longer than expected before dropping to the floor. "If you don't, the authorities win. This tech will continue to control our lives. Taking away more and more liberties until we're prisoners of this world and everything in it."

"How do you know that?"

"Because we already *are* prisoners. Most people just don't know it yet."

I blinked, unable to speak. The tracker network was hardly a prison. It was knowledge. It was an instant worldwide connection. It was freeing.

"There are a billion new laws related to tracker technology. The authorities rule with an iron fist, above the law, and don't give a crap about anyone." He waved his arms, indicating the people around the room watching us, who nodded in agreement. "They just want the damn tech to work, to keep us passive. If that's not prison, I don't know what is."

"Last time I checked, access to unlimited knowledge was the opposite of prison." The part of me desperate to grasp on to the familiar piece of my life refused to give in. If anything, the hive was a prison, no windows, one exit, and no options.

"Unlimited knowledge? Is that what you call a heavily monitored network and blocked searches?"

I clamped my mouth shut, a good comeback just out of reach. I knew the frustration of blocked searches all too well. "What about the lack of crime?"

"That world is a myth. No one is perfect. We proved that yesterday."

"You're taking credit for that? Someone died!"

"No, I'm not. It's just…"

Maybe I was getting to him. Maybe I'd get the help I needed on my terms.

Before I could fire back again, Bailen said, "Do you think you can take one step without the authorities knowing where you are? Whom you're with? What you're doing?"

"That's common knowledge."

"You want common knowledge? The authorities, our government, Global Tracking Systems—they all work so closely together."

"So what's your point?"

"The lines are blurred."

He could say that again. Everything was blurry mess. But it wasn't anything the world didn't already know.

"They gave everyone this present but refuse to let anyone

79

open it to see what's inside. There's a reason they don't tell people about the history of this tech or what it's potentially capable of."

"We all know the benefits outweigh the bad stuff." I spewed the lines they'd always told us in school like a reflex. I'd been spoon-fed all the wonderful things about trackers my whole life. And there was no denying parts of it were great. But in the last few days alone, between the restricted access, the annoying blinking lights, and the invasion of privacy, I had to wonder if it was worth it. But it was my life. I didn't know the world any other way. If the tracker network was gone, how would I talk to my friends? Try to keep in contact with Jake?

"Benefits? They give you a shiny picture about infinite knowledge, health monitoring, and protection. But if you stop for one minute and consider the possibilities, it's downright terrifying."

"Terrifying how?" I couldn't stop myself.

"Global Tracking Systems put a chip in your brain. Your brain! The center that controls every function in your body. They took away a piece of your free will. One slip, one malfunction, you're done. That's a risk we should have never been asked to take. And don't even get me started on tracker diagnostics."

His words pounded into me. Some of what he was saying rang true. The authorities had hurt me, but there were rules around trackers for a reason. The world was more connected with trackers in it.

"Let's say that I believe you." I didn't know what I believed anymore, but I humored the guy. "How is your messing with my tracker any different than what the authorities have already done?"

"Human decency. We aren't in this for the tech. We want to protect people. From the tech, from the authorities, and from themselves. Give the world their free will back, return them their privacy."

"And if I help you, you'll protect me from the authorities?"

"With everything we have."

Hiding from the authorities was one thing, but it was only a matter of time before they caught up to me with their unlimited resources. Unless no one knew where I was. And even then, trusting the Ghosts was a huge risk.

He could still be jerking me around. "If I say *yes*, I can't go home, can I?" I doubted they would let me go home if I said no, but I had to ask.

He shook his head. "If you go back, the authorities will experiment on you and try to figure out what happened. If you're lucky, they'll replace your tracker and let you go on with your life. But I'm guessing they'd rather throw you in lockup and study your chip, make you disappear. You're too big of a threat to them."

He was right. My options sucked. Never go home or go home and let them turn my brains to mush. Jake's refusal to answer messages was bad enough. But my parents, my friends, Harlow—they'd all try to cover for me if I went home. I couldn't let them risk their lives. But if I stayed here, it was only a matter of time before these goons were lobotomizing me as well. I couldn't trust the Ghosts. Both options led to torture if I was lucky. And if I wasn't? I couldn't face that realization.

The room spun like a tornado. I gasped for air. I heaved, but only a dry cough erupted. I swayed as the room closed in around me.

"Kai." The distant voice sounded familiar, but the rest of the sentence evaporated into the fog, engulfing me. It was the last thing I heard before everything went black.

Nine

I awoke in a darkened room. The only furniture beside the bed was a dilapidated dresser with an empty slot for a drawer, a chipped wooden table with a single lamp, and a gray folding chair. I blinked, trying to access the tracker clock—nothing. I tried again.

Emptiness.

My head was empty.

When I rolled over and saw the concrete wall next to the bed, my Ghost encounter came rushing back. Was I their prisoner?

I wasn't sure I wanted to help them, but I didn't have a choice. Even if I snuck away, I couldn't hide from the authorities without help. At least the Ghosts would feed me and put a roof over my head. They wouldn't let the key to their whole plan die. I had a headache just thinking about it.

After a few ragged breaths, I wished for something familiar. I didn't get to say goodbye to anyone.

A void formed in my mind, ripping through the place where

those I loved resided. Lydia was my sounding board, Harlow always knew how to comfort me, Mom made me smile, and Dad could run circles around these primitive techies.

I'd give my left arm to get my hands on a scrap of paper and some charcoal. I could draw them before they faded from memory. But finding that was as likely as regaining access to the network. All I wanted was five seconds on the tracker network to watch my videos and see my pictures. But my bum tracker was what had gotten me into a giant mess in the first place. Funny how you take something for granted for so long, and you don't really appreciate it until it's gone.

I sat up and pushed my bare feet to the rough, concrete floor. I still wore the T-shirt and jeans I'd arrived in. My body ached with exhaustion and was slimy from a lack of shower. At least they hadn't violated my privacy. I found my tennis shoes in the corner by the only door to the room. I pressed my ear to the cold, steel door, straining to hear.

Silence.

Nothing was getting through that.

I pulled the lever and it jerked to the left with a metallic shriek. *Great. I'm sure the whole world heard that.* The door lurched open a few inches with a clang. I peered out the crack at a guy wearing torn jeans and a white T-shirt. He slouched in a chair next to the door. His scraggly blond hair fell over his cheeks, covering his eyes. When he lifted his head, I gasped. I covered my gaping mouth to avoid drawing attention.

What kind of sick mind games were the Ghosts playing?

My heart exploded into a spastic rhythm. My breath caught in my chest. Not ready to find out what kind of torture this might be, I scrambled to slam the door. How could they dangle him in front on me?

Jake.

The one thing I needed most for so long staring back at me. The impossibility was too convenient, and yet perfect all at once.

He shot up from the chair and reached for the door but screamed as his fingers crunched between the door and the frame. I backed away and fell onto the bed, trembling. My memory instantly transported back to one of our worst fights as kids that had ended with his fingers smashed in a closing door. But the memories weren't the same as the video recall on my tracker. And I wasn't sure if I should be shutting him out or letting him in.

The door flew open. The dirt smudges on Jake's wrinkled T-shirt stood out as he stomped across the room, yanked the chair away from the table, and dropped into it backward. His stalking angry routine was the same, but his longer hair and thinner frame were different. He massaged his fingers, glaring at me. I stared back, unblinking. He was waiting for me to speak first. While I wasn't content to sit in silence forever, I couldn't let him win, either. It was good to see him, but the hurt of him ignoring me was like being suffocated.

Finally, he broke. "Kai, talk to me."

I jerked at my nickname. For the first time, it sounded awkward coming from his lips. I shook my head and started pulling fuzz balls off the blanket on the bed. After so much time, I didn't know what to say to him.

He stood from the chair and sat on the far side of the bed. "You and I both know you can't stay mad at me forever."

Funny, he didn't know how stubborn I'd gotten since he'd left, since he'd stopped answering my messages.

Out of the corner of my eye, I saw a devilish half-smile cross his face. "Don't make me resort to the ketchup joke."

A snort escaped before I could stop it. Something about that stupid joke got me every time. I studied him. His pale blue eyes were full of the same love and kindness they'd always held. He didn't look like a prisoner, but his mere presence set off waves of confusion in my mind. How had he ended up here?

Despite my confusion, a smile tugged at my lips. I'd missed him. He was the one person I wanted more than anyone right now. The one person I needed when shit hit the fan. He was my comfort zone.

If he was here, then things were far more complicated than I'd imagined. "What are you doing here?"

"I could ask you the same question, but I already know the answer."

"You haven't returned any of my messages. You've ignored me for months. What kind of mess are you in?" The real question I wanted to ask was what kind of mess had I gotten myself into?

"They need me." He inched closer. "And we need you."

"We? So that's it? You're one of them?"

His single nod sent ripples of anger through me that left me seeing red. After everything we'd been through together, he was ready to throw it all away.

"How could you do this to me?" I asked. "You've lied about everything."

"Just give them a chance."

"A chance?" He had to be kidding. This wasn't a ball toss at a carnival. "You want me to betray everything I've ever known?" But I didn't need an answer from him. He'd already betrayed our former life. Not only had he ignored me, but he'd joined the Ghosts.

"You already have just by being here." His tone had a hard edge.

He was trying to drag me down with him. "I didn't have a choice. They were going to turn me into a lab rat if I stayed. You have no idea what they did to me." I shook as I tried to stave off the painful memories of the needles and the probe. At a time I needed him most, he hadn't been there. And the painful realization was written all over his face. Maybe I hadn't lost him.

Jake moved closer, pulling me into a hug.

My muscles eased, but I drew away. "How I can trust you? Trust them?" He was a terrorist.

How could the one person I needed most be a terrorist?

He laughed—not his usual carefree laugh, but a deep, menacing one. I shivered.

"You've questioned me your whole life," he said, "but you've always loved me. Isn't that enough?"

"No. I refuse to be the Ghosts' guinea pig."

"You wouldn't be a guinea pig."

"Then help me understand why I should help them."

He opened and closed his mouth three times, then he shook his head. It was like he wanted to tell me something but couldn't find the words. Just like that note. He never seemed short on words when he was writing, and yet here we were.

"Fine. If you can't tell me why I should be here, then tell me how you decided it was the right place for you?"

His gaze dropped to the floor. I prepared myself for the lie about to slip from his lips, but when he lifted his head, tears welled and were seconds from spilling down his face. I wanted to reach out my hand, but I wrung my fingers in my lap instead, still unsure what to make of Jake's decision.

"After the accident, I lost my best friend. It changed my priorities."

Of course he meant the motorbike accident. The one that had prevented me from ever getting on a bike. Mom and Dad never tired of reminding me. Everything always went back to the accident with Jake. It was his go-to excuse. But it was also why we'd gotten so close. Despite everything, I wasn't going to let him get away with that excuse. Not like Mom and Dad did. "Denny's in a coma. He's not dead."

"He might as well be." Jake's mouth snapped shut, as if he hadn't meant for that to slip out. He rubbed his face in his hands. "I can talk to him, but he can't respond. It's not the same thing as having him here."

The words stung, as if our bond was second to his with Denny's, like I'd been a place holder all that time. "But why the Ghosts? What do they have to do with accident? How does losing Denny lead to you thinking life as a terrorist is the path forward?"

"I found something here. Something I lost when Denny…"

I let the silence persist because it helped mend that void, even if it never fully healed. When it was clear he wasn't going to finish his sentence, I said, "So that's it? You found something that was missing? That's not a lot for me to go on." I sighed, my brain racing to understand, but the answer kept slipping from my grasp. "What happened to our unstoppable duo? Conquering the world together. Never abandoning each other." He'd promised we'd always be there for each other. But breaking promises was his new default. "What part of becoming a terrorist seemed like a good idea?"

He flinched when I'd said the word *terrorist* again. Maybe I was getting to him. Maybe I could make him remember what we'd done for each other.

"Denny and I were supposed to go to college together, but when it was clear he wasn't going with me, I couldn't face it alone."

"So you didn't go to college at all? You just went off the deep end?" I let out a long breath. "Does Dad know about this?"

Jake froze, like I'd just caught him doing something more illegal than joining the Ghosts.

"So Dad doesn't know. Got it." There was something I was missing. A piece of the puzzle that that was preventing me from seeing the whole picture. I needed a new tactic if I was going to get any answers.

"Why should I want to help them?"

"Because there's something you don't know about the accident."

I shifted on the bed. Now we were getting somewhere. "What?"

"It was the authorities' fault."

"What do you mean? They said you were inexperienced new drivers without proper training on flying motorbikes. No licenses. It was an accident."

Jake's gaze slowly moved to meet mine, like he was taking in every word I said. He shook his head once, then a single tear dripped down his cheek.

As mad as I was at him, I squeezed his pinky. Our little symbol to each other that we were listening, that we were here for each other.

"I started it." He opened his mouth, but no words came out.

"I don't understand."

"It was so stupid." He put his hand over mine and squeezed.

"We were taunting the authorities. Flying by the station and revving the engines on the bikes so they would rumble the windows. Denny and I were competing to see who could get the closest to the window. I dared him to get the head authority to spill his coffee." Jake sucked in a breath and let out a half-laugh. "The guy spilled his coffee, but it wasn't because of Denny's engine. At least not directly."

"So what happened?"

"Denny shot past the window, only he revved the engine so loud and screeched the tires against the side of the building at such a high pitch, it shattered the glass window."

"No, Denny lost control of the bike and shattered the window when he crashed into it." At least that was the story I'd been told every time I'd asked if I could get on a flying motorbike.

Jake shook his head.

"They found him unconscious in the station." I kept telling the story as if Jake hadn't gotten it right. As if he hadn't been there and didn't know what had happened.

Jake grabbed his hair and pulled, as if that would release the pent-up frustration. "That's what the authorities said happened. But Denny recovered from the shattering glass and came around for another pass. As he did, the head authority took control of Denny's tracker and froze him. The bike's momentum forced him to crash through the adjacent window into the station, making it seem like he'd lost control of the bike. When Denny landed, his helmet flew off and his head slammed into the wall. He never got up."

My heart sped up. That couldn't be real. We all knew the authorities pushed the boundaries, but they never outright abused their power. Not like that. "Why didn't you say anything?"

"I wanted to. So many times. But who was going to believe a teenager? Especially one without a license for a crotchrocket. One that was out way after curfew. And one that had contributed to destruction of property. The authorities cut me a deal before Mom and Dad picked me up. They agreed not to press charges if I kept my mouth shut. So I did."

"The authorities just got away with putting Denny in a coma?"

"That's exactly why I'm here." A smile tugged at his lips. I knew it well. That was the devious, I'm-up-to-something expression. The smile he used to give me when he lied to our parents after taking me for ice cream right before dinner. But it held a slight difference now. The smile he wore was so tainted with darkness, it smelled of revenge.

I pulled my knees up to my chest. None of it made sense. My head was exploding. Everything I'd thought I'd known about the accident, my brother, and about what had happened to Denny had been a lie. Even if Jake and Denny were complete idiots, the authorities had crossed a line. One that couldn't be uncrossed.

I'd watched Lydia and her parents suffer through Denny not waking up. It had been hell on all of them, Jake included. And it had been completely avoidable. It was a gross abuse of power. How many other times had the authorities abused their privilege? They had certainly walked a fine line when they'd run me through tracker diagnostics.

"Please tell me Denny was the only incident."

Jake stared ahead like he was playing the scene over and over again on the tracker network, then shook his head a single time.

"How many?"

He remained silent as if lost in thought.

"How many?" The exact number seemed important, even if it wasn't. Once or countless times, it didn't matter. No one should have the power to ruin someone else's life.

"Hundreds, maybe thousands, of others. There's no way to know for sure. We don't have a ton of proof. It's our word against theirs."

Part of me wanted to fight Jake, but after seeing the distant look on his face and the tears, I knew the accident had been eating away at him for a long time. I didn't know how he'd lived with such a massive secret for so long.

His dark, discarded poetry and unfinished note made perfect sense. He hadn't been living with it; it'd been eating away at him. And he'd hidden it from me, not let me help him. Shielded me. I squeezed his pinky.

"If the authorities are abusing their power, then why not fight the legislation, or better yet, get the bad ones fired?"

"Why should the authorities even have that power to begin with? Why should anyone have that kind of power? The power to control, the power to spy on others, the power to get away with it under the law?"

"Laws can be changed."

"Perhaps over time. But how many more people have to die or get seriously hurt before these things stop happening? There's this pretty picture of how a tracker is supposed to work, and it sounds great, but when you see how it's actually being maintained, how it actually executes in the world, the risks far outweigh the benefits. This tech is not worth losing what makes us human."

Now he was sounding like Bailen. Was the whole Ghost

hideout brainwashed? "What they did to Denny was unforgiveable. But this all sounds crazy."

"That's exactly it. The authorities are crazy. Crazy drunk on power. And I hate to think what they will do to you knowing that your tracker doesn't follow their rules. They won't hesitate to bend the rules when it comes to you. I'm afraid for you, Kai."

My body shook. I hated him for making me come to terms with it. Part of me didn't want him to make sense, but he did. The authorities had nearly hauled me off twice. They'd left me with a scar I could never mend. They prevented my family from observing a tech-free Shabbat, our ability to be Jewish at our very core. And worst of all, if they had messed up my hard reset, my brain could have been turned to goo.

"The way I see it, you have two options. One, go back into the world and let the authorities show you how little they care about their protocol." He paused, as if giving me time to think.

And in that short span my mind overloaded. The authorities left a trail of pain and torture wherever they went. They ruled by fear. And everything that seemed so great about trackers was carefully wrapped in laws that were only there to keep everyone in line. Perfect obedient minions, imprisoned to the tech. Our perfect little world wasn't so perfect after all. It was a concrete, windowless cell.

And in the whole world, the only people who had come to terms with it were the Ghosts.

"What's my other option?" Although I knew, I didn't want hear it. Because if the words were out in the open, then I'd be forced to face the truth.

"Fight them with everything you have. Help us get the ammo to bring down this tech and destroy everyone who abuses its power. Because they won't stop coming after you until you're dead."

Dead.

That word was a punch right to my gut.

He was right. About all of it. If they could put Denny in a coma and silence Jake, how long would it be before they killed me and made it look like an accident? Over something I had no control over. That hardly seemed fair. And yet I knew it was true in my core.

"I miss home." I didn't even know why I said it. It didn't make sense to miss home anymore. Even if I went home to Mom and Dad, they couldn't protect me from the authorities. At least if I stayed here, I had Jake. And in a room that felt like I had nothing, having Jake back meant everything.

"This could be your home, if you let it." He put his hand on my shoulder. "And if you help us, you can have your life back—or whatever life you choose—when this is all over."

His unsaid words spoke louder, though. We had to survive the hoard of authorities who were hunting us first. And then we'd make them pay for what they'd done.

But none of it mattered because he pouted at me—the same expression that had always managed to sucker me into some crazy scheme when we'd been younger. Something that had ultimately led to our best adventures. Despite my life spiraling out of control, he anchored me to reality, making things feel almost normal. Almost.

I threw my arms around him. He squeezed me so tightly, I struggled to catch my breath. *Who needs air?* "I've missed you so much."

"I missed you, too."

I trembled in his arms. I didn't have any answers, but at least there was some peace of mind in his comfort. My safe space.

When my breathing calmed, he said, "And in case you've been wondering, I wasn't ignoring you. I've just been a little... incommunicado."

I pulled away from our embrace and smacked him playfully on the arm. "Joining a terrorist group is no excuse for not calling."

"Well, do you see any carrier pigeons around here?"

"Excuses, excuses." And just like that, we were back to our old carefree selves. It was the thing I loved most about Jake. We had terrible fights sometimes, but we always snapped back to normal as quick as a rubber band.

We both laughed like we were little kids with no worries in the world. When we stopped, his lips pulled tight. "We really need you, Kai. The world is only going to get more twisted and painful. You can help us stop the pain trackers have caused. Help us make things right."

The blanket fuzz pile I'd created was much larger than I'd expected. "I know," I whispered.

"Does this mean you'll help?"

All of Bailen and Jake's arguments swirled in my head, followed by the horrible torture I'd been through. I thought of my friends. Harlow had experienced painful tests. What if they did the same to Lydia, or Mom, or Dad, or anyone else? I couldn't let the authorities harm the people I loved, not in the way they'd hurt Denny. They'd taken so much. I wouldn't let them have more.

The decision that should have been difficult suddenly became simple. It was *Jake* asking, after all. I trusted him with my life.

And if I wanted to live, I had to stay with the Ghosts, fight with them. At least now, I understood why. My path was with the Ghosts. With Jake.

"Dad's going to kill us."

He laughed, his carefree usual laugh. "Some things never change."

Ten

I didn't know how much time passed, but Jake and I quickly fell back into our old routine of talking over each other. Even though the days ran together, on Friday night he brought candles, wine, and challah so we could celebrate Shabbat. We lit that candles and said all the blessings. And for the first time, it was quiet, no tracker messages, no interruptions—just the two of us sharing stories. On Saturday night, we did a short Havdalah service. I didn't know where he'd managed to find a braided candle, but it was almost like we were home. Almost like he'd never left.

The lack of all the usual distractions made things better than I ever could have imagined. It lifted a huge weight off me to have Jake nearby. Now that I had him back, things started to make sense again. But we'd lost so much time. I was thankful for the few days we'd gotten back.

Unfortunately, his run-ins with the authorities not only rivaled mine but far exceeded them. His experiences only added to the horrors I'd experienced and cemented my decision to stay. Hopping on the back of the bike with Peyton may not have been such a giant mistake, after all—especially if it had brought Jake and me back together. It was easier to swallow the pain knowing I hadn't been the only one to experience it.

"So, what now?" I kept my voice lighthearted but secretly shuddered at the possibility of them cutting into my head to remove my tracker. Even after all of Jake's stories about the Ghosts, my nerves were still on edge.

"Funny you should ask. Bailen wanted to check your tracker readings and run some diagnostics."

I cringed, knowing that the brother-sister time couldn't last forever. I was with the Ghosts for a reason. "No more tests."

He furrowed his brow as if saddened I'd been so hurt. "Oh, Kai, no. Not that kind of test. This is different. It won't hurt a bit."

"Are you sure?"

"Positive. He's done similar tests on all of us. The authorities' methods aren't the only way. Unfortunately, their fear tactics have worked on you." He blinked a second longer than normal. The fear tactics had worked on him as well. But he'd never admit it. I squeezed his pinky, and we shared a moment of understanding and solidarity. "The information we learn from your tracker could show us how to outsmart Global Tracking Systems."

"Promise you'll stay with me?"

"Of course. There's nowhere else I'd rather be." He stood up, squeezing my hand back. "I'm glad you're here."

"Me too." I'd be lost or lobotomized by now if it weren't for Jake and the Ghosts.

He pulled me from the bed and led me down the hall to the large computer room I'd visited the night I'd arrived. Not much had changed, but the vibe was completely different. The machines whirled and hummed around me, but no one stared.

Bailen turned from his monitors. "Ah, Kaya. Ready to cooperate, I see."

"Who said anything about that?" I crossed my arms for added effect.

Bailen's smile faded like a kid who'd just lost his favorite toy.

Jake nudged me with his elbow then turned to Bailen. "She's got some demands before we finalize our arrangement." Jake turned his back on Bailen and winked at me.

And just like that, we were back to our old antics. Jake would play along while I pulled a fast one on Bailen.

"Wha—?" Bailen swallowed and tried again. "Jake, we don't exactly have a lot of capital here. What kind of things is she demanding?"

It was hard to tell in the light, but there may have been sweat beading up on Bailen's forehead.

I choked down a laugh and tried to keep a straight face. "My brother doesn't speak for me. You'd do well to get that straight right now."

Bailen turned to me. "Okay, what can I do for you?"

"I want a room with a view, for starters." I rubbed my nose to block the smile exploding across my face.

Jake stepped closer to Bailen. "You heard the girl. Knock a wall down if you have to."

Bailen's gaze darted between me and Jake as if he wasn't sure if the whole exchange was actually happening. "You know we're underground, right?"

"That's a whole lot of not my problem," Jake said with a completely straight face.

I didn't know how he did it, but the laughter burst from my mouth before I could control it. "Sorry," I spit out between giggles.

"I leave for a few months and you lose your edge. You're out of practice." Jake cracked a smile at me.

Bailen's gaze continued to dart, but his body relaxed. "Real funny."

"You should have seen your face." Jake slapped him on the back like he used to do with Denny when he'd pulled one over on him—proving Jake had come to respect Bailen.

"Can we get back to business?" Bailen rubbed his palms together. "I'm excited to see what's under her hood."

"My *hood*? I'm not a car," I said.

He looked me up and down. "No, but I can't wait to inspect—"

"Back off, killer. That's my sister." Jake grabbed Bailen's T-shirt and shoved him against the table.

"Look, dude, I just meant I wanted to check out her tracker, that's all," Bailen said.

Jake lunged at him with a grunt but stopped short of punching him. Bailen's eyes bugged out as he leaned away. "Watch yourself." He stepped back and gave me another smirk.

"Relax! I'm just trying to do my job," Bailen said. "We get one tiny break, and everyone goes on high alert."

I stifled another laugh. I loved Jake's protective-big-brother routine. It was fun to watch guys squirm. The first time Harlow had taken me out, I'd thought Jake was going to make him wet his pants. He'd threatened to make Harlow's life hell if he wasn't a perfect gentleman. And Harlow had been ever since. Sometimes I wondered if that was the only reason Harlow was always a perfect gentleman to me, but such as ass with his friends.

Bailen sidestepped Jake and turned to his computer. Several black windows with green text popped up. Bar graphs shifted up and down. "Everything seems to be in order. I'm ready for you, Kaya."

I tensed. *I can do this... I think.*

"Have a seat." He pointed over the monitors to a padded lounger. His attention briefly flicked to Jake, whose gaze followed him like a tracking beam. Bailen moved around the table toward the chair. I slid into the lounger. It hummed as the upper half reclined until I was almost lying down.

Bailen pulled three circular discs out of his pocket and peeled off the paper backing. He placed one on each of my temples, and the last at the base of my neck below my hairline. The cold surface sent shivers through me.

He strung wires over me that weighed me down and shoved me deeper into the chair. A large group, not much older than me, crowded around the table and watched like I was a viral vid on the network. A few folks as old as my parents leaned around their monitors but didn't gather like the younger Ghosts.

Peyton pushed through the crowd and plopped down in Bailen's chair behind the monitors. I craned in the chair to see what she was up to.

"Come to watch the mastermind at work?" Bailen asked.

"Nope. I refuse to miss a potential opportunity to gloat."

"What is this, Pick on Bailen Day?"

Peyton smirked at Jake, like she was in on the joke.

"So this is a regular occurrence with Bailen?" I asked.

"I'll never tell." But Jake nodded ever-so-slightly—his silent code to me that he'd been practicing the fine art of screwing with people even though I was rusty.

Peyton leaned back in the chair with a devious expression and then tapped on the keyboard next to the computer attached directly to me.

Bailen screeched and ran to his desk. "Stop it. You're ruining my settings."

Seriously? It wasn't a joke. That stuff was about to scan my brain. There was a time and place to mess with people, and while I was hooked up to a ton of equipment wasn't it. Jake certainly took things too far sometimes, but now I'd have to keep an eye on Peyton too.

Bailen shoved her out of the chair. "Go stand over there where you won't damage anything. You wouldn't want to break a nail."

"The only thing I'm going to break is you." She took a few steps to the side, crossing her arms.

Bailen sat in his chair, pounding on the keyboard. "Almost there," he muttered in a trance-like state.

Jake pulled up a chair on my right, grabbed my pinky, and squeezed. "See? Nothing to worry about."

"Just do something to make me laugh," I whispered so only he could hear.

"Ketchup."

I snorted, then watched Bailen examine his monitors.

"You ready?" he called from behind the desk.

I sucked in a breath and nodded, too afraid to talk. Jake patted our clasped hands. There was no way I'd be doing anything without him.

Bailen hit a single key. The discs hummed to life, vibrating my head. My teeth chattered to the rhythmic hum, but it didn't hurt. A high-pitched whine buzzed in my ears—a minor annoyance. Hushed whispers of the crowd were drowned out by the tone in my ears. I closed my eyes and breathed in slow and deep, falling into a daze. The cushy chair pulled me in. I wiggled, fighting the wave of exhaustion. When the whine and vibration stopped, I opened my eyes.

Without moving my head, I focused on Bailen. His fingers flew over the keyboard while he fixated on the monitors. The computers beeped rapidly.

That couldn't be good.

The crowd glanced between me and the monitors, confirming my worst suspicions. I had a faulty tracker, a stick of dynamite in my brain with an unknown length of fuse. It was a realization that should have terrified me, and yet the finality seemed infinitely better than the authorities' tracker diagnostics. A broken tracker presented possibilities I'd never thought possible.

"Kai." Jake's quiet tone drew my attention. "Don't think about them. It's just you and me. Nothing to worry about."

He was right. It was the two of us. That was all I needed.

When the keys stopped their rhythmic clicking, Bailen peered over the screens. "The data is still uploading, but I think we got what we need. If not, we can get more later." He slid around the desk and began unwinding the massive tangle of wires. Even though the scan was harmless, I took a deep breath, relieved it was over. I didn't have any answers yet, but I no longer had the uncontrollable urge to find them. Where the authorities created problems, the Ghosts were working toward solutions. What these tests might show was potential knowledge the network could never give me.

Jake stood up and released my pinky. "All right, show's over." He pushed his arms out, shooing away the crowd of people. One more thing to add to my growing list of reasons why I couldn't be here without Jake. He knew exactly what I needed without asking.

Everyone cleared the area, whispering as they went—only Jake, Bailen, and Peyton remained. I sat up in the chair, letting my legs dangle over the side. The wires draped over me like a heavy blanket.

"Wait, Kaya. Stop moving." Bailen waved his arms frantically then knocked me back into the chair with a surprising jolt. "You're going to tangle the wires."

"Oh, sorry." As he untangled the wires at my feet, I sucked in a deep breath that seemed to last forever.

"Now you can sit up," he said, removing the final one.

I exhaled, thankful that the hard part was done. "What about these?" I pointed to the disks still stuck to my skin.

"Let me get those." He moved in so close, his warm breath beat on my cheek. I pressed into the chair, trying to put some space between us before my face erupted with color. He peeled them away from my skin, like a Band-Aid.

Clutching the tender spot on my temple, I noted Jake's concerned-big-brother expression. "Are you going to be okay? I have some work to take care of, but if you need me, I can stay."

"I'll be fine. Go take care of your stuff."

"You sure?" He eyed Bailen, who stood by Peyton behind the monitors.

"Yeah. I'm fine. Really."

Jake tilted his head ever-so slightly, silently asking if I was afraid to say I was scared out loud.

I was thankful for the extra out but waved him off. "I want to see what they learned from my tracker. Besides, we need Bailen in one piece… for now at least."

His lips curled into a half-smile, indicating he had ideas stewing on how next to catch Bailen in a gullible moment. "Okay. I'll catch up with you later." With a quick wink, he left me alone with Bailen and Peyton.

I hopped off the chair and joined Bailen in front of the screens.

"I can't believe there're two of you," he muttered under his breath.

"What was that?" I didn't try to hide the smile forming.

He grit his teeth. "Nothing."

Bailen returned his attention to two monitors containing multiple black windows. Each one had scrolling green text, while a few others had maps of the city with numerous blinking red dots.

"So what'd you find out?" I asked.

"Unfortunately, nothing yet. It's going to take a while for the data to process. We might get a preliminary view in a few minutes." Bailen pointed to the screen with the black windows.

"What's the rest of this stuff?" I asked, indicating the four large monitors with the map and blinking dots.

"That is TROGS."

"Oh, here we go." Peyton rolled her eyes. "Kaya, I suggest you brace yourself."

"For what? I don't know what a TROGS is."

Bailen rubbed his hands together in excitement and plopped in the chair. "Of course you don't. It's a secret. But one day, everyone will know who is responsible for this fabulous tech."

"Oh, please. We'd be in serious trouble if the authorities found out about TROGS. But if it makes you feel better, I'll make you a trophy out of cable ties."

"Whatever, Pey. You're just jealous you aren't going to get any of the glory."

"Ha! Don't make me gag. Then again, the result of that might be more interesting than TROGS."

"Not even close. But it would make you more entertaining."

"You wish you knew the meaning of that word."

"At least I know what a dictionary is."

It was like a ping pong match as they hurled insults at increasing intensity. When the insults reached lightning speed, I yelled, "Hold on a sec."

They both stopped mid-sentence.

"Who cares who invented it? What the heck is it?"

"This is important," Bailen said with a hurt expression. "We should all care about it."

He opened his mouth to continue, but I cut him off. "If it's so important, then you can explain it."

Peyton choked down a laugh. "She has a point."

"Fine, we'll settle this later." His face lit up as he focused on the monitors. "TROGS is an acronym standing for Tracker Redirecting Off-Grid Ssystem."

I blinked, trying to process the words.

"It's phase one of our plans. All of the Ghosts are what we call off-grid. It's how we hide in plain sight." He paused. "Well, for our purposes, anyway. The authorities see something else entirely."

"Why build all this? Couldn't you just use a radio wave

generator?" I asked.

"While a radio wave generator can block the signal, which is part of TROGS, there's nothing to stop the authorities from being alerted due to the tracker signal being interrupted. We needed something to keep the authorities off our backs."

"So you tricked them? How?" After everything the authorities had put me through, raising a little hell for them was something I could get behind. It was exciting to think that we didn't just have to accept the pain because that was how things were. There was another way.

The right side of his mouth pulled up into a devious half-grin. "The tracker, under normal circumstances, outputs a signal anyone can track, right?"

"Yeah, that's common knowledge."

"I hijacked the signal and told it to report what I want the authorities to see." I scrunched my nose, and he must have picked up on my confusion. "Take me, for example." He pointed to a blinking dot on a map display on one of the monitors. "Right now, if the authorities were to ping my chip, they'd see I was at the gym." He pointed to another blinking dot. "And Peyton is at the salon getting her hair done."

"Fat chance." Peyton whacked Bailen on the head before swiping an apple off the desk. "I wouldn't be caught dead in a salon. Your snazzy code is just a tad unrealistic." She repeatedly tossed the apple in the air and caught it. "And I hope you aren't boring her with all your techno nerd babble."

I couldn't help but smile. Bailen had some serious genius level intelligence. He'd taken the authorities' tech and had thrown it back in their faces. It sounded a little like something Dad might do—find a way to work the system to his advantage while staying within the laws. Of course, if Bailen got caught, he'd be executed for treason.

"No," I said. "I find it fascinating."

"*Right*," spat Peyton. "There is absolutely nothing fascinating about my brother."

"Brother?"

She rolled her eyes and continued tossing the apple. Bailen reached for it midair, but she beat him to it. Then, as if to rub it in, she leaned close to his face and took a giant bite out of it.

"Hey, that was mine," he said with a slight whine.

"Not anymore." She took another large bite, sidestepping his second attempt to swipe the piece of fruit.

"But—"

"I'm sorry, were you saying something important?" She waved the apple in his face but yanked it away as he made another grab for it.

"If I'm boring you so much, why don't you leave? No one is forcing you to stay."

"Good point." She bent over him, took one more giant bite from the apple then, jogged from the room.

Stifling a laugh, I asked, "You going to let her get away with that?"

He shrugged. "It's not worth fighting over."

"But if you keep letting her get away with stuff…"

"Yeah, yeah, I know. You give a girl an edge, she'll run away with it, but give her a rocket, she'll fly to the moon."

"Exactly. At least you know it."

The poor guy had just been outplayed again. No wonder he was sick of Jake's antics.

"When you grow up with a twin like Peyton, you have to

pick your battles wisely. She's stubborn as hell."

"You guys are twins?"

"Yeah, I know. It surprises most people because we couldn't be more different."

"So who's older?"

"She is, and she definitely doesn't let me forget it." He slouched in his chair, propped his feet up on the desk, and laced his fingers behind his head. "But I'm smarter, which is more dangerous," he said, acknowledging all the technology around him.

It was becoming clear why Peyton gave him so much hell. She took pleasure in beating him down a peg or two. It was the same reason Jake jumped on the bandwagon. He liked to put people in their places.

I sat in the empty chair next to him. "So, where am I on your map?"

"Nowhere. You don't need the algorithm."

"Why not?"

"Because…" He focused on the screen with the black windows and scrunched his face. Several images popped up among the scrolling streams of data. He dropped his feet to the floor and inched closer to the monitor. "Hmm."

An icy chill raced through me. "Is something wrong?"

"No, but this is going to be a lot more complicated than I originally anticipated."

"What's going on?"

"Even though your tracker isn't working, you're still sending out a signal."

My gut twisted into a tighter knot, afraid of what that might mean. "I am? Does that mean they're going to find me?"

"I don't think so. This isn't the normal signal. It's extremely complex. Not like anything I've seen before." He rubbed his face in his hands. "At first glance, it appears this signal is overriding your tracker's function. But I have no idea how it works."

"What do we do?"

"I don't think we need to redirect your signal with TROGS. But we'll keep a close eye on it. In the meantime, this code needs to finish analyzing. It could delay phase two of our plans. It's going to take a lot longer to decipher this than I thought."

"How long?" The faster they figured everything out, the faster I could start getting back to something that felt like *normal*.

He shrugged. "This will probably take us days to crack. Possibly a week. Depends on if we can get our hands on enough computing power to beef up our tech. Stuff that would allow us to slide into Global Tracking Systems during a small open window."

"A week? What am I supposed to do around here for that long without seeing sunlight?" It had only been a few days and I was already stir crazy.

"We have a supply run tomorrow night. You want to tag along?"

Eleven

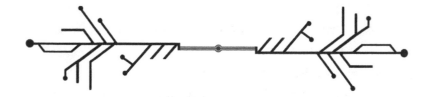

"**S**he's not coming," Jake protested.

Inside the barn, I stood next to five motorbikes in varying colors, wearing clothes that weren't mine and a pissed-off expression. I'd borrowed boots, cargo pants, and a black T-shirt from Peyton. They didn't hug me like my usual clothes, but I didn't mind. At least I fit in with the others, assuming Jake didn't throw a fit and get me kicked off the trip.

"Lighten up, Jake. I want to protect her chip too, but it's a routine run." Bailen squeezed Jake's shoulder in an attempt to calm him, but Jake twitched ever-so-slightly. This would be harder than I thought.

Jake leaned in inches from Bailen's face. "Don't you tell me to lighten up."

"Says the guy who turns everything into a joke," Bailen spat.

"She's *my sister*, not some anomaly tracker chip. It's bad enough she's on a wanted list. But that aside, she's not trained to evade the authorities. And you know what they do to people they

111

catch stealing."

"My dad's just lying low; he'll be back soon." Bailen's voice quavered, like he was hiding something.

Jake nodded, but a glint in his eye said he didn't fully believe Bailen, either. Their exchange aside, I didn't know what it had to do with me tagging along.

"Don't I get a say in this? It's my life." I hated when Jake talked about me like I wasn't there.

"Stay out of this, Kaya. You have no idea what you're getting into." Jake sounded like Dad when he was about to ground me. "We've lost good people to less dangerous missions."

There was something about the way he said the word *lost* that hung heavily in the air, but I scowled at him anyway. Pretending to be responsible was the part of the big-brother routine I hated. He couldn't protect me from the world, but that wouldn't stop him from trying.

"It's an easy run. We know all the layouts and where everything is. A simple snatch and run. If she's with us, she's got to learn. Plus, it's really her decision, not yours." The edge of Bailen's lips twitched into a half-smile, as if he were enjoying the payback.

Although Bailen treated me like some prized piece of tech, he at least respected my ability to make decisions. He really knew how to push people's buttons. At least they weren't mine.

Bailen continued. "The Ghost life is dangerous. Shit's going to happen. But now's as good a time as any to have her join."

"Yes, it's dangerous, and we don't need *shit* to happen with her there. Which is exactly why *you* shouldn't be going. We can't afford to lose you, either." Jake said it like he might lose the argument.

"I need to look for very specific components. It's not like I can write you a grocery list. Besides, I'm trained for this."

"And Kaya's not."

Peyton stepped next to her brother, but her attention remained on Jake. "Trained or not, as much as it kills me to say this, Bailen's right. It's Kaya's choice. Besides, we have Jeremy and Gavin, two of our best guys. Nothing bad should happen." She put her hand on Jake's shoulder but quickly pulled it back.

Jake frowned with a hint pleading in in his eyes. A lame attempt to guilt me into siding with him. "Fine. It's up to you."

"Really?" I said, excitement bubbling inside me.

"Yes." He grabbed my shoulders and twisted me so I had to face him. "But remember this isn't a game. You know what's at stake with your tracker if you get caught."

"I want to go," I said without hesitation. There was no way I'd let him leave me again. I wanted in on the action. It wasn't like the Ghosts had any rules. They lived to break them. And if I was going to be one of them, I'd have to learn to live outside the law.

Jake's intense gaze fixed on Bailen, the warning it held remained unsaid. "If she's going, she's riding with me."

"That cool with you?" Bailen asked.

I nodded, afraid to say anything that might jinx the situation.

"Good. Let's not waste any more time," Bailen said.

Jake climbed on his silver bike and offered me a hand up. I pulled on a black helmet that, unlike the others, lacked the Ghost symbol, then gripped Jake's waist.

The roar of the engine and the rush of wind whisked away the argument. The group rose into the night sky, headed toward the city. For someone who'd supposedly taught himself to drive a motorbike, Jake had amazing control.

The city lights glimmered in the distance as we flew over vacant farmland. Everything seemed so peaceful from far away, but the closer the city grew, the more my nerves did too. The floating highway signs and lights illuminating the edges of the skyways felt like a spotlight on what we were about to do.

As the lit-up skyrises filled the horizon and the noise of the city picked up, so did my heart beat. I had no idea how the Ghosts were going to get away with heading into the city unnoticed. Especially not with me. The authorities routinely patrolled the cities in addition to monitoring tracker activity.

But we took a lightly traveled skyway toward the outskirts of the city. Ten minutes later, we landed on a narrow, skyrise rooftop. I climbed off the bike, handed my helmet to Jake, and took in the view at the edge of the roof. The lights around the outside of the city were starting to shut off for the evening. Only a small section of downtown remained heavily lit. I loved St. Louis, but practically the whole town shut down at 10 P.M. An occasional car flew by in the distance, but it was too late for heavy traffic. No wonder the Ghosts had waited until now for a supply run.

"All right, this should be a quick in and out." Bailen's voice drew me back to the group. "We need processors, memory, and storage devices. If you find anything else you think will be of value, run it by me. Otherwise, grab whatever you can carry and leave. We don't anticipate any trouble, but you all know the risks. If the authorities catch you, you're on your own. Do the best you can to not give up any intel and hope they give you a quick end. 'Cause we've all heard rumors about the alternative."

I whispered to Jake, "What's the alternative?"

He waved his hand to shush me, turning his attention back to Bailen. If he wasn't telling me, it was as bad as I suspected.

"Gavin, get the door."

A tall, lanky guy with shaggy, brown hair snatched a toolkit off his bike and headed for the roof access door. After whipping out a series of screwdrivers and wrenches, Gavin opened the wall panel and hacked into the locking mechanism with a small black computer. It was amazing what he could do in a short amount of time with such primitive tech.

"Check the route," Bailen said.

When Gavin disappeared down the stairwell, Bailen turned to the group. "Peyton, you're with me, Kaya is with Jake." The smirk on Jake's lips told me he was pleased he'd gotten his way, but Bailen didn't notice. "Jeremy, you keep watch. If anything out of the ordinary happens, radio me." Bailen tossed an old-fashioned police radio at Jeremy. It never occurred to me that without trackers, they needed some other form of communication. I wondered how secure it was. Less monitored than trackers, I hoped.

Jeremy caught the device and headed to the edge of the roof, scanning the skies. Perched on the ledge, he was not someone I'd want to mess with. For a short guy, he had some serious muscle bulging out of his shirt. His dark skin further accentuated the muscle lines of his biceps.

Gavin reappeared in the doorway. "It's empty the whole way down. We're good to go."

"Jake and Kaya head down after Gavin. Peyton and I will bring up the rear," Bailen instructed.

I followed Jake through the doorway. The concrete stairwell was lit by moonlight from a single window. Shadows stalked us as we began our decent. I brushed against a cobweb along the wall and rolled my shoulders as shivers shot up my back. Rusted paint chips embedded in my palm as I grabbed the railing for extra support. I yanked my hand back and plucked the paint from my skin.

I'd never broken into a building before, let alone been somewhere ominous at night. The scariest place I'd ever been was a haunted house, and nothing here compared. It was much worse. At least in haunted houses, you expected stuff to jump out at you.

A musty smell clogged my nose and settled in the back of my throat. I swallowed, but it only made my throat dryer. I was starting to regret coming. No one had said anything about crypt-like stairwells.

Jake slid his hand behind him, and I stuck out my pinky. He gave it a quick squeeze and I relaxed.

Several flights down, we picked up the pace, which didn't give me time to keep thinking of all the things lurking in the dark corners. We stopped on a landing with a large, white number sixty painted on the door.

Gavin cracked the door with a quiet creak and peered inside. After a few seconds, he pulled open the door and held it for us. I inched through the doorway, thinking the whole scene resembled a bouncer letting a group into a secret hangout.

"I did recon earlier today. They have a lot of the things we need," Gavin said. "Memory and processors arc down those two aisles in the storeroom. Storage devices are behind the counter in the shop."

Rows of metal shelving almost reaching the ceiling housed wire, broken computer monitors, cables, and other mysterious, rectangular equipment—many things I'd never seen before. Boxes hung from overstuffed shelves, threatening to fall off the edges. Wire coiled around everything like a spiderweb.

"Good," Bailen said. "You grab the stuff behind the counter. Peyton and I will search the far row. Jake, you and Kaya check out the second-to-last one."

I trailed behind Jake, squeezing into the tight row, checking out the antique equipment with curiosity. "So, what are we looking for?" I asked as he rummaged through a shelf. Items scraped together like silverware across a metal pan. I shuddered and clenched my teeth.

"Memory."

I scrunched my face.

"Stuff like this." He held up a green, flat, rectangular object for me to see. Small, gold rectangles ran one length of the finger-sized component. Black raised boxes with silver prongs ran along the other side. The object was so foreign, it amazed me that Jake knew what it was. The knowledge he'd gained about mysterious tech in his time with the Ghosts made the time we'd spent apart feel like an eternity.

I pushed aside a small but heavy, blue box. I saw a few of the flat pieces similar to what he'd shown me entangled in some wiring. As I unwound the cabling, a shiny, square object drew my attention. The shimmer reflected as if to say, "Pick me!" I grabbed the small item, letting the meager light catch it at various angles. Scooping up my finds, I positioned the attention grabber on top of the pile.

"Like this?" I asked.

Jake stared blankly at the shelves as if lost in thought. I nudged him with my elbow and tried again. "Like this?"

He jumped as if coming out of a daydream and raised his

eyebrows. "Yes, but where'd you find this?" He picked up the shiny object and rotated it in the light. "Bailen, look at what Kaya found."

Bailen rounded the corner and held out his hand. Jake dropped the square into Bailen's palm. Bailen shifted the small square delicately in his hands. "Is this what I think it is?" he asked, scraping his fingernail across some rust flecks on the surface.

"Yep," Jake said. "A five thousand series chip."

"I thought they destroyed these!" Bailen resembled an excited puppy drooling over a new toy. "What made you pick it up, Kaya?"

"I don't know. Something about it seemed important."

"Nice find. You've got good instincts." Bailen handed the chip to Jake, who shoved it in his pocket.

"Thanks," I muttered, unable to form any additional coherent words. The praise caught me off guard. Why was it so hard to talk to him all the sudden?

"See, Jake?" Bailen nudged him with his elbow. "If we hadn't brought Kaya, we might not have found that chip."

A hint of a frown crossed Jake's lips before he returned to the shelf and became engrossed in an uninteresting spool of wire. He hated to be proven wrong.

Gavin appeared at the far side of the aisle holding a small box. "Bailen, I found a dozen or so USB sticks. I haven't seen any of these in ages."

"What's a...?" Before I could finish my sentence, the box started beeping, slowly at first, then in rapid succession. Expressions of horror appeared on both Jake's and Bailen's faces. They launched at me, knocking me to the ground. Pain shot through my knees first, followed by my elbows, which hit next.

A deafening explosion tore through the room. I struggled to move, but Jake and Bailen smothered me. With each increasing second, the pressure weighed down heavier and heavier like a trash compactor. I gasped for air as they crushed my chest between their bodies and the hard floor.

"Kaya, stop moving." Jake's scream sounded like he was inside a bubble. The clanging of metal made my ears ring. When the roar died down, the immense pressure eased off my back. I let out a long breath now that my chest wasn't compressed and immediately coughed from inhaling the flying dust and debris. After a few more deep breaths, I hoped to get some fresh air, but it was nearly impossible to avoid choking.

When the dust cleared and my lungs were sufficiently filled with air, I stood up, eyeing the room in horror. Torn-apart shelves were knocked on their sides like a pile of dominos. Most of the equipment was blown apart or damaged. Rubble surrounded us. I'd never seen so much destruction. The room resembled a war zone.

Jake lay on the ground face-down next to one of the toppled shelves. I stumbled over and collapsed next to him, shaking his shoulders.

"*Jake!*" I yelled, but with my ears still ringing, it sounded like I was underwater. He groaned and turned his face toward me. He blinked rapidly, as if trying to focus on me, then pressed his hands to the floor. A scream escaped his lips as he tried to push up from the ground. He crumpled to the floor, clutching his abdomen.

"Are you okay?"

He nodded as he rolled onto his back and let out several short breaths. "I'll be fine." He inhaled deeply, sat up, and said, "See, no big deal."

I offered him a hand, and a slight wince crossed his face as I helped yank him up. Jake pulled me into a hug.

"Are you okay?" he asked with a cough.

My heart hammered for what seemed like an eternity before I was able to answer. "Yeah, other than a few sore muscles, I think I'm fine." Jake had a large scrape on his cheek and several more on his arms but otherwise seemed good now that he was standing again. He pushed me away at arm's length and checked for injuries. When he was satisfied that I was unharmed, he let go.

I turned and nearly tripped over Bailen. He sat against a fallen shelf, taking ragged breaths. He seemed distant, as if thinking about another time and place. It wasn't until I saw him cradling his arm that I noticed the large chunk of metal protruding from it.

My stomach lurched at the sight of all the blood, and my knees buckled, sending me toward the floor. Jake caught my arms and helped steady me before I hit the concrete. He grunted and coughed as he bore my weight and lifted me back onto my feet.

"Are... Are you okay?" I stumbled, trying to get the words out.

Bailen's face was ghostly pale. "Peyton." His voice was hoarse. He cleared his throat and tried again. "Peyton, where are you?" he screamed with a hint of terror in his voice.

Metal debris crunched and scraped. Peyton limped around the corner with dirt covering her face and several large cuts on her arms and legs. "I'm right here. Stop your holler..." She stopped as soon as she noticed his arm. She fell to her knees next to him and clutched his shoulder. "What can I do?"

He winced. "The metal has to come out, or I'm not going anywhere."

"Whatever you need." Peyton turned away from Bailen and shot us an expression that pleaded for help. "Jake, hold him down. This isn't going to be pretty."

Jake grimaced as he knelt beside Bailen and held his shoulders in place. Peyton's hands hovered over the metal like it was a bomb about to go off. "I'm so sorry about this." She grabbed the metal and pulled. Bailen's scream tore through the room. Collapsing onto Bailen's heaving chest, Peyton embraced him, muttering, "I'm so sorry," over and over again.

In that moment, none of their bickering mattered. Their strong sibling bond shined through. If that were Jake lying there, despite wanting to lose my lunch, I'd have ripped the metal from his arm too.

Peyton pulled off her T-shirt, revealing a black tank top. She wrapped the shirt around Bailen's arm to stop the flow of blood. He gave her a slight nod of gratitude, and that one action told me more about him than all our encounters over the last few days combined. When it came down to it, he wasn't just a ball of technobabble; he knew how to appreciate the things around him.

A low rumble drew my attention away from Bailen's injury. Shelves rattled and fell along the opposite side of the room, sending more equipment crashing to the floor.

"Where's Gavin?" I asked, staring at the spot where he had once stood. It was now covered by a mountain of concrete and various computer parts.

Jake dropped his head, but no one said a word. A knot formed in my throat, the realization flooding over me. Somewhere in the pile of ash and debris were parts of Gavin. It seemed unreal, and putting it into words would force me and the others to face the truth.

Gavin was dead.

The blast originated from the box he'd been holding. There was no way he'd lived through that explosion. I didn't know him, but it didn't seem right that he'd been there one minute and gone the next.

"Guys, what the hell happened down there?" called a frantic voice from Bailen's pocket. "We have to move. The authorities are headed this way. It's too narrow for them to land on the roof, so they'll come in through the main floor of the shop."

Peyton pulled the radio out of Bailen's pocket and pressed the button on the side. "Long story. We'll be up there soon. Get the bikes ready." She clipped the radio to her belt. "Can you stand?"

Bailen struggled to push off the ground, making little progress. Jake grabbed his uninjured arm. As Bailen stood, a grunt escaped between his lips.

Trying to be helpful, I opened the stairwell door so Jake could guide Bailen through it. If I didn't know better, I'd have thought Jake was as hurt as Bailen. The pair of them hobbling together was a sorry sight.

Inside the stairwell, Jake clutched his abdomen and doubled over, leaving Bailen leaning against the wall. "Are you sure you're okay?"

"Fine, just a bruised rib, I think." He reached for Bailen's arm and guided him up the stairs. Peyton limped past me.

Just before I pulled the door shut, sounds of breaking glass erupted behind us.

"We've got company," Peyton said, removing a baton like the ones the authorities used from her belt. She wedged it through the door handle, across the frame and part of the wall. "Time to go. That's not going to hold them for long."

We stumbled up the stairs. I tried to comprehend everything that had just happened, but it didn't seem real. Images of the authorities barging into our living room flooded my mind. My body shook with fear at the thought of them capturing us.

Despite my screaming joints, I offered Jake a hand with Bailen, but the stairwell wasn't wide enough for the three of us, and Jake waved me up the stairs. I jogged up the remaining steps, eager to put plenty of space between me and the storeroom, as if that would erase the horror that had occurred there. I pushed through the rooftop access door and gulped the cool night air.

Two bikes hummed quietly. Jeremy, already wearing his helmet, worked on starting a third. When he saw me, he tossed me my helmet before returning to the bike. The others emerged through the doorway, bracing it behind them. Peyton ran for her bike, jumped on, and took off into the night sky.

"Where's Gavin?" Jeremy asked.

"Never mind. Just head back!" Bailen yelled at Jeremy.

Jeremy climbed on his bike, revved the engine, and tore off after Peyton.

Bailen lifted his arm, still wrapped in the bloody T-shirt. "Kaya's going to have to drive my bike."

"What? Are you nuts?" I shouted. As much as I'd always wanted to, now wasn't the time to learn.

Jake shook his head. "Out of the question. She has no idea what she's doing."

"We can't afford to lose two bikes. Since Gavin…" Bailen swallowed, as if the right words were stuck in his throat. "I'm not leaving my bike here. I'll talk her through it. She'll be fine. Now go before you put more of us in danger."

Jake froze, no words forming on his lips. I silently pleaded that he'd do something to stop what was about to happen. The thought of flying a death cycle made me want to hurl.

"I promise I won't let anything happen to her. I know how important she is to you. I'd kill anyone if they hurt Peyton. Don't worry. I'll keep her safe."

Jake pointed a finger at Bailen. "You better keep that promise." He hopped on his bike and launched into the sky after the others.

What had just happened? Jake's bike faded into the distance. The Jake I knew never would have put me in charge of such a dangerous situation. But here we were. Bailen was offering to help me, and Jake had let him? I was in some kind of alternate hell.

I turned back to the bike, but Bailen stood frozen in place. Was he in shock? No, that was sheer terror. An expression that said he couldn't afford to screw anything up. That he'd do whatever it took to get us both back safely. He wouldn't let Jake down. And it was all I needed to know.

"Uh, Bailen, we've got to go," I said.

He jerked and moved closer.

I climbed onto Bailen's bike and he slid behind me, wrapping his uninjured arm around my waist. I flinched under his light touch as he cradled his injured arm between my shoulder and his chest.

I pulled on my helmet and grabbed the handlebars so tightly, my knuckles turned white.

"Breathe," Bailen said through the speaker inside my helmet. "I'm right here. We'll do this together."

"Okay, what now?" My voice trembled to match my quivering body.

"I need you to hold the brake while I kickstart the engine."

I lifted my cramping fingers and clutched the brake handle. Bailen kicked down with his foot, and the bike rumbled to life.

"See? That wasn't too bad," he said. I could feel his chest rise and fall rapidly behind me. "Now, release the brake, twist the throttle, and yank the handlebars toward you."

I gulped. My body froze as an icy chill ran through me. Who was I kidding? If our escape depended on me, we were dead. I moved my feet from the footrest to the ground to steady myself. "I can't do this."

"You can. Because I know you won't let anything bad happen to either of us." For the first time, his voice was soft and kind.

"No pressure there," I muttered under my breath.

A loud banging on the rooftop door drew my attention behind us.

"I don't want to rush you, but we don't have a lot of time," he said.

My heartbeat quickened. That barricade wouldn't hold long. "Okay. So release the brake?" I asked, confirming the next step.

"Yes, but put your feet on the bike. I'll hold us steady."

I let go of my iron grip on the brake.

"Good. Now the throttle."

I twisted the handle, and the bike roared. Bailen must have lifted his foot off the ground because we were rolling toward the edge of the roof.

"Now yank back on the handlebars."

I tentatively pulled on the bars, not knowing how far to go. The bike lurched and the engine sputtered beneath us.

"More!" Bailen yelled as we continued to roll toward the ledge.

"More what?" I yelled back. Over Bailen's shoulder, the door crashed open and two agents burst through.

Twelve

"Face forward and pull!" Bailen screamed then released his hold on my waist. He grabbed my left hand and yanked the handlebars back. In moments we lifted off the roof, inches from toppling over the edge. The agents shrank into the distance as we sped away.

"Hold it steady."

"I'm trying," I said, panic filling my voice. My arms shook so violently, it was impossible to keep a straight path. I pulled the bike to the left to avoid a nearby high-rise, but Bailen shoved us quickly to the right to correct my wide turn and avoid a floating street sign. Wind whipped around us as we missed a second building by inches.

Once we were on a steady course, I blinked twice while thinking *MAP.*

Nothing.

Right. No tracker. "Which way?"

"Keep us low between the buildings. It'll be more difficult for the authorities' beams to find us."

I eased the handlebars forward, allowing the bike to tilt down.

His calm voice came through the speaker in my helmet. "There. See, I think you're starting to get the hang of it."

My sweaty palms made it difficult to maintain my death grip on the handlebars. Coasting was easy. It was the not-getting-us-killed part that wasn't. With a slight tilt of the handlebars, I attempted to level the bike. It jerked up then down. My stomach jumped into my throat. With one final adjustment, I managed to keep the bike steady.

"I think I need a lot more practice." I let out a nervous laugh. "And I thought Peyton's driving made me sick."

"Nah, you're doing fine," he said. "This is the easy part. It's the starting and stopping that's tricky."

My muscles relaxed, but my heart kept pounding. Stopping was exactly what I was worried about.

"Turn toward the river. We need to head back." He slid his hand farther around my waist. His touch sent a tingle through me.

Angling the bike, I followed Bailen's directions to the Hive. I gripped the handles tighter as I caught sight of the barn in the distance.

"Breathe," Bailen said. "I'll handle the flight controls. You just keep us steady."

"Okay," was all I could manage to get out.

"Now ease up on the throttle."

I twisted it, and the engine settled to a dull hum. Bailen nudged the left handle down, angling the bike toward the forest. As the trees rushed toward us, he returned his grip to my waist, and I inhaled sharply. As the bike hit the ground, I let it out. We bounced into the air again, and on the second hit, the bike stayed on the ground. The front tire swerved. Bailen clutched the handle and yanked it to steady us as we glided to a stop inside the barn.

Jake paced silently, though his pale face relaxed the minute he saw us. His normally well-combed hair stuck up. His eyelids were heavy, but his shoulders were drawn tight near his neck.

I pulled off my helmet and hung it on the bike, waiting for Bailen to get off first. As soon as he did, Jake grabbed him by the shirt collar and hauled him over to the far wall. Jake attempted to yank Bailen into the air but coughed and shoved him into a pile of gardening tools instead. Bailen used his uninjured arm to catch himself against the wall before whirling to face Jake, who stood inches from Bailen.

"Don't you *ever* do anything like that again," Jake said.

Bailen cradled his injured arm. I tried to separate them, but there was no space to squeeze between. I dug my nails into Jake's arm. "Enough! He's already hurt. You pounding his face in will only make things worse."

"Maybe, but it'll make me feel better." Jake's eyes lit with fire. He bared his teeth like a rabid coyote. "What do you have to say for yourself?"

Bailen grimaced and furrowed his eyebrows, a sure sign he was gearing up for a fight. "We were in a shitty situation. I'm not sorry about my decision. We got back here safely."

"Tell that to Gavin," Jake said, rubbing his abdomen with his free hand. "You put everyone at risk, especially Kaya. I never should have let her come."

"She's fine. I told you I wouldn't let anything happen to her, and I didn't. What's your problem?" Bailen yelled with such rage, he spit in Jake's face.

Jake didn't wipe it away, but his chest rose and fell with increasing speed. Before he could argue further, I crossed my arms over my chest and used my best pissed-off voice to say, "Jake, leave Bailen alone. You aren't mad at him. You're mad at me for wanting to go."

I scowled and tapped my foot in an attempt to show my impatience at Jake's overreaction. Jake froze with a stunned expression then slowly backed away from Bailen. Bailen ducked around Jake and took off for the trap door. Moments later, it slammed shut behind him.

"Let it go. He just saved my life…twice."

Jake scoffed. I wrapped him in a tight hug. When he winced, I eased up slightly. "I'm fine," I said into his chest. As he stepped back, his normally pale blue eyes seemed more glassy and distant than usual. "I'm not as fragile as you think. Besides, Bailen was there the whole time."

Jake took another step, swaying slightly. He dug his feet into the ground and wrapped his arm around his midsection. "I know. But we lost…" He winced again and shook his head. "I don't want anything bad to happen to you." He coughed. "I'm supposed to protect you."

"Oh, trust me. You protect me a little too much."

He cracked a weak smile, telling me I was right, and gently hugged me again. As he rested his chin on my shoulder, he coughed again. It was a slow rasp at first, but as I let him go, his cough grew violent until he heaved, throwing up blood.

"*Jake*! Somebody help me!"

His face paled. He staggered in circles and swayed. I caught Jake by the armpits and lowered him to the ground, placing his head in my lap. He continued to hack, blood splattering his lips. I ran my hands over his chest, searching for a wound or some other cause. As I grazed his stomach, he inhaled sharply. I peeled back his shirt to reveal a dark bruise across his midsection.

"*Somebody help!*" I cried, but I wasn't sure there *was* anyone to help.

"I'm...fine," Jake choked out, his eyes hollow.

"This isn't the time to be heroic." I nudged him, but he didn't respond.

"*Somebody! Please help!*" I screamed again, praying for someone to burst through the trap door.

He shook his head. "I need..." Aa short raspy breath escaped his lips. "More time."

"We have plenty." *Why did he think we were out of time?*

He lifted his arm and pointed toward my head. "You're... a smart..." He squeezed my pinky, but it wasn't as strongly as usual.

"I'm a smart what?"

Jake coughed, releasing my pinky to cover his mouth. Harder and harder, he hacked like he was struggling to get air.

"Don't talk. I'll get help."

I stood to leave, but he tried to grab my leg and coughed out a word that sounded like *stay.*

I knelt beside him, my heart pounding while my brain stalled, unsure what to do. I'd never been so helpless.

Jake's breathing grew raspy. I tried to cradle his head again, but it seemed to make things worse, so I lowered him back to the floor. His hand reached for mine again as a quiet groan escaped his lips. His arm fell slack, his pinky lightly brushing past mine as it hit the ground.

"Jake?"

Nothing.

"Jake?" It would be just like him to joke about something serious. I shook him. "Stop messing around."

Nothing.

"*Jake*!" I shook him again. "Wake up!"

I kept shaking him, expecting him to laugh with a twinkle in his eye and say, "Gotcha" at any minute. But the minutes ticked on and no amount of shaking made him say anything. His eyes remained open.

Glassy.

His head hung back with no resistance. Jake's arms lay limp at his sides. His chest didn't move. No throbbing vein in his neck.

"Jake." I shoved him. "This isn't funny."

I picked him up by his shoulders.

"Jake?"

His body flopped like a ragdoll.

Body.

It was just a body.

My thoughts swirled as my brain tried to process the word. What it meant. How had this happened? He'd been fine a minute ago. Well, not *fine*, but walking and talking, just a bruised rib like he'd said.

What was here wasn't Jake. Not anymore. He was lifeless.

It was lifeless.

My heart clenched, then crumbled to dust. It was like someone had sucked out my insides. I gasped for air.

Nothing existed in that moment but Jake and me.

I bent over him and screamed into his chest.

"No, you can't leave me here alone. I need you." The weight

of the words brought my world crashing down.

Dark shadows loomed around me like walls closing in.

For the first time, I noticed the blur of people around me. They tried to rub my back and comfort me, but I pushed them away. "Leave me alone!" I screamed and buried my face in Jake's chest.

People grabbed my arms, trying to pry me away. I slapped at them and kept my face buried.

I squeezed Jake's pinky but met no resistance. This had to be some kind of joke.

I whispered into his ear, "I can't do this without you."

But here I was.

Alone.

Again.

And the longer I stayed, the more real it was. I pushed off his chest, shoved past a blur of people, and bolted to the trap door. I didn't stop running until I reached my room. The metal door slammed shut behind me with a horrific *clang*.

I collapsed to my knees. The full magnitude of the evening slammed into me like a speeding motorbike. My body shook as I tried to stave off the impending tears.

Against the wall, I drew my legs into my chest, taking ragged breaths. I couldn't catch my breath. I gasped over and over and over again. The noises coming from my mouth didn't sound human, or like they were even coming from me.

I collapsed, my cheek pressed against the ground, staring straight ahead. The world spun around me and my brain struggled to process everything. Jake was gone.

Dead.

The words of the Mourner's Kaddish slipped through my lips

almost on autopilot. It wasn't under the right circumstances, but what was right when someone you loved was gone? As the final words of the prayer escaped my lips, they took with them my last bit of strength. Unable to move myself to the bed, I curled into a ball and wept until I ran out of tears.

Thirteen

Food came and went. I couldn't remember if I ate any of it or how it appeared and disappeared. I spent more time asleep than awake. And the waking hours were only long enough to rip me from the nightmares haunting my slumber—authorities torturing my family and friends, agents carving into my skull, Jake coughing up blood.

When the bed grew uncomfortable, I curled into a ball on the floor again. The cold surface nearly froze the wetness on my cheeks. Dirt and dried blood cracked off my clothes. The misery and filth cocooned around me until the smell became too much to ignore.

I tore the clothes off and tossed them into the far corner. If I never saw them again, it'd be too soon. Searching the dilapidated dresser, I pulled out a towel and wrapped myself in it before heading down the hall to the bathroom.

In the shower, I let the hot water pound on my aching head. The water dripped off me, splashed across the floor with a pinkish hue, and swirled into the drain. It was just like my life, slowly peeling away and being sucked into oblivion.

I leaned against the wall and slid to the floor. Pulling my knees into my chest, I cried into my hands. As the water continued to rain down, my ribcage shook in time with my wracking sobs. I hoped it would wash away the grief like it did the blood, but the sadness kept coming just like the water—a never-ending supply.

I wanted to go home. In that moment, I missed my family and friends more than ever. And there wasn't a thing I could do about it. I needed my safe space and no one at the Hive could provide that.

I needed Jake.

I pushed against the wall and shut off the shower. In my room, I dressed in a T-shirt and jeans I found in the dresser then headed to the computer room.

It was surprisingly empty, except for one person. Bailen spun in his chair. "You're awake. Can I get you anything? Maybe something to eat?" He tried to smile but avoided eye contact.

"I'm not hungry." Falling into the chair next to him, I pulled my legs up to my chin. I didn't know what to tell him because I had no idea what I needed. Instead, I asked, "What day is it?" I shook my head. "Never mind. I don't want to know." It felt like an eternity, and I'd need much more than that to forget.

"Are you sure?" he asked.

"Just find something to distract me."

He eyed me cautiously, almost like I might break. I didn't want his pity, but luckily, he returned to his monitor. "Well, the good news is, the first code is almost done running, but the decryption is going to take a while."

"I've got nothing but time," I said solemnly, knowing it was an utter lie. Everything needed to end so I could get out of here as fast as possible. But I was thankful to Bailen for humoring me.

As if sensing my mood, Bailen continued. "There's a lot of interesting things in the diagnostic report from your tracker. Even without the full picture, we have a sense of how to replicate the code. Unfortunately, it's going to be a logistical nightmare."

"Great. I was hoping for some good news." Although I doubted positive news could bring my spirits up when I had a giant cloud suffocating me. My whole body was numb.

"But there *is* good news."

"Oh?"

"The guys think they discovered a loophole in the tracker network. They're digging in to see if we can exploit it with the info we're learning from your chip." He had that excited I-love-tech expression again. Anything was better than the pity look.

"A loophole? Like what?" I just needed to keep him talking. The longer he talked, the less time there was for painful memories to creep into my mind.

"Something that might allow us to turn off our trackers for large chunks of time without the authorities noticing."

"Really? You learned all that from my tracker?"

"Yep. And hopefully we'll be able to use the data to our advantage." He tapped on the keyboard with lightning speed, unaffected by his bandaged arm. "With all this intel, we might be able to hit Global Tracking where it hurts. Plant some small chunks of code that can slowly eat away at their system, eventually allowing us behind their defenses." Several windows popped open on his screen and minimized in seconds.

An older man approached us and grabbed the back of Bailen's

137

chair. "Working hard or hardly working?" He let out a deep laugh.

Bailen whirled around in his chair and threw his arms around the man. "Ha. Working hard." He released his tight hold and plopped in his seat again. "Welcome back, Dad. How'd your trip go?"

I could see the resemblance. They had the same oval face and wild, brown hair. His Dad's piercing green eyes bore into me with a sense of familiarity I couldn't place.

"As good as any trip, but it wasn't without a small incident."

"You scared us. I'm glad you made it back safely."

The simple words were laced with fear. I didn't know the specifics of his trip or the exact consequences of capture, but I knew enough about the authorities to infer what could have happened.

"You know I do my best, but there are things at stake that are more important than my life." Bailen's dad faced me. His features were jarring. It was like an older version of Bailen and Peyton staring at me. They all had the exact same eyes.

"And you must be Kaya."

"Yeah, it's nice to meet you, Mister…uh…." In that moment, I realized I didn't know Bailen and Peyton's last name. How little I knew about all of them was painfully brought to the surface.

"Overland, but you can call me 'Myles.'"

"Myles, right. It's nice to meet you."

He put his hand on my shoulder and squeezed, a gesture I was sure was meant to be soothing but didn't manage to take away any of my pain. "I'm very sorry to hear about your brother. He was a valuable member to the team. He will be missed. We lost two great guys."

His apology was like an asteroid collision on my chest. All the air left my lungs. "Thanks," I muttered, not knowing the appropriate response for the situation. Was there even a good response to a statement like that? It wasn't like words could bring Jake back.

Myles dropped his hand and sat in a chair on the other side of Bailen. "Any idea how this happened? We never miss explosives in our initial sweeps."

"No. The intel was good—too good. The authorities showed up right after the bomb went off. Like clockwork. Something about it still doesn't feel right." Bailen scratched his head then returned to his computer.

My lips quivered, and my hands shook in a similar rhythm. "It's all my fault."

Bailen pulled me into a hug. I flinched at first but was too emotionally drained to fight it and fell into him.

"No, don't say that. You had nothing to do with it."

I stumbled over my words as my body quaked. "If I hadn't come…"

I shook my head in an attempt to clear my thoughts.

"Or maybe if I'd gotten help sooner." I squeezed my eyes shut before any tears leaked out. "If I'd noticed something was wrong…"

"Shh." Bailen eased out of the hug and positioned himself in a manner that forced me to give him my full attention. "It's is not your fault. You hear me?"

"It just doesn't seem fair. You both dove to protect me, but he…" I choked on the last word "Died." And it hung heavily in the air. Part of me wished it was Jake here now and not Bailen, but I knew that wouldn't feel right, either. While Bailen probably only tolerated me because of his interest in my bum tracker, he didn't deserve Jake's fate. No one did.

I shook my head then focused on the ceiling, blinking away the tears. "I didn't get to say goodbye." I paused, regaining some composure. "Oh, hell! How am I going to tell my parents?"

"As soon as everything is over, we will help you tell them. I promise," Myles said. "In the meantime, I'm concerned we have a mole."

"A mole? Seriously?" Bailen shook his head. "We've been so careful. Small circles, spread-out facilities."

"I know, but we can't rule out the possibility."

"You mean to tell me, my brother may have died because someone betrayed the Ghosts?" Rage bubbled inside me as they both acknowledged my worst fear. If I ever found out who, I'd make them pay.

Myles rose from his chair, his attention on Bailen. "I sent you some files to review. Let me know what you think." He pointed to the monitor. "And if you need help with the analysis, give me a holler. I've got some guys coming back soon who can lend a hand."

"Sure thing. Thanks."

Myles walked to the far side of the room and sat down at a computer that was segregated from the main group.

Bailen leaned back in his chair and stared at me.

Why is he staring at me like that? Do I have snot on my face? I wiped my nose and cheek, but my hand came back clean. I rose from my chair, side-eying him as I stepped toward the exit. I needed some time to digest all the new information.

"Hey," he said in a quieter tone than usual. "What do you say we get out of here tonight? Do something fun?" As he finished

140

the question, his voice trailed off, like he'd already been rejected. "Maybe get your mind off things."

"I don't know. I think I'm just going to hang around here." As much as some fresh air might be good, I didn't have the energy to do anything. But I appreciated his attempt at misdirection.

"You want to be alone?"

I nodded, too tired to speak. He slouched into his chair. Somehow, he knew I didn't want to talk about it. I appreciated it more than he knew. Too bad so many things brought back the pain. I wasn't ready to go back into the world. I needed to forget that night had ever happened. The one bonus of being with the Ghosts was I could crawl into my bed and let things go on without me. I didn't have to face reality, didn't have to have it crammed down my throat through my tracker.

"You sure?"

"Yeah." I turned from his chair and headed out muttering, "I'll catch you later." But a small part of me wanted Bailen to stop me so I wouldn't feel so alone.

Fourteen

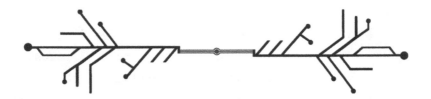

I wove through the tunnels, lost in my thoughts. Despite wanting to crawl into bed and hide from the world, the idea of fresh air sounded better and better. When I reached the barn, I yanked open the main door and took in as much of the outside air as my lungs would allow. It was only slightly less suffocating than the Hive. But the sun was peeking through the trees, and the orange glow warmed my skin. If only it could warm my heart.

I sifted through the old, rusted equipment and broken wood at the back of the barn. In the heap of junk, I found several beat-up cans of paint. After prying open the musty cans, I grabbed a thin piece of broken board and poked through the dried top layer, hoping the paint hadn't dried all the way through. The wood passed through and returned black from the paint below. I did the same for the white and red. Both of those were good as well.

Shoving a rusted barrel aside, I uncovered a couple of crusty paintbrushes lodged underneath some rotting boxes. The broken bristles were far from perfect, but the brushes would work.

I outlined an intricate pattern on the barn wall in black. I wasn't sure what it was. My hand flowed through the brush strokes. After a while, a pattern emerged. When I got bored with my doodles, I headed for the opposite wall, but the silver gleam of Jake's bike called to me.

I sat on the ground facing the front of the bike and outlined a shape in white. Adding in some black for contrast and shading, the Ghost symbol of a skull took form. My hand moved in large brush strokes on either side of the skull. When I finished with the black and white, I picked up a clean brush and dipped it in the red paint. After a few quick strokes, I leaned back to admire my work. Two large, flaming wings emerged from the sides of the skull.

I dropped the red brush. It was missing one thing. I picked up the white again and with a couple of brush strokes added a חי between the flaming wings. I smiled for the first time I could remember because it reminded me of Jake's free spirit and fire for life. The Hebrew symbol *Chai* was a perfect tribute. But it would have been more perfect if he were still here.

"Nice work."

The sound of Bailen's voice made me drop my brush. "Sorry, I... got a little carried away."

"Don't be sorry. You're really talented."

My cheeks warmed. "Thanks. But I wasn't apologizing for the art, just for where it ended up. I have a bad habit of doodling all over the place."

"Don't apologize. The bike is yours now. You can do whatever you want with it."

"Really?"

"Yes. Including learning how to drive it."

"I…" I swallowed, trying to find my words. "I don't know if that's a good idea."

"Why not?"

I took a deep breath to collect my thoughts. "After my last attempt at flying." *What if I got in an accident like Lydia's brother?* Or not like Lydia's brother. It felt so long ago, but the pain of my conversation with Jake was still as fresh as the paint on the bike.

The left side of his mouth curled upward. "That's exactly why I think you should learn. You could use the practice."

I stood up to appear more intimidating, despite being eye level with his chin. "Hey, I doubt you did better your first time driving. Plus, I'm sure the authorities weren't chasing you at the time." I wasn't sure where the sudden anger came from, but it felt right in the moment. Not that I was mad at Bailen. I was mad at life, or the lack of it.

"All right then. Show me what you're made of."

"Now?" I gulped, regretting the anger that opened the door for a challenge.

"Yeah, the sun's coming up. I'll take you somewhere we can practice."

Hands shaking, I moved the paint cans against the wall. I'd wanted a distraction and here was a huge one. Bailen tossed me a helmet and started the bike. I climbed on behind him. We rode through the barn doors. In the woods, we stayed on the ground, weaving around the trees and allowing the wind to whip around us.

As we stopped in a clearing nestled between the woods, he cut the engine. Bailen removed his helmet and climbed off the bike. I stood, but he tapped my shoulder, sending a shiver across my collarbone into my chest. I melted back into my seat.

"Let's start with the basics."

Starting on the bike didn't seem very basic to me, but I did as he asked.

I clutched the handles. Bailen kicked up the stand. An eerie silence filled the air as I waited for further instructions. The trees rustled around us, but the usual horn honking and cars whooshing by were absent. Although it was awkward, I didn't miss the bustle of the city or the demanding tracker lights and messages popping up in my vision. The quiet was a nice change of pace. In all the simplicity, it was easier to forget about all the crazy things happening around me.

Bailen straddled the bike behind me. "Your left hand is your clutch." He ran his hand over mine and grabbed for the silver bar above the handle. My hand tingled under his touch and I tensed. Not trusting my voice, I nodded.

"The right hand controls your throttle." His breath beat on my neck as he spoke. "Above the handle is your brake."

I shook my head and dropped my hands to my jeans, wiping the sweat on them. So much to remember already and we were still on the "basics."

Bailen backed off the bike. I let out a long breath now that there was some space between us.

"Put the bike in neutral so you can get a feel for it. Then ease up on the clutch, and let the bike roll."

His pinky brushed against my thumb as his hand pulled away. I released the clutch a bit too quickly, and the bike lurched forward. That seemed easy enough.

"Walk the bike around. Get a sense for how it feels

underneath you."

I pushed off with my right foot and rolled the bike forward then gave a second push with my left. I wobbled a bit, but after a short time, I was powering around using my feet and turning in large circles. The experience was freeing.

"See, you're a natural. Now let's turn the bike on."

I stopped in front of him and froze. I was thankful the helmet hid my face. My expression was surely betraying the terror building up inside me.

Putting on his helmet, he climbed onto the bike behind me. His firm chest brushed against my back, causing my breath to quicken. His voice came through the speakers in my helmet. "Put your feet on the pedals. I'll steady the bike while you start the engine."

I pushed the *start* button. The bike hummed beneath us. I hoped the slight vibration hid the fact that I was shaking. I gripped the handles tightly. I'd do it for Jake. And if I was going to honor his memory, I needed to be strong on my own.

"Now twist the throttle slowly."

I turned my hand, and the bike roared. The unexpected sound made me jump back into Bailen. I clutched the handles and inched away from him before we touched for too long.

"That's okay. Try again. It's a bit sensitive."

I squeezed the handlebars again and twisted my hand much more slowly. The engine hummed a little louder.

"Good. Remember that feel. Now shift into gear."

My muscles tightened, but not because of the bike. He was so close to me. Attempting to block Bailen from my mind, I pushed the lever down with my left foot.

After a few deep breaths, I let out the clutch. The bike

lurched forward and died. I dropped my hands to my thighs and wiped them again. My nerves twisted into knots. Driving wasn't easy, and Bailen's presence was making it that much harder to concentrate. *This is for Jake. You can do it.*

"That was a good first attempt. Try again, but next time, add some throttle."

I restarted the bike and as it hummed to life, I repeated the steps to shift into gear. The bike rolled forward slowly, and my heart pounded as Bailen wrapped his arms around my waist.

"Good. Now ease up and shift to neutral using both brakes."

I let everything he said sink in. When the bike stopped, I dropped my feet to the ground, trying to slow my breathing— which became infinitely easier when Bailen got off the back of the bike. There were so many things to think about while trying to not think about Bailen, and his closeness. No wonder Dad never wanted me to learn to drive a crotchrocket. It was so easy to get distracted, especially when Bailen was around. Even if I was glad he was distracting me from my sorrow.

"Now for turning."

I gulped. More things to remember. But if Jake had learned how to do everything, I could too. If I was going to be a Ghost, I needed to prove I could keep up with them.

"It's all in the counterbalance. You'll want to lean a bit away from the direction you turn." He grabbed my hip. My insides trembled. I hoped he couldn't tell I was shaking. "Use your butt to steady yourself."

I clenched both sets of cheeks. The last person whose hand had been that close to my butt had been Harlow. *Crap!* Harlow. When was the last time I'd even thought about him? He should have been here now, not Bailen. Harlow had promised to teach me to ride one day. The situation weighed on me like a huge betrayal. I might not see him again, but was it really fair to take something that was supposed to be ours and share it with a near stranger?

I shoved the thoughts aside and focused on the bike. Driving it was more than enough to worry about.

Bailen climbed on the bike, and I tensed again but started the engine. Soon we were rolling around the field. I eased in and out of turns. Turning came much more naturally to me than the other parts.

After dozens of laps and zigzags around the field, Bailen said, "How about we go a little faster?"

Feeling more confident, I twisted the throttle, shifting into a higher gear, and the bike sped up. As we headed toward the edge of the clearing, I squeezed the clutch and tried to slow the bike into the turn. The back wheel spun out to the side. My heartbeat quickened. I released the brake and pulled the handlebars to straighten out, but the bike was falling.

I landed flat on my back with Bailen on top of me. I ripped off my helmet, gasping for air. But there was none because Bailen seemed to be consuming any that remained.

He removed his helmet. "Are you okay?"

I took several large breaths just to be certain. "Yeah." My heart still pounded in my chest, though. And not because of the crash.

He brushed a strand of hair out of my face. His touch left a trail of goose bumps across my cheek.

"Good." He smiled, continuing to stare at me, but not with his usual *I'm interested in the tech* expression.

I lost myself in the moment. It felt good to have him so close, smelling like fall leaves. It was intoxicating. As the wind blew through his hair, I wondered if I was more than just a shell for his precious glitchy hardware, or if I should even be having these thoughts.

He leaned in, but at the last possible second, a single name pierced my mind.

Harlow.

I turned my head to the side, and Bailen planted his lips on my cheek.

"Is something wrong?"

I scooted out from underneath him and sat up, still trying to catch my breath. "I can't," I said as a thousand thoughts raced through my head.

"Oh. Because of…?"

I could if I really wanted to, but it wouldn't be fair to Harlow. It wasn't right. I shook my head. "No. It's not like that." I paused, hoping a better response than the truth would come, but it didn't. "I have a boyfriend… Or at least, I did before I came here."

Bailen fixated on his hands, plucking grass from the soil like it was suddenly the most interesting thing he'd ever done.

"Oh, sorry." He stood up and righted the bike. "Want to give it another try?"

I wasn't sure how to respond. There was too much going sideways. But all I could think about was how I may have ruined any chance I had with Bailen. And part of me wasn't sure I was okay with that.

Fifteen

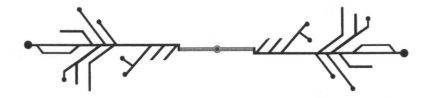

climbed on the bike and waited. Bailen hesitated before he sat behind me and this time, he didn't hold me as tightly. My heart sank. I wished I hadn't told him. But it was the right thing to do, even if it felt like eating gravel.

After many awkwardly silent laps, I stopped the bike in the center field. "I think I really have the hang of this. Thanks, Bailen."

"You're welcome," he said. "But you still have one more thing to learn."

"What?" Hadn't we done enough for one day?

"Flying."

Ugh! In all the confusion, I'd completely forgotten that. "Now?"

"Yeah, why not?" He placed his hand on my shoulder, sending tingles through me. I resisted the urge to shiver, even though a part of me wanted him to know I enjoyed being closer. The closer I was, the more I forgot the awful parts of my life. The part where I lost everyone I cared about.

"Besides, you know everything except how to go up and

down. That's the easy part."

Sweat formed on my forehead. "Okay, what do I do?"

"Move the lever in front of the handlebars. That releases the yoke and engages the flying mechanism."

I thrust the lever to the right, feeling it lock into place.

"If you pull back on the handlebars, the bike will go up. If you push forward, it will go down."

"Easy enough," I said, glad the hard part of crotchrocket training was over. The hard part of my *life* was something else entirely.

"Now build up enough speed to get off the ground."

After everything today, that sounded simple. I started the bike and increased the throttle. As we rolled toward the edge of the clearing, my sense of adventure returned.

"A little faster, then pull back on the handles." Bailen tightened his grip around my waist. My insides warred. A mixture of guilt and excitement swirled.

I shifted into the highest gear. As we neared the trees, I pulled back on the handlebars, sending the bike into the air. My stomach tightened as the ground sank beneath us and wind rushed around me. I was doing it. The skyrises in the distance had never looked so beautiful before.

Bailen's voice sounded in my helmet. "See, simple."

I laughed and twisted the throttle. The biked sped on. My worries whisked away with the wind.

Hours later, we pulled into the barn as the sun set behind us. I took off my helmet and hung it off the handlebars.

"Thanks. I don't know how I can repay you."

"It was nothing." He shrugged and took a step away from me. I wanted him to stop backing away. Unfortunately, things were too complicated. I gave him a weak smile, but his expression remained even. I hoped it was enough to convey how I was feeling, but deep down, I knew it wasn't. How could I show him what I wanted if my emotions were a swirling, confusing mess that I couldn't even understand?

Before I could open the trap door and escape the awkwardness, it swung open and Peyton emerged.

She pointed her finger at Bailen's chest. "Where have you been? I've been searching everywhere for you."

"I was teaching Kaya to ride." Bailen put his helmet on the seat of the bike.

Peyton gave Bailen an *oh please* expression, grabbed his arm, and yanked him down the stairs.

"We need you to do some coding. You have to come too. We finally understand how to use that loophole we found."

"Can it wait?" Bailen asked, gazing at me like we'd just been interrupted, even though we hadn't been.

"No. We have a thirty-minute window before Global Tracking Systems finishes their upgrade and locks the system down even tighter than it already is."

Bailen's shoulders slumped, which I never expected to see from him in a conversation about tech. "I thought the upgrade wasn't until next week."

"They must have suspected an attack. They started it ahead of schedule."

"We can never catch a break." Bailen bolted to the trap door with Peyton on his heels, leaving me several paces behind them.

Before I knew it, I was back in the chair in the computer

room. Wires draped from my arms, legs, and head. A dozen people stood around Bailen, who tapped on the keyboard behind his row of monitors. His dad sat on one side, periodically pointing to things. At the station to their left, Jeremy was engrossed with his work.

"Is this really necessary?" I sat up from the lab chair, trying to ignore the people staring at me.

Peyton pushed me into the seat. "Yes. Now stop moving. We don't have much time." As I was about to ask *time for what*, she pulled up a chair next to me and watched me like I was a prisoner about to escape.

I huffed and tried to remain still, but my feet shook, restless to get out of the room. Her scrutiny bore into me, making me squirm. But it wasn't what it implied that made me uneasy. It was my thoughts, my emotions, and my guilt. Shouldn't I be holed up in my room crying over Jake and not worrying about boys? But when my grandmother had died, the rabbi had told us to mourn in whatever way felt right. Being alone felt wrong, alienating, and lonely, like the last person on Earth. Bailen filled an empty void. Kept my mind off things.

It had started as an escape from reality, but I'd never expected to enjoy it. To crave his company. I wanted Bailen to fill the void Jake had left, have him do something reassuring like Jake would have, but on a whole other level.

I closed my eyes to block out the room. I took a few deep breaths in a futile attempt to expel the churning guilt.

Maybe if the loophole worked, I'd be able to see everyone again, pick up where I'd left things. Well. almost. Harlow would be there, but Jake wouldn't.

And I still owed Harlow the truth—why I'd run instead of trusting the authorities. What I'd done with Bailen. Telling him wouldn't be easy. But did I even want things to go back the way they were? So much had changed. The world and the people I cared about no longer had a filter on them.

I shifted in the chair, searching for an escape route. There wasn't one. The wires weighed heavily on me, but my thoughts were heavier. Going home also meant telling my parents about Jake. Even if Myles helped, the thought of the conversation numbed my body. What if they blamed me? No matter what Bailen said, it was my fault. Things would have turned out very differently if Jake hadn't tried to protect me.

Now I wasn't sure if I wanted to go back to my old life. It seemed easier to hide out with the Ghosts. The absence of my tracker felt simpler in a lot of ways, but other parts of my life were much more complicated. I couldn't hide by turning to the network. Staying with the Ghosts meant never seeing my family again—or what was left of them. It also meant dealing with Peyton and Bailen.

But none of it mattered if the exploit didn't work. I had to clean up the mess I'd created—all the pain I'd caused. My brain moved a million miles an hour, matching the swirling feeling inside me.

The sudden hum of the discs on my temples brought the conversations of the room to my attention.

"We're online. Jeremy, start cloning Kaya's signal. I have to finish the application code."

Jeremy hit several keys at his station. The discs buzzed in my ears—a sound that normally would have annoyed me but instead slowed my horrible stream of thoughts.

"Is there anything I can do to help?" I asked.

"Yes, stay still. We have fifteen minutes to clone your signal and apply it to our trackers before the system maintenance completes. If we can mimic your signal and send the data to the network, we'll be able to disconnect people without the authorities knowing. But if the maintenance finishes before we do, game over." Bailen peeked over the monitors at me with a quick grin that should have been reassuring but wasn't.

"Game over? What do you mean?" I asked, hoping the discussion would distract me.

He continued to type and didn't answer. I turned to Peyton, who was still glaring at me like she saw through some ruse I didn't know existed. I wished I were a mouse so I could scurry through a hole and hide between the walls.

"Game over, as in the authorities will be able to track what we're doing. Then they'll know where we are." She pulled her hair into a messy ponytail. "We have to finish and get out of the system before it's back online."

"But if we're really lucky, I might be able to sneak in some sleeper code that can start unraveling their defenses from the inside." Bailen's devious, I-love-tech grin appeared on his face.

Despite the high spirits, my muscles tightened. It was a huge risk they were taking on me and my faulty tracker.

Several others came in and sat down at their stations, murmuring to one another and pointing at their screens occasionally. There was no escaping the tension swimming in the room. I bit the inside of my cheek, trying to diffuse some of my anxious energy. It didn't work.

"I'm almost done with the cloned signal," Jeremy said to Bailen, breaking the long silence.

"Great. Send it over the second it finishes," Bailen said, his attention glued to his monitor. "I need a time check."

Peyton illuminated her watch. "Seven minutes."

"Seven? That's it? Please tell me you're kidding."

"I wish I was, but this is no joke."

He bit his bottom lip and I forced myself to look away before I had any more inappropriate thoughts about him. "We aren't going to make it."

She stood from her chair and joined him on the other side of the monitors. "I'm not a coding prodigy, but can I do anything?"

"Do you remember when I showed you how to install memory?"

"I think so." Her voice sounded confident, but her deer-in-headlights expression betrayed her words. I'd never seen Peyton so terrified.

"Good." He reached across the desk and held up a small silver chip.

I recognized it immediately. It was the chip I'd found at the building where Jake... I stopped myself from allowing the memory to persist. If I did, I'd have lost it.

"Install this five thousand series chip in the secondary server. We need all the power and speed we can get." Bailen passed her the chip.

"Don't you need to shut down the server so I can install it? Can you afford to be down a server for a minute or two?"

"Not really, but if you're fast enough, the new chip should more than make up the difference."

"Okay. I trust you. You're the tech genius."

"The server will be offline in ten seconds."

The fact that Bailen didn't acknowledge the compliment told me how much was riding on the exploit.

"You know I like a challenge, but this is insane. Kaya, keep the time." She tossed me her watch then bolted to the far corner.

I caught it and peeked at it. The countdown showed five minutes and thirty seconds left. My heart pounded in rhythm to the ticking seconds.

"The cloned signal is on its way to you," Jeremy said before heading to where Peyton was pulling a large rack out of a huge metal box.

"Great. I've got it." The clicking of Bailen's keys increased in speed. "Time check?"

"Four minutes and forty-five seconds," I said.

Why was it when I wanted a class to end, the clock crawled, but now that every second counted, it zoomed by?

Peyton shoved the rack into the metal box and slammed the door shut. "The chip is in!" she yelled across the room.

"I'll bring it back online." Myles stepped up to another terminal and his fingers passed over the keyboard with a speed that rivaled Bailen's. It was like they were racing each other instead of the clock.

"Good. Just in time to enable the cloned signal," Bailen said. "How much time?"

"Three minutes fifty seconds," I said, watching the seconds tick away.

"Five percent complete." Bailen rubbed his hands together. "It's going to be tight. Let me know when we get to one minute and again at thirty seconds."

I gulped, trying to ease the giant lump forming in my throat. All attention was glued on Bailen's monitors, but I fixated on the watch, letting the changing numbers hypnotize me. For every second that passed, my gut squeezed tighter.

When the watch hit the first marker, I could barely choke out, "One minute."

"Eighty-two percent complete," Bailen called out.

Peyton moved next to my chair and watched the clock with

me. I opened my mouth to call out the next time marker, but Peyton beat me to it. "Thirty seconds."

"We're at ninety percent complete," Bailen replied.

As the final thirty seconds ticked down, the walls crawled toward me and the ceiling lowered. My chest tightened, making it difficult to breathe. Everyone held their breaths, including me, as Peyton and Bailen tracked the final seconds and percentages. When twenty seconds remained, Bailen said, "Ninety-five percent... Ninety-six."

"Ten seconds."

"Shut it down!" Myles yelled.

"What? Dad, are you nuts?"

"There's no time. It won't complete, and we can't risk them finding us." Before Bailen could protest further, Myles flipped a switch, and the computer fell silent.

My heart sank to my feet as I watched the final seconds tick away.

Bailen slammed his fists on the desk. "Ninety-eight percent. We had it!"

But the room fell silent as the main screens went black and green text scrawled across them.

I KNOW WHO YOU ARE AND WHAT YOU'RE AFTER.

YOU MAY THINK YOU'RE CLEVER, BUT I WILL HUNT YOU DOWN.

CROSS ME AGAIN AND THERE WILL BE SEVERE CONSEQUENCES.

-R.S.

Bailen slumped in his chair. Myles put his hand on his son's shoulder. "See? They were onto us. Luckily, they didn't get much from their location trace."

"We lost our window by sheer seconds."

"I know, son."

"It'll be weeks before there's another upgrade or maintenance. And who knows if we'll be able to catch it in enough time."

"I know. We will beat them." But his words didn't feel like enough.

Bailen shot up from his chair. "How? They're always ten steps ahead of us. They know our plans before we do. They got in our system! We're never going to be able to take down the tracker network and free people if we can't get inside their defenses. When are we going to catch a break?"

"We'll find another way. We always do."

Despite Myles's hope, Bailen's reaction had me wondering if the years of dodging the authorities were catching up with them, if they were running out of chances.

Sixteen

very time I closed my eyes over the next few nights, I was transported back to the explosion. No matter what I did differently in my dreams, they always ended the same, with Jake coughing up blood in my arms. I tossed and turned, trying to prevent sleep from taking me, but each time, my eyelids grew heavy, and the nightmare returned.

As time went on, the nightmare expanded. My brain added the signal cloning, but then Jake turned into a zombie authority and shut the program down before it could complete.

I flicked on the light, but my memories still went to Jake. Whether I was awake or asleep, there were reminders of him everywhere, reminders of what I'd lost. I let out an exasperated scream and threw off the covers. I pulled on a hooded sweatshirt and plodded across the room to the dresser. I opened the top drawer searched the emptiness then slammed it shut with a thud. As I reached for the next drawer, a soft plop caught my attention. I pushed the dresser aside and found a black-and-white notebook folded in half, held that way with a rubber band.

I pulled off the rubber band and flipped through the pages, instantly recognizing Jake's handwriting. I shuffled back to the bed and leaned against the wall, turning the pages but not really reading. There were lots of poems early on. Words like *pinprick of light in a fog* stood out. He'd obviously found something small worthwhile here. But the more I examined through the pages, the more erratic the writing became.

Some pages had very few words, or just big question marks. Until I found the final pages with writing. Four words spanned the two pages—WHY CAN'T I REMEMBER?

More puzzles from Jake. Who or what was he forgetting? With distance from the tracker network, maybe he was missing his videos and family images.

I flipped backward through the writing and found phrases like *lost chunks of time* and *extreme exhaustion*, but no answers to the mounting questions. Maybe it was the stress of the Ghost life, or the fight against the authorities. There was no way to know for sure. I thought we shared our secrets, but the journal was something else he'd kept from me.

I held it to my chest and curled into a ball. It was the last piece of him I had, and it didn't make sense. Just like his death.

A soft knock at my door made me jump. I hid the journal under my pillow, trudged across the room, and wiped my snot-covered face. I heaved the door open to find Bailen standing wide-eyed. His messy hair stuck out of his sweatshirt hood.

"Trouble sleeping?" he asked.

"Yeah, you?"

"I can't get it out of my head. We were so close. I feel like we lost everything."

"Tell me about it."

"Sorry. I didn't mean to—"

"It's fine." I cut him off. I'd thought about Jake enough. I didn't need to talk about it too. "What time is it?"

Bailen checked his wristwatch. "8:00 P.M."

"You mean we both slept a whole hour?" I'd turned into a pathetic loser sulking around and going to bed at seven.

"Seems like it." He paused. "Also seems like we both need a distraction."

I was starting to get stir crazy. I needed out of this room before I lost it again.

A smile tugged on Bailen's lips. The first hint of one I'd seen in days. "Good. Meet me in the computer room in half an hour. And dress nice. I've got an idea on how to get us out of here."

"Done." I shut the door and collapsed on the bed again, exhaustion washing over me. Maybe it was a bad idea.

<hr />

"So where are you dragging me?" I stood behind Bailen's chair with my arms crossed over my chest. Even after our brief agreement about distractions, I wasn't sure a little outing would help keep my mind off things. Leaving the Hive seemed like mixing too many paint colors into a muddy mess.

Bailen was the only one left in the room, but his focus was glued to his monitor. Either he loved the tech way too much or was obsessed with what happened and couldn't let it go. After several minutes, I wondered if he'd heard me or even noticed I was behind him. He continued typing with a rhythmic clicking of the keys. I inched away and crept toward the door, hoping to escape.

Before I made it more than a dozen steps, he said, "Oh, you know, somepl—" He spun in his chair. "You… look, uh…" He paused, his face paling.

My cheeks flushed. It was weird having someone compliment me after I'd spent most of the day alone in sweats, having nightmares and sobbing. Especially someone who wasn't Harlow. "Uh, thanks. Peyton gave it to me." I fidgeted with the hem of the black-and-silver, sequined tank top over a pair of tight-fitting jeans. "She said she didn't wear it anymore. Am I overdressed?" But what I really wanted to ask if I was still a ball of snot.

Smiling with a hint of deviousness, he shook his head. "It's perfect," he said.

"Where are we going?" I asked again so I had time to mentally prepare. Peyton had managed to avoid that question when she'd thrown her tank top at my head and slammed the door in my face. I wasn't sure what I'd done to deserve that response.

"It's a surprise." Bailen jumped from the chair and motioned for me to follow him down the corridor toward the trap door.

"I hate surprises," I muttered under my breath.

Inside the barn, I reached for a helmet.

"Oh, you won't need that." Bailen took the helmet from my hand and placed it on the bike. "We're walking."

I arched my eyebrow. "Oh?" I said. "Mind giving me a hint?"

"You'll see." He activated a small light on his watch. As he dropped his hand, the outside edge brushed against mine, sending a flutter rippling through my stomach. The brief contact somehow made the void inside me seem slightly smaller.

I followed Bailen through the main barn door into the

darkened forest. The underbrush crunched beneath our feet. The moon barely peeked through the treetops and with the nearest farmhouse likely miles away, it was hard to see inches in front of us. It was a stark contrast from how illuminated the city was, so I was thankful for Bailen's light.

As we walked, my mind wandered to Harlow. I wished I could fall into his arms and tell him everything while he ran his hands through my hair. He'd listen and, by the end, I'd know what to do. And then things would return to a calm state, almost boring. I needed boring. Anything that resembled my life. Anything that kept the thoughts of Jake from creeping out of the dark corners of my mind. But that wasn't my life anymore.

I was lucky to have Bailen. But he was someone I barely knew. Despite that, we'd already shared so much. Even with all the crazy, I had to give him credit for trying. There was an ease about hanging around him. And although hiking through the woods in the middle of nowhere wasn't exactly my style, it kept my mind off things. Jake would be happy that I wasn't sitting around drowning in a pool of tears.

"We're almost there," Bailen said softly—so much so that the hooting owls almost drowned out his words.

"Do I need to close my eyes for this surprise?" I asked sarcastically. I secretly hoped he'd give me a clue as to where we were headed, but I embraced the mystery that kept my mind guessing instead of the infinite loop of Jake's death playing through my head.

"If you do, you might trip on a tree branch," he said. "And we wouldn't want that, even if I promised to catch you."

I scoffed and kicked a rock to avoid showing I secretly thought the comment was charming.

"Besides, it's not necessary. You have no idea where we're going."

"Wow. Just rub it in, why don't you?"

"If that were my intent, you'd know it."

"Then just tell me."

"I could tell you," he said. "Or I could show you." He pointed ahead to a rundown shed, illuminating it with the light from his watch.

The slanted roof seemed like it would slide off at any second. Its deep red paint chipped off the walls. Several of the wooden boards were broken or missing, and a giant crack ran the length of the lone window.

"Uh, what is this place?" I asked, goose bumps forming on my arms.

"You'll see." He tapped his fingers together, then ran his palm across the crack on the window. A green light traced the path of the crack. The entire wall slid to the right with a series of creaks, revealing a set of concrete stairs.

"More secret hideouts?"

"Something like that."

He led me down the stairs into a small corridor. There was barely enough space for us to walk side by side without knocking into the walls or each other. The close proximity to Bailen made my muscles tense, but my heart warmed. Around two turns, we stood in front of a large steel door. I gulped, wondering what secrets were locked behind it.

Bailen pounded on the door three times. A small slit near the top of the door screeched open. Two brown eyes appeared. Retro club music spilled out from the slot. The eyes scanned us up and down then stopped on me, making me feel like I was under a microscope.

"She's with me," Bailen said.

The guy snorted, and the slot scraped closed.

With a metallic clang, the door swung open, and Bailen pulled me inside. We stood on a wrought-iron balcony overlooking a small concrete dance floor packed with people. Who knew there were so many Ghosts?

Leading me down the staircase on our right, we walked past a series of booths toward the circular bar. Strobe lights panned and changed colors. The heavy beat of the music vibrated off my chest and pounded in my ears, muddling latent memories from a time that seemed so far away and so close all at the same time.

"Where are we?" I shouted over the music.

"Neon Nectar, the hottest hangout around."

"How come I've never heard of it?"

"'Cause it's a secret."

Bailen winked and straddled a bar stool. He motioned to the one next to him, and I climbed on. A series of illuminated, large clear tubes running floor to ceiling lined the wall behind the bar. Each tube contained different neon-colored liquids. I watched the bright bubbles rise in the tubes then pop once they hit the surface.

"If it's a secret, why are there so many people here?"

"Because the Ghosts have hideouts all over. People come from everywhere to interface with headquarters."

"This club is headquarters?"

"No, but the Hive is. And while they're here, they usually need to blow off some steam."

"Aren't you afraid they'll find this place?"

"Did you see the outside?"

"All right. You've got a point."

"Can I get you a drink?" Bailen asked without missing a beat.

"Uh, yeah," I said, unsure what a drink here entailed.

He waved down the bartender. "Two purple nectars please." The bartender moved to the purple tube and filled two tall, skinny glasses. After dropping a straw in each, he slid the drinks in front of us. I grabbed the cool glass and sipped a bit of the liquid. It was surprisingly sweet, with a grape flavor. I took a larger swig. My head felt lighter, like I'd drunk in a giant breath of pure oxygen. For the first time in days, my head cleared.

"Good, huh?" Bailen asked, his gaze lingering on me over the top of his glass. He gulped down half his drink in one go.

I took another large swig, enjoying the sense of freedom and clarity the drink gave me.

"Care to dance?" Bailen hopped off his stool and offered me a hand.

I shrugged. "I'm not much of a dancer." Harlow never would have asked me to dance. Soccer players didn't dance. But I'd never cared. Now, everything was different. A different time. A different place. A different guy. I wasn't sure what different meant, but maybe I needed it.

"Oh, come on. I bet you could dance circles around me."

"I don't know about that."

He laughed, the first carefree thing I'd heard from him in days. His loose-fitting jeans and collared, green shirt—although not his usual attire—accentuated his tall, boney frame. Despite his clean-cut clothes, his wild, brown hair still hung in his face. Part of me longed to reach out and brush it away so I could see him better. Not that it would matter. I could never read him anyway.

He moved his hips almost to the beat as he waited for me, clearly not taking *no* for an answer. He wasn't a good dancer, but something about his awkwardness made a smile tug at my lips. One that I didn't know I had desperately needed.

Sliding off the stool, I accepted his outstretched hand. We weaved through a sea of people to the center of the dance floor.

He continued to move slightly offbeat, and I hesitated before matching his swaying. Reaching around me with his left arm, he placed his hand on the small of my back. My skin prickled underneath my thin tank top. I suddenly wished I had on more clothes. Then maybe I wouldn't want to forget I had another life, forget about Jake, forget about those I'd left behind, and forget Harlow was waiting for me. A life I might not get to return to.

I wasn't supposed to feel like I wanted to destroy everything from my past before it had been taken from me. But Bailen was trying so hard to help me. To be sweet. Maybe he wasn't trying; maybe he actually was. Or maybe there was more to him than what I'd originally seen. Like the glimpse on the roof where he and Jake had switched places momentarily. My heart pounded.

There was a fine line between his obsession with technology and genuine interest, and Bailen flirted with both.

Flirted with me.

His intense gaze locked with mine, and I inhaled sharply. He grabbed my belt loop and pulled me closer to him. My awkward dancing settled into hip swaying that matched the heavy beat, and his hips soon found mine.

Bailen leaned in. His warm breath tickled my ear. "I'm glad you came."

"Me too."

But despite my acknowledgement, he pulled away. As the

space grew between us, the void inside me expanded. I inched closer, and the ache in my heart eased.

Somehow, beyond all impossibilities, he was exactly what I needed, the thing I'd least expected to help. I stared into his eyes as if they held some kind of secret message for me. The crowd of people surrounding us faded into the background. I lost myself in the swirls and various shades of green in his irises.

I draped my arms around his neck and pressed my forehead to his to get even closer.

But my brain kicked in and I eased back, butterflies swarming inside. *What am I doing? I have a boyfriend.*

Bailen cupped my cheeks, drawing me closer to him. Time slowed. He leaned toward me. I did nothing to stop it. I'd always followed the rules. Now I wanted to break them.

Our lips brushed against each other, and I pulled away slightly, my pulse beating in my neck. Bailen leaned in again, and I met him halfway.

Our lips crashed together in a wild fury. A kiss like none I'd ever experienced. A kiss that made me forget everything I didn't want to remember.

My hands roamed to his waist. He wrapped his arms around my hips and pulled me closer. I stretched up on my tiptoes to be closer to him. All sense of time flew away as I lost myself in the moment. A moment so far from everything I knew—in the best possible way.

"My god! Get a room!"

Peyton's voice ripped through the fog and returned me to reality. Jerking away from Bailen, I faced her. She had her head cocked to the side with a sly grin plastered on her face. When I could no longer stand it, I dropped my attention to my hands.

My life came crashing back to me. *What had I done?*

I'd always hated cheaters. Now I was one. And Peyton's face said she knew my secret.

Without a word, she turned to Bailen.

"We have an extraction."

"Now?" Bailen asked.

Peyton propped her hand on her hip. "No, next year, loverboy."

My cheeks burned, but Bailen didn't notice because he was too busy giving Peyton a death stare.

"Believe me, I wouldn't have gotten within a fifty-mile radius of this horrific display if it weren't absolutely necessary." Peyton spun on her heel and headed for the door.

Bailen took my hand and kissed me on the cheek before I could twist away.

Seventeen

"**W**hat's an extraction?" I asked once we were back in the barn. The name alone sounded unpleasant.

"We have to take someone's tracker off-grid. I wish we could do more of these, but they're risky. Once we find that loophole..." He shook his head as if to say he didn't want to remember what had happened during their last window. "Want to come?" Bailen asked.

I shrugged. It wasn't like I had other plans. And if I hung out by myself, I'd sink back into a dark hole and try to sort through the mystery of Jake's crazed journal entries.

"You can drive if you want."

I hesitated. "By myself?"

"Sure. You know how to handle the bike. Besides, we don't have to go far."

"Okay." I smiled, not sure if I was happy for another distraction or something that would keep Peyton off my back about what she'd just witnessed. She kept staring at me like an animal playing with its dinner.

I grabbed Jake's bike—no, not Jake's, *my* bike. I shoved my head into my helmet and climbed on. "Where to?"

"You can follow me." Bailen started his green bike.

I swallowed to calm my shaky nerves—alone on the bike and no tracker to navigate. As if I didn't have enough on my mind already.

My bike hummed beneath me. I shifted into first gear, proud of myself for getting it right on the first try. Jeremy climbed out of the trap door with two large boxes. He fixed one to Bailen's bike and the second to his before starting it. Bailen secured his helmet and pulled out of the barn. I took off behind him, my gut twisting. It was a lot easier with someone else on the bike.

Ahead of me, Bailen launched into the air. I switched on the flying mechanism and headed skyward. We flew close to each other, so close, I could almost reach out and touch the others. Almost. One wrong move, and I could take out the whole formation. The thought frazzled my nerves more.

In my head, I repeated the step-by-step process of shifting gears and flying the bike, while keeping an eye on Bailen's path. We swooped around a couple of buildings, headed for a familiar gray-bricked building in midtown. Bailen circled the roof, then landed. I put my bike down next to his. Of all the rooftops in the Central West End, I was surprised to be on that one. I'd been there hundreds of times—with Harlow.

We used to hang out on the roof gazing at the stars or watching the bikes fly in the nearby city. It was the one place we'd gotten some alone time. A pang of regret filled me. I'd messed everything up. And being there couldn't be a coincidence.

The guys opened their black cases, pulled out large knives,

and affixed them to their belts. They slammed the cases shut without a word. I guessed we weren't taking any chances. But what was a knife against another bomb going off? I blocked every thought surrounding that night out of my head.

We took the roof access to the stairs. As we continued down, my heart quickened. We stopped on the fifty-second floor. The floor Harlow lived on. The thought of seeing him again brought butterflies to my stomach, but not the first-kiss kind of butterflies—angry, psychotic butterflies. I wanted more than anything to see him, to know he was okay. But a run-in with Harlow would mean telling him what I'd done. It would have been a happy reunion if I hadn't been so stupid.

Bailen swung open the door and turned left. My heart sank— the opposite direction of Harlow's place. We weren't here for him. *Who were we here for?*

Three doors down, Bailen knocked softly. After a few moments, the door cracked open. A young girl peeked out beneath a gold chain.

"Bailen?" The voice sounded hesitant.

"Yes, it's me. Do you remember your Uncle Dave said we'd be by? Is he here?"

"No." The door closed with a quick click.

"She wasn't supposed to be alone. Dave promised her mother he'd take care of her right before she…" Bailen trailed off, the words understood by everyone. "We promised we'd take her off-grid, even though we don't normally for kids this young. The Ghosts owe it to her."

"That jerk is probably gambling again," Peyton said.

"Hey, it's got to be tough for the guy. He didn't want to be a dad, but he got stuck doing it. Death creates difficult circumstances," Jeremy said.

Bailen's focus flicked to me, as if he were checking my reaction to the word *death*. It was quickly becoming clear the Ghosts dealt with it a lot, and I'd have to as well. But it didn't make it any easier.

Peyton crossed her arms over her chest. "Well, we shouldn't have let him join the Ghosts. I don't care how much his sister insisted."

"Now that he's in, it's not like we can remove him. He knows too much," Jeremy said.

Peyton slammed her fist into her palm. "I'd like to pound his face in for leaving his niece here alone."

After a jingling sound, the door swung open. A thin, brown-haired girl stood in the threshold of the dimly lit apartment.

Bailen squatted so he was eye-level with the girl. "Can we come in?"

She nodded, causing her tangled hair to flop in her face.

Bailen stepped inside and waved us in. Jeremy placed his case on the coffee table in the living room. He pulled out small boxes and wires. Bailen set up a small portable computer.

I turned from the flurry of activity to the shaking girl. I felt bad for her. "What's your name?"

"Em-Emily," she whispered.

"Hi, Emily, I'm Kaya," I said. "Are you scared?"

She nodded, not very talkative.

"Let's go sit over here. I promise we'll keep you safe." I held out my hand. Emily accepted. I led her over to the couch near the spiderweb of wires emerging from the cases. Peyton stayed by the door, periodically checking the peephole.

"How old are you?" I smiled, trying to appear reassuring.

"Eight."

Emily reminded me of myself at that age. I'd wanted to be like Jake. Do everything he did. Everyone had always told me I was too little, including Jake. I tried to shake off the thought of all that wasted time. Time we'd never have again.

Bailen sat on the end of the coffee table in front of Emily and me. He held out three round discs like the ones he'd used on me. "Emily, can I put these on your temples? I promise it won't hurt."

As Bailen moved closer, she flinched away.

"It's just like a Band-Aid." I grabbed one of the discs from Bailen and pushed my thumb on the sticky side. "See? Feel it. It's sticky."

Emily hesitated then reached out and stuck her index finger to it. She pulled it off slowly then looked at me and smiled for the first time. "Okay," she said.

He brushed her hair behind her ears and stuck a disc on both of her temples, followed by a third at the base of her neck. When he finished, she sunk into the sofa cushion. "What's it going to feel like?"

"It's going to buzz like a fly in your ear and make your teeth chatter a little. Kinda like going to the dentist. Only less scary," I said in my most reassuring voice.

She grabbed my hand and squeezed. It made me wish I had some way to comfort her further like Jake had always comforted me with his pinky. Bailen moved to his computer resting on the coffee table.

"Uh, we have a problem." Peyton backed away from the door as something slammed against it.

"What now?" Bailen unhooked his knife and pivoted toward the door in anticipation of a fight.

The door flew open, slamming into the opposite wall. A scruffy, middle-aged man lurched into the room, nearly falling on his face.

"Dave's back. And he's drunk." Peyton closed the door.

Dave stumbled into the kitchen and rummaged through the cabinets and drawers, slamming each one shut when he didn't find what he wanted. He yanked open the refrigerator, stuck his head inside, then shoved the contents around.

"Who drunk my beers?" He whirled around, knocking a glass ketchup bottle to the floor. It shattered and ketchup splattered everywhere.

"You did, you dick!" Peyton said.

"Pey, keep him quiet," Bailen said. "We don't need the neighbors barging in on us or alerting the authorities."

"Fine. I'll take drunk duty," Peyton said. "But I'm not a babysitter."

Dave lumbered toward the door, but Peyton blocked his path. She grabbed him under the arm and guided him to a chair in the living room. He fell into it but immediately tried to stand again.

Peyton pushed him back like a bouncer at a club trying to control the riffraff. "Stay there."

Dave raised his fists in the air, ready for a fight. "No little missy's gonna tell me what to do." He pushed up from the chair a second time, but Peyton grabbed the pressure point in his neck. A moment later, he collapsed into the chair without another word.

"Nobody calls me 'little missy.'"

"We don't have time to deal with him. If he's still out when we finish, we're leaving him," Bailen said.

"What happened to him?" Emily asked.

176

"He'll be fine. Maybe we should let him take a nap," I said, running my hand through her hair in an attempt to comfort her.

She squeezed my hand tighter. It reminded me of when I'd sat in the chair at the Hive. Jake had held my hand while they'd run tests. I shoved down the pang of regret welling inside me. I wouldn't allow myself to lose it again. Not in front of everyone. I had to be strong, for Emily and for myself.

"Her signal is good," Jeremy said, staring at his device.

"Great. Keep an eye on it," Bailen said. "Are you monitoring the authority network?"

"Yep, you're all set. I'll let you know if anything pops up. Peyton, get ready to track the time."

Peyton hit several buttons on her watch then checked the peephole again.

Bailen squeezed Emily's shoulder. "Emily, your head is going to vibrate. Then there'll be a buzzing sound. You ready?"

"I think so."

"Here we go." Bailen's fingers flew over the keyboard.

I studied Emily's expression for signs of a panic attack. She crossed her arms over her chest and squeezed her eyes shut. I lifted my arm to pull her into a hug. But instead of tensing, she giggled. "It tickles."

"See, it's not so bad." I relaxed into the couch and watched the guys in action.

"I've got a lock on her signal. I just need to redirect the output. Mark the time... now," Bailen said.

"Five minutes counting down." Peyton tapped her watch.

Part of me wished I had the timer app, but the other part of me didn't miss my tracker or its contents. That was what had started my whole mess.

"Her signal is shifting to the TROGS network. How's the read?" Bailen asked.

Jeremy checked his device. "This is the cleanest switch I've seen. The authorities don't seem to be watching."

"I think we lucked out. They don't monitor kids as closely," Bailen said.

"It's about time we had some luck on our side." Jeremy tapped a few keys then sat back, as if satisfied with what was there.

Peyton checked her watch. "Three minutes left."

Bailen shrugged like it was no big deal. "That's plenty of time. The switch is eighty-five percent done. Another minute and it should be over."

Finally, we could breathe a little easier. And yet something deep down told me not to let my guard down yet.

Peyton squinted out the peephole. "Hallway is clear. Kaya, we should head to the roof and get the bikes ready. It's better if we're prepared."

"Nah, I'll hang back with Emily."

Peyton frowned briefly, indicating I'd messed with her well-thought-out plan "All right, we can stay, but you need to be ready to move."

"No problem. I'm ready."

"That's it. Pack it up." Bailen closed the small computer and wound up the wires.

Jeremy stuffed everything in the kits. I helped Emily remove the discs. We moved to the door with the others close behind. Peyton opened the door, peeked out, then stepped into the hall. Holding Emily's hand, I followed. When we got to the door at the end of the hall, a girly giggle drew my attention around the corner into the next corridor.

A guy in a soccer jersey was making out with a skinny blonde. "Stop it, Harlow." The girl laughed and playfully poked him.

I choked on my next breath. The blood drained out of my face and into my feet. I couldn't stop watching the scene. Maybe it was karmic payback for what had happened with Bailen, but there was something about seeing your mistakes reflected back at you. And I didn't like the image in the mirror. It tore at my core. Part of me wanted to march over and slug Harlow—to end the pain. A pain I shouldn't have been feeling. Just because I'd messed up didn't mean I'd stopped caring for Harlow. But now he'd done the same. Confusion fogged around me, freezing me in place—as if the authorities had gotten to my tracker.

Eighteen

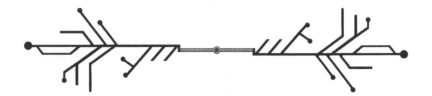

"**K**aya, we have to go." Peyton's voice tore me from the horrible scene. She peered around me at Harlow and the blonde. "Ugh, some people need to get a room."

Harlow pushed the blonde away. His eyebrows rose. A hint of a smile briefly crossed his lips before his mouth pulled tight, probably remembering his current situation and that I shouldn't have been witnessing him cheat. My jaw clenched. We stared at each other, at an impasse.

"Kaya?" His expression filled with confusion, sadness, and regret, the very same things swirling inside me.

I opened my mouth to say something, but words failed me. Peyton grabbed my free hand and dragged me into the stairwell with Emily at my heels.

I yanked away from Peyton's grasp and stumbled to the corner of the landing. I buried my head in my hands, my chest heaving. My emotions pulled me in two separate directions. I needed to clear the air with Harlow, figure out our confusing mess, but I couldn't risk staying behind. What if someone called the authorities? I took a long, deep breath. *Not now, Kaya.* I turned from the wall.

"What's gotten into you?"

I tried to wipe away the vision of Harlow shoving his tongue down another girl's throat. "Nothing. Let's go."

"Fine by me."

We bolted up the first flight of stairs as the door crashed open behind us. Jeremy and Bailen spilled into the stairwell on the landing below. I was so glad Bailen hadn't seen me almost lose it.

"Why aren't you on the roof?" Bailen asked.

"We would have been if your girlfriend hadn't just lost her shit."

My cheeks grew hot, and I pounded up the concrete stairs. If we weren't in a hurry, I might have paused long enough to deliver a witty comeback.

As we emerged onto the roof, I gulped in the fresh air, relieved to be out of the building.

"Emily, come with me." Bailen reached for her hand. She jerked it away and wrapped her arms around my waist.

"I want to go with Kaya."

The hairs on the back of my neck stood on end. I peeled her arms off me but held on to her hands, meeting her line of sight. "I need you to go with Bailen. He's a good guy. I promise."

"But..." Her bottom lip quivered, and her big eyes turned sad and doe-like.

That was the worst expression I'd ever seen. No wonder Jake had always caved to my puppy-dog eyes. Every part of me wanted to cave, but there was no way she could come with me. I was still figuring out what I was doing on the bike. It was too dangerous to bring a kid along.

Peyton crossed her arms over her chest. "We don't have time for this."

"I... I..." I couldn't say *no*. How could I tell her *no* when she needed me? "Fine, she can come with me."

Bailen grabbed my arm and pulled me off to the side. "Are you sure?"

"Peyton's right. We don't have time. And if riding with me is the only way she'll go... I'll take it slow. It's not that far." Hopefully, he believed me, because I wasn't sure I believed myself. But I was eager to put distance between me and Harlow.

"Okay. I'll ride right behind you. You guys go on ahead."

Everyone else hopped on their bikes and took to the sky.

I climbed on my bike. Putting on my helmet, I realized we didn't have one for Emily. As if reading my mind, Bailen grabbed his and placed it on her head. He picked her up and positioned her behind me.

"Hold on tight," I said into my helmet.

She wrapped her arms around my waist. I breathed heavily. Even though Bailen couldn't see me through the dark visor, I focused on him. The right side of his mouth curled into a half-smile, as if he knew what I needed. He squeezed my shoulder and leaned close. "You got this."

I gulped then started the engine. His bike roared to life as well. Before I lost my nerve, I revved the bike and launched into the sky. The rumble of a second bike told me Bailen was close behind.

I stayed low and maneuvered around the buildings at a slow pace. Authority searchlights shined a dozen blocks ahead. I squeezed my eyes shut for a brief moment and prayed they weren't headed in our direction. Luckily, they were hovering in one place, meaning they were involved in a tracker investigation. Even still, I wished I had the first responder app to confirm. It would ease my mind a little.

The roar of a familiar engine caught my attention, but it wasn't Bailen's bike.

Harlow.

Over my shoulder, the orange streak of a fast-moving crotchrocket caught my attention. *Great. He's the last thing I need right now.*

"Kaya, wait." Harlow's voice came through my helmet speakers.

He'd hacked my helmet? What the hell? I revved the engine a little harder and sped forward without checking to see if Bailen kept up.

"Talk to me." Harlow's voice was in my helmet again. Talking to him was the last thing I wanted right now. I wished I didn't need my iron grip on the bike so I could mute him.

"You could at least respond to your messages. You can't expect me to believe that fake auto reject app you're running."

Auto reject app? Another reason I was glad for my bum tracker.

"Nice bike. You look hot on it." Harlow pulled up on my right and kept pace with me, nodding his head in silent approval.

I scoffed. *Really? Ugh!* I wanted to scream and ditch him, but I wasn't sure how. He was a much better driver than me. Unfortunately, Bailen didn't have a helmet, so I had no hope of asking him for help.

But before I could motion for him, Bailen rode up on my left side and furrowed his eyebrows. I shook my head to tell him to let it go. How had I ended up on a flying death cycle sandwiched between the two guys vying for my heart? It was almost like an invisible rope was wrapped around me and each guy had an end. If one pulled too hard, I'd fall off.

As if sensing trouble, Emily squeezed me tighter. "Hang in there, Emily," I said, trying to take my mind off the guys.

Heavy breathing erupted in my helmet speakers.

"You ran away and disappeared. What was I supposed to think?" Harlow asked.

He was right. And then I'd kissed someone else. How could two people who cared about each other do such horrible things to one another? But the moment to discuss that had passed, left hanging in that hallway. I had to focus on getting Emily back to the Hive.

"I stopped by to see your parents," he said.

I kept my focus on the path ahead. I wouldn't let him get to me.

"They skipped town. They couldn't bear the thought of you running off. Of not finding you."

"You're lying," I yelled into my helmet microphone.

"You'll never know unless you talk to me," Harlow said.

An icy chill crept through my body. It took everything in my power not to ram my bike into his. It was a boldfaced lie. It had to be. I kept my focus ahead. I couldn't cave to his vicious trick, but I also couldn't ignore the possible truth invading my thoughts. Could I trust him after what he'd done with that Barbie wannabe? Could he trust me after what I'd done with Bailen?

We'd never lied to each other—until now. There was a lot of hurt and confusion between us. Neither of us deserved what we'd done to each other, but here we were. And I had no idea what to say.

What if I ignored him, and he was telling the truth about my parents?

Before I could respond, Harlow's engine thundered louder. He whipped his bike directly in front of mine. I yanked my handlebars to the left to avoid him, forgetting that Bailen was on my other side. As the bike tipped, I felt little hands slip from around my waist.

"*Emily!*" I yelled. I reached for her, but my hand closed around air.

I slammed on my brakes and hovered. Twisting around, my stomach unclenched, but only for a moment. A new foreboding tightened its fingers around me. Bailen leaned off the side of his bike, which was also frozen midair below me.

Emily dangled in his grasp.

She screamed and flailed as he tried to lift her onto his bike. I spun my bike around and sped toward them. As Emily continued to struggle, her legs flew upward and knocked the kit off the back of Bailen's bike.

"*No!*" Bailen yelled with a horrific scream that echoed off the buildings. "My computer!"

The kit plummeted to the ground below and smashed into a million pieces. On cue, a garbage truck inched past, sweeping up the debris.

With a large grunt, Bailen hauled the still-kicking Emily onto his bike. She immediately threw her arms around him and locked her fingers together. I let out a deep breath in relief. At least we hadn't lost her.

"Kaya, will you talk to me?" Harlow yet again in my helmet.

"Go away, Harlow," I spat. "You've done enough damage."

"But, Ka—"

"No, Harlow. It's over. Get out of my way."

"Fine. You weren't worth the wait, anyway." He whirled his bike around and ripped off toward his apartment, taking my shattered heart with him and leaving nothing but a smoke trail in exchange.

Nineteen

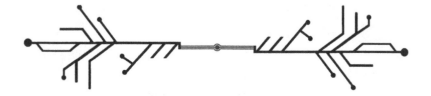

flipped up my visor. "I'm so sorry."

I wasn't sure if I was sorrier about Emily, my inexperienced driving, Harlow, or Bailen's broken computer, but my gut churned so fast, I wanted to hurl. It was all my fault. I never should have let Emily ride with me. And that was the smallest of my mistakes.

Before I could say anything more, Bailen twisted his throttle and tore off. I knocked down my visor and did the same, trying to keep up. "Slow down!" I shouted, doubting he could hear me.

Minutes later, he dipped beneath the treeline, headed for the abandoned barn. I followed, still trying to get him to acknowledge me. When we pulled into the barn, Peyton was leaning against the door with her arms crossed over her chest.

"About time!"

"Save it," Bailen snapped. He climbed off the bike then turned to lift Emily off. He removed her helmet. "Go with Peyton." Without another word, he spun on his heel and stormed down the trap door steps.

Emily glanced between me and Peyton, seemingly unsure what was the better option, then backed against the wall.

"What bit him in the ass?" Peyton asked.

Parking my bike, I pulled off my helmet. I stood my ground, determined not to show any guilt. "Don't give me that look. He's pissed he lost his computer."

She froze, realization washing over her. "The one with TROGS on it?"

"I don't know. Whatever he had strapped to his bike. It's gone."

"Gone as in *lost* or gone as in *destroyed*?"

I shrugged. "I don't know. Some garbage truck swept it up. What's the big deal? It's just a copy, right?"

"Losing TROGS is a shitstorm! If someone finds that computer, we're all screwed."

I hadn't thought of that. Emily inched closer to me, as if she knew I'd protect her. I couldn't let Peyton find out exactly what had happened. She'd kill me.

Mouth dry and tongue swelling, I swallowed hard. "I'm sure it will be fine. That thing smashed into a billion pieces when it hit the ground. I doubt any of it is recognizable." But I didn't believe that, so why should Peyton?

"You better hope so." Peyton flicked her hair over her shoulder and stomped to the trap door. She disappeared, leaving Emily and me alone in the barn.

I pulled out the paint cans again and dipped my brush into the black. I continued with the design on the barn wall while Emily sat with a paintbrush on the barn floor. My strokes started out choppy but slowly transformed into smooth, effortless lines.

Even though the patterns meant nothing to me, they were soothing.

I had nothing to lose myself in but painting. No tracker messages, no blinking lights, nothing but my art with no lenses or filters. Despite all the chaos around me, it was amazing how calming it all was. Everything Dad had ever said about unplugging and taking time to reflect made sense. I finally understood the meaning of Shabbat, and it wasn't a sacrifice at all. It was about allowing myself to experience the world in a different way than my everyday routine—to be myself without all the distractions. To rest. I leaned in and embraced the quiet calm.

Lost in my thoughts, I didn't know how much time had passed. It must have been a while, though, because Emily ended up curled in a small pile of hay, fast asleep, peaceful. And now I was thankful I knew how to find that kind of serenity too.

The trap door creaked, causing me to jump. Jeremy appeared, followed by Bailen.

"We've been looking for you," Jeremy said.

Bailen scowled but didn't say anything.

"I was painting." A hint of a smile briefly crossed Bailen's face before his scowl returned, as if he were forcing himself to remain mad at me. "Emily was too, but I think she's worn out." I pointed to the corner.

Jeremy craned his neck then moved around me and cradled her in his arms. "I'll get her to bed." He gave Bailen a mischievous grin before leaving the barn.

I dug my foot into the ground, more interested in my shoes than Bailen. "I'm sorry about your computer," I mumbled.

Bailen ignored me and climbed onto his bike.

"Wait." I grabbed his arm, more because I needed to touch

him than to stop him from leaving. "Talk to me."

He shrugged my hand off, taking my last shred of hope to turn his mood around away with it. "What do you want me to say?" From his slouched back to his tense jaw, the hurt oozed out of him. Even his eyelids drooped, as if they had given up. He'd lost everything because of me.

"I don't have time to chat. I have to get the computer." He winced as if he were watching it tumble to the ground and shatter all over again. "Or what's left of it."

I wanted so badly to hug him, but I doubted he would let me. "At least let me come with. It's partially my fault." No, that was a lie. "Okay, all my fault."

"It's not your fault. It was my responsibility."

"I still feel bad. Let me help." Besides needing to rid myself of the guilt, I needed an excuse to forget what had happened earlier. All of it.

"Fine. Just be ready to get your hands dirty."

"What? Why?"

"Hop on. I'll show you."

I climbed on the bike as he revved the engine. We shot through the open barn doors before I could get my arms fully around Bailen's waist. The wind whipped past as we headed for the sky.

"So, how did you find the computer?" I asked as we flew. "I thought it was swept away by that garbage truck."

"The good news is I was able to hack the city's logs and find out where the truck makes its drop-offs."

"What's the bad news?"

"Maybe I should let you wait and see."

Great! More surprises. As we emerged from the wooded area,

I saw the local fly-in movie theater at the edge of town. I knew it well. My friends and I went there often because it was too far for our parents to chase us down, but it was a parentally acceptable activity because despite the name, we could walk and enjoy the movies from the picnic benches. Harlow and I frequently made out there—or used to. The once happy thought gave rise to an uneasy feeling I had to shove deeper down to avoid.

Bailen pitched the bike downward, landing in a lot next to the fly-in.

"The town dump?" I asked, gagging on the stench of rotting food and dead animals.

"Yep. I warned you that you might get dirty."

"I didn't think you were being literal."

"I don't joke around when it comes to my computer equipment." He extended his hand to me. "Come on. Let's get this over with."

I accepted his hand. His touch sent tingles through my fingertips, but he let go far too soon. We walked through the main fence into the dimly lit junkyard. I scanned the trash heaps. Each of the piles around us seemed to contain a random assortment of junk, everything from metal scraps to rotting food to broken furniture. "How are we supposed to find TROGS in all this?"

"With this." He pulled a small blue box from his jacket pocket and flipped it open. When he turned the switch on, a small window display lit up. "If we get within one hundred feet of TROGS, my device should pick it up."

"What's to stop the authorities from being able to track that signal?"

"It's modified old tech. The authorities wouldn't know to

look for it. Not to mention, you basically have to be on top of the box to find it." Bailen slowly moved the device in a large arc.

In the dark it was hard to tell how far the piles of trash went, but I imagined a never-ending field of garbage. "Great. We're sunk."

"We are not." He paused to pick something off one of the heaps. "It just might take a while."

We'd be junkyard diving all night. I walked into the distance, but honestly, I didn't even know how to begin to find TROGS. It was hopeless.

"This place is a dump," I said, gagging on the smell of something so rancid, I couldn't begin to identify it.

"No kidding," Bailen called from behind one of the trash heaps. "But you never know what gems you'll discover."

When he rounded a giant pile of crumpled plastic bottles and old clothes, I couldn't help but laugh. He was wearing giant gold-rimmed glasses that were missing a lens, a sideways red mesh hat, and a hot pink plastic clip-on earring.

"You look ridiculous," I said, trying to stifle my giggling. It wasn't supposed to be a fun trip. We had equipment to find. The longer I spent in the dump, the sicker I felt.

"Yeah, but I made you laugh, didn't I?"

"Sure," was all I could manage to get out through my swirl of mixed-up emotions.

With everything that had happened, I'd forgotten how to have fun. It felt good to let go a little. It was strange, almost like I was watching a new person. Or maybe I was seeing him in a new way, without a filter.

I ran to the next pile of trash, kicked an apple core aside, and picked up a torn floppy green hat with giant purple and pink flowers. Putting it on my head, I turned to Bailen. "What do you think?"

"Beautiful, my lady. Care to dance?" He held out his hand, palm up. When I grabbed it, he pulled me in close. We performed a mock tango down the aisles of trash, giggling as we went.

In the center of the dump, we collapsed onto a pile of trash, our chests heaving from laughing so hard. The stars in the sky shined brighter at the edge of town. My hand sat inches from his in an infinite limbo. My head went into an immediate tug-o-war. Part of my brain said, *Take his hand!* while the other part thought, *No, you've lost your chance.* I went back and forth for what seemed like an eternity. My fingers crept toward his then pulled back in an awkward dance.

I took a deep breath and started to make my move, but Bailen sat up and pulled out his device again. He circled it around, checking the screen. "I don't think it's here."

I pulled the green hat off my head, wishing I could bury my face in it. If it didn't stink so bad, I might have.

"Come on, let's keep searching." He stood and reached out to me. I let him pull me up, but he quickly turned his attention back to the device.

We wandered the dump in silence with the trash below our feet crunching in rhythm to our steps. I opened my mouth a million times to say something but always thought better of it. A strange energy buzzed between us, almost as if we'd get zapped if we moved any closer to each other.

After an eternity of silence and searching a majority of the trash piles, he said, "The device would have beeped by now. Either that or TROGS was too badly damaged."

"I'm sorry. I thought we'd find it." A lame attempt to lift his mood, even though I knew it was an impossible task.

"It's okay," he said. He grabbed my hand and squeezed, sending a shiver up my arm. Maybe my mixed-up feelings weren't so crazy after all. Maybe he was still interested. Maybe I was, too.

"I'm guessing it's completely destroyed. There's no way it fell from that height and still works. Even if the authorities found it, I doubt it would be useful to them now." He shrugged, but I wasn't sure if he really believed everything he said. He was rationalizing the loss to himself.

I stood in silence, unsure how to respond. Odds were, if we couldn't find it, no one else would, either. At least I hoped that was true.

After a long while, Bailen broke the silence. "Can I ask you something?"

"Yeah. Anything."

"Who was that guy chasing us earlier? You seemed to know him."

"Just some jerk from school."

Bailen put his arm around me, pulling my shoulder into him. "Really? 'Cause it seemed like you knew him pretty well."

I shuddered then took a deep breath, preparing myself. "He's my boyfriend," I said. "Or at least he was. Now, I don't know what he is. It's a mess, like everything else in my life."

"If you want my opinion, he sounds like an asshole. But he's whatever you let him be."

As much as I cared for Harlow, Bailen was right. I could choose whether or not I wanted Harlow in my life. How could two people cheat and hurt each other and still think they fit? I wasn't sure Harlow and I were right for each other. Maybe we never had been.

Bailen's deep green eyes held a hint of sadness that told me he cared despite everything that was happening. I had something great right in front of me. I wouldn't let it go again.

Bailen leaned down and kissed me, dragging me out of my worried thoughts. I let the warmth and kindness pull me into the moment. Every painful thought and uncertainty drained out of me into the trash heap below us, exactly where it belonged. I was safe with Bailen. I didn't have to worry anymore in a moment that felt more right than any other. Despite everything changing at lightning speed, Bailen had become the one person who always seemed to be next to me at the right times. The one constant.

And without another thought, I knew my answer.

I pulled away from the kiss but leaned into him, watching the giant movie screen at the fly-in on the other side of the fence. "Man, I miss the movies," I said in a hushed voice, trying to change the subject.

"Really?" Bailen asked.

"Yeah."

"Then what are we doing in this trash heap?"

A couple of minutes later, we were on the opposite side of the fence. We parked in the far lot away from most of the other vehicles.

"Are you sure it's safe to be out in public?" I asked.

"I think the authorities have much better things to do then stakeout the local fly-in," Bailen said. "But we can hang back here just in case."

Climbing off the bike, I handed my helmet to Bailen. "Wait here. I want to go clean up a bit. I smell like a dumpster."

I headed for the bathroom. Once inside, I grabbed a wad of paper towels from the dispenser next to the sink. Flipping on the faucet, I checked the dimly lit mirror. My face was red, puffy, and streaked with brown, like I'd been crying dirt for a week, which was perfect because that was exactly how I felt.

A frantic knock on the door made me jump. I turned as the door opened and Bailen slipped inside.

"You know this is the ladies' room, right?"

"Yeah, but that's the least of my concerns. We've got company."

"What?"

"A couple of agents just showed up. I guess they proved my theory wrong."

"Crap."

"I think it's just a routine check. We'll lie low and sneak out before they see us."

I knew our little detour had been too good to be true. I dropped the paper towels in the trash and shut off the sink. Bailen cracked the door and scanned outside. "They're gone for now."

As Bailen pulled the door open all the way, he put his arm around me. We stepped out of the bathroom and kept to the shadows. I laced my fingers through his. He led me to the far side of the building. At the corner, we stopped. Pressing a finger to his lips, he peered around the side of the building but jolted back.

"There's an agent," he whispered, his hot breath beating into my ear.

Twenty

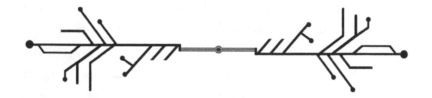

Bailen backed against the wall, and I leaned into him, inching closer and closer until our bodies met. I tensed as his chin rested on my shoulder, his breath tickling behind my ear. I buried my face in his neck. He left a trail of soft kisses starting from my earlobe down my jawline. I wrapped my arms around his waist and didn't bother to pretend I wasn't enjoying it.

"Is it clear?" he whispered. His hot breath made me shiver.

I rose on my tiptoes and slowly peeked around the corner, struggling to focus as Bailen pulled back the collar of my sweatshirt and caressed my shoulder with his lips. I shook my head. Bailen pulled me in. His heart pounded in time with mine. If I hadn't been freaking out about a million things, it might have been hot.

"Now?" Bailen's voice ripped through my uneasiness. I peeked around the side of the building. The agent rounded the corner toward the front of the building. I let out a long breath in relief.

"Let's go," I said.

Bailen grabbed my hand. We tore across the parking lot. Moments later, we were on the bike and in the air.

The whole way to the Hive, I didn't know whether to be more concerned that the authorities were so close to me or to TROGS. As much as I wanted to believe it was an awkward coincidence, part of me knew it was no accident the agents had been at the fly-in. Not only did many kids from school hang out there, but it was right next to the dump. There were too many places to search for clues. I'd have to be more careful. If I got caught, what would they do to me? What would they do to my parents? My parents.

Flying crotchrockets.

I'd been so worried about Harlow, Bailen, Emily, TROGS, and everyone else, I'd completely forgotten about what Harlow had said—that my parents had left. Or had they? Where would they have gone? And why leave when I was missing? It didn't add up. And that fact ate away at me. I needed answers before the awful thoughts fogging my mind took over.

I was so distracted, I didn't realize we'd landed in the barn until Bailen shut off the bike. He opened the trap door but paused. "You coming?"

I wanted to, but I couldn't let the horrible feeling go. I shook my head. "I need to paint some more." It was a lame excuse, but hopefully he'd buy it.

"Okay. Don't stay out here forever. I may need you."

I stifled the growing smile because I wasn't sure if he meant my tracker or me. "I'll come down in an hour or so."

"I'll be watching the clock." He smirked, letting me know it was more than just my tracker, then disappeared through the trap door.

The minute it slammed shut, I bolted to my bike and rolled it silently out of the barn. When I was out of hearing range, I started it and took to the sky. An hour didn't give me much time, but I had to follow my instinct. As I flew over the river toward the city, I wished the wind swirling around me could blow away all my uncertainty.

Ten minutes later, I landed beside my apartment building. I hid my bike behind a dumpster then jogged up the fire escape. I couldn't risk entering the building on the main floor or the roof, there were too many cameras and tracking sensors. But if I could peek in the windows, I'd hopefully get my answer. When I reached the thirtieth floor, I paused to catch my breath.

Now came the fun part. With the fire escape ending there, I had to scale the last five floors. Many buildings in midtown had this feature. When they decided to add additional housing on top of the existing buildings, they built extra internal stairwells instead of expanding the external ones. Something about improving the external aesthetic of the building, but they never removed what was already there which was to my benefit.

Although I'd snuck out and climbed from my window to Lydia's more times than I could count, I'd never attempted to crawl up the side of my building. I jumped on the railing and grabbed on to the window ledge above. Kicking my feet up, I pulled myself onto the concrete lip that was barely wide enough for my feet. From there, I wiped my sweaty palms on my jeans and searched for hand and footholds between the balconies. Slowly, I moved toward my window. I shifted in and out of the shadows cast by the single bulbs lighting every few floors. Luckily, most people were asleep; otherwise, they might have screamed and alerted the authorities of a creepy figure outside their windows.

As I continued, it was tough to find secure holds. Sweat dripped, blurring my vision, but I didn't dare move my arm to wipe it. My palms grew clammy. With every reach upward, securing a grip became more difficult. My fingertips began to slide on the bricks. I risked a quick swipe on my shirt before stretching to the next position. Legs wobbling, I paused to balance myself then judged the distance to my window. Just a few more arm lengths and I'd be there.

I stretched for the next good crevice in the side of the building, but my sweaty fingers slipped off the edge. I grabbed for my previous hold then waited for my pounding heart to slow. After wiping my palms on my shirt, I attempted to pull up again and successfully secured the hold. Two more moves. I struggled up another arm length. One more move and I could reach the windowsill.

When I grabbed on to the ledge and hauled myself up, I was sweating through my clothes and gulping in air. Despite that, the climb was exhilarating. From the height, the cars and sidewalks below seemed so trivial.

"Damn," I muttered. Why had I left my curtains closed?

Pressing my ear against the cool glass of the window, I listened for signs of my parents. Silence. Maybe they were on some kind of temporary assignment or were sleeping. A pang of regret passed over me. I'd give all my art supplies to see them just for a second.

I paused again to listen for movement. Still nothing. I scaled across the building toward the living room balcony. I reached for secure hand and footholds. It wasn't much different than climbing to Lydia's window, except I was moving in the opposite direction. Ten reaches later, I jumped over the railing to our balcony.

I squatted by the edge of the window and peered inside. The whole apartment was dark. Not a single item in the living room was out of place, as if no one lived there. How strange. My parents were never neat.

I crept along the balcony to catch a glimpse down the hall toward my parents' bedroom. The digital displays of family photos hung on the wall. Darkness loomed on glossy screens holding my family's smiling faces.

I couldn't see the images from outside the window, but I knew them well. Family dinners and birthdays, Thanksgiving, and Chanukah. Snapshots of all the best traditions, things I'd never thought I'd miss. But now having lost everything, I clung to the memories.

Everything I'd grown up with and believed in carried so much more weight. I'd lost all the best parts of myself, the happy moments, and my most favorite of all—us by the lake.

We'd go for Tashlich to cast our sins away. Jake had never missed it until a couple of months ago, the first time he'd missed it. At the time I had assumed he went to the campus Hillel to celebrate. Now I knew the real reason why. It wasn't the same without him secretly throwing the bread at the ducks, even though he was supposed to cast it into the water. He'd chuck it right in the middle of the ducks and laugh as they scrambled to be the first to get it. Not even Dad's stern insistence that we take it seriously scared us.

Jake and I would struggle to control our snickers. And even

after getting a few quiet moments to reflect, Jake would side-eye me, and we'd lose it all over again. My gut twisted knowing I'd never hear his laugh again.

I couldn't even remember what it sounded like anymore. If it weren't for my bum tracker, I'd pull up a vid to remind myself, but all I had was the memory. And the next time I cast off my sins, I'd have a lot more to be sorry for.

My insides ripped apart.

I needed to find my parents. But what then? Would I rush inside, hug them, and tell them everything, including what had happened to Jake?

I didn't know.

The shadows in the hall threatened to envelop the happiness oozing out of the photos and squash it forever.

I climbed on the opposite railing and reached for a hold on the side of the building. My fingers cramped, and I released my hold. I kneeled down and leaned against the building for support. Flexing my fingers a few times, I waited for the cramping to stop. I just needed to check my parents' bedroom then I could head back. No one would know I'd been here.

When the ache in my hands dulled, I grabbed the handhold again. I shoved my foot into a gap on the wall and pulled myself onto the building. My whole body shook as I slowly made my way toward the windowsill outside my parents' room. My fingers tingled and I paused to steady myself before proceeding through the last few maneuvers.

Balancing on the window ledge, I peered inside. Their bed was made perfectly, as if no one had ever slept in it, but there were suitcases lying open on the chairs next to the bed. Clothes and shoes spilled out of the cases and some items had fallen to the floor. Dread coursed through my veins like an IV full of acid. *Why would they leave in the middle of packing?*

I rested my forehead on the cool glass. It seemed like they'd been trying to pack in a hurry, but if they weren't here and their clothes were, where had they gone? Or maybe the better question was: Who or what had made them leave without their stuff?

My heart pounded. The hour I'd promised Bailen was nearly up. I'd have to find those answers later. I climbed back to the living room balcony and bolted across it. I sat on the railing and reached for hand and footholds leading me back to my bedroom window. As I stepped onto my windowsill, a red light with a blinking *TW* chat bubble appeared in the corner of my eye.

Twenty-One

Goose bumps erupted on my skin. Cold, spidery fingers twisted in my gut. Why was my tracker active again? There was only one way to find out. I knew I shouldn't, but I blinked twice to open the message.

17:00

Honey,
Are you okay? We miss you.
They hurt you Kaya. We are so sorry.
Let us help. Even if it means more tests, let's fix this.
Please come home. We're really worried about you.
Love you lots,
Mom and Dad

I blinked twice. The message collapsed out of view. Were they nuts? More tests? That didn't sound like them. And I was already home. Where were they? I froze, framed in my window staring at the concrete thirty-five floors down. I waited for signs of life from inside the apartment. I wanted to see them more than anything. But the voice of doubt whispered in my mind, *It's a trap.*

The familiar click of the front door sounded from the entryway. Heavy footsteps padded closer to my bedroom, accompanied by muffled voices I didn't recognize. An icy chill swarmed my body. A voice screamed inside my head.

Run.

With the familiar click of my bedroom door, I snapped back to reality. I kneeled, clinging on to the edge of the window with my hands. Swinging, I dropped onto the balcony below then immediately vaulted over to the next window ledge. From there, I scaled the wall down three more stories to the fire escape.

Chat bubbles with the initials *LW* flooded my vision. Lydia. I caught glimpses of OMG YOU'RE ALIVE and WHERE HAVE YOU BEEN? before I minimized them from view and focused on my escape route.

I risked one final glance at my window and locked eyes with an agent wearing a wicked expression that told me he would catch me no matter what it took. Another moment passed before he yelled something into my apartment. I jumped over the railing and landed on the floor below. I continued to catapult over railings until I reached the ground.

Despite my cramping leg muscles, I sprinted to the dumpster and grabbed my bike. My head filled with crazy theories and possible truths while I started the engine. The tires squealed as I pushed the bike to its limit. The moment I had enough space, I engaged the flying mechanism and soared into the sky, checking to make sure the authorities weren't tailing me as I turned toward the Hive.

My worst nightmare was a reality. If my parents weren't home, and they weren't on transfer, then the authorities had them. I said a quick prayer for their safety. I'd never forgive myself if I'd gotten them killed.

I lowered into the woods toward the barn. My body stiffened and bile ran up my throat. A wave of horror whipped through me. If the authorities were at my apartment, and they had my parents, then there was only one thing left for them to hunt.

Me.

The authorities were using my parents as bait. And they'd only found me because of my tracker's mysterious reincarnation. Or maybe they had been watching my place? How could I have been so stupid?

A second wave of horror wrapped itself around me, making each breath more difficult. If my tracker was active, I'd just lead the authorities right to the Hive.

I wanted to vomit. The tires squealed in protest as I skidded into the barn and nearly ran over Peyton.

"You idiot! Watch what you're doing!"

A group of Ghosts in dark gear with flashlights surrounded me.

Peyton stared daggers at me that threatened to cut me in two, then rolled her eyes at Bailen. "See, I told you she'd be fine. Kaya's a big girl. Chill out."

My chest tightened. "We've got a problem," I blurted out before anyone could say anything else.

"What kind of problem?" Peyton raised her fist in my face. "If you bring harm to the Hive, I will make your life a living hell."

"I'd never intentionally hurt anyone." But despite my best

intentions, we were moments from being overrun by authorities. And it was all my fault.

Bailen stepped between us. "Enough, Pey. Let her talk."

He spun around, grabbed my arms, and looked me square in the eyes. "What is it? Whatever it is, we'll fix it."

"My... My tracker... It's back..." I shook my head, trying to clear out the haze, but it didn't help. "I'm not sure what happened. I got a message from my parents. I think it was a trap. The authorities showed up at my place as I was leaving."

"You went home?" His expression twisted into a mixture of confusion and horror.

"Yes, but I didn't go inside."

"Crap! Code Nine. We gotta move." Peyton shot me a death stare then followed the others through the trap door.

Bailen remained behind. "What were you thinking? You knew you couldn't go home. That's the first place the authorities would watch for you."

"It was something Harlow said about my parents. That they're gone. I didn't feel right about it. I thought if I just got a peek inside." My shoulders slumped like I'd just been caught sneaking out. I should have told him, let him help me. But I knew if I had, he would have tried to stop me. "Then I got this strange message. I'm sorry. I didn't know what to do or where to go."

His expression hardened. "Peyton's right. We have to clear out." Clutching my hand a little too tightly, he dragged me through the trap door.

When we reached the computer room, people were tripping over each other. A blue light near the ceiling swirled ominously over the chaotic scene.

Bailen led me to his desk. He pushed me into a chair and pulled a kit out from one of the desk drawers. I flinched at the sight. It resembled the kit the authorities used to jumpstart my tracker.

"What are you doing?"

"Masking your tracker signal. We don't have time for TROGS. And the only version I have right now isn't mobile." His eyebrows furrowed. "This will hurt."

The needles gleamed, daring me to run, but I knew I couldn't. I swallowed hard as he picked up a needle and filled it with an orange liquid. "Where are you putting that?"

"Your arm."

"Do it." I rolled up my sleeve and squeezed my eyes shut. After a tiny prick, it was over. The traces of the tracker windows faded to a ghostly transparency. A few moments later, they disappeared from my vision completely.

"How long will this last?"

"I flooded the programming in your chip. It should hold for a few hours then come back slowly. As soon as we're moved, I'll switch you over to TROGS. Assuming we all make it."

"I'm so sorry. I didn't know what else to do."

He pursed his lips as if he were trying to avoid yelling at me. "It's fine."

Before I could say anything further, Bailen disappeared into the chaos of people, leaving me alone in the mess I'd made.

I searched for some way to help, but every time I bent down to grab something, someone else swooped in and took the item before I could. After a few attempts, I gave up and watched them scurry like ants coming out of an unearthed hill.

Across the room, Jeremy carried Emily on his back. She

reached out to me. "Kaya." I shoved into the sea of people. Everyone bumped me and pushed me toward the exit. Before I knew it, I'd lost sight of them. I couldn't do anything. I couldn't find Emily. Everything was my fault.

As the equipment disappeared, the people cleared out with it, making it easier to pick out individuals. I ran across the room to Bailen.

"What can I do?"

He plopped a heavy black-and-silver box in my arms then spun me around without a word.

"Would you talk to me?" I asked.

He grabbed another box and stormed toward the exit.

I hurried after him. "Bailen, wait. I said I was sorry."

"And I said it was fine."

The edge in his voice struck me hard. I wished he'd yell at me and get it over with. I'd screwed up, and that guilt was more than enough. But Bailen icing me out was too much.

When we reached the barn, he dumped the equipment into a container on the back of the bike. Outside, a giant truck hovered a foot off the ground. Peyton stood in the back, taking tools and computers that people passed her.

"Where will we go?" I asked.

The only response I got was the sound of the container on the back of my bike slamming shut. I grabbed Bailen's shoulder.

"Talk to me, please."

"Start the bikes. I have to grab more gear."

Not exactly what I'd hoped for, but it was a start. Before I could respond, Bailen had vanished again. I didn't like the sense of loneliness that filled me every time he took off. I knew everyone had a job to do, and the authorities could show up at any second. If Bailen hadn't flooded my tracker, I'd have been able to see how close the authorities were. But it had to be done, and here I was left in the middle of chaos, completely alone. And yet I felt suffocated by his silence and I couldn't handle it. Bailen, on the other hand, remained focused on the task. Like some kind of warrior instinct had kicked in—a warrior who wanted nothing to do with someone who had betrayed them.

The commotion in the barn dwindled. Fewer and fewer people remained. Bailen's father scurried around with spools of wiring and then disappeared behind the truck.

I climbed on my bike and secured my helmet, waiting for Bailen. A minute later, he emerged from the trapdoor with another load of gadgets. He dropped them into the storage container on his bike. He hopped on and his voice filled my helmet. "Follow me. Stay close."

He revved his engine, burst through the barn doors, and whipped around the truck. I tailed close enough to see steam rolling off his tires, coiling like a cobra. We wove through the trees, keeping to the shadows. Branches tore at my shirt and jeans. The cool night air burned the newly formed scrapes on my arms and legs. I wanted to inspect the wounds but didn't dare lose sight of Bailen.

My head throbbed. A slight buzzing rang in my ears. I gripped the handlebars tighter and continued to plow through the underbrush. The deeper into the forest we went, the more my head pounded. Then the buzz shifted to a whistle like a wind blowing through my ears.

"Bailen, I'm getting dizzy," I said into the helmet.

A long silence persisted before he said, "Hang in there. We'll be there soon."

If I could hold on a little longer. But I didn't have time. The outlines of apps started to glow in my vision. *No. It's too soon!* My hands and feet tingled. I squeezed my hands into fists in an attempt to regain feeling, but the tingling moved up my arm. The thudding in my head became unbearable. I couldn't focus on anything. The rhythm of the pulsing pain flooded my mind. I had to keep going. It was just a little farther. But I wasn't sure I could do it anymore.

A chill ran through my body. I tried to hit the brake and pull to the side, but my body was completely rigid. I'd lost the ability to move. My bike sped on under the weight of my unmovable foot. My voice screamed inside my head as the bike narrowly missed tree after tree. I struggled to form coherent thoughts. The throbbing made it impossible. The authorities had control of my tracker.

My muscles trembled. Sweat beaded on my forehead. I fought against my tracker for control of my body. If only I could get Bailen's attention. But even he couldn't stop the rollercoaster of insanity.

The trees around me blurred. All sound morphed into a horrible buzzing in my ears. I tried to pry my hands from the handlebars to grab my head, but they wouldn't budge.

My foot lifted off the accelerator against my will.

The bike's engine stalled. It ripped through the underbrush. Twigs cracked underneath it. The bike groaned. I plowed deeper into the woods, whipping through shrubs. Leaves and dirt spewed up on both sides of me like a geyser. I silently pleaded for the bike to stop.

It kept rolling.

Jump off!

I mentally commanded my body to move.

No response.

Shit!

My breath caught in my throat. My pores filled with sweat as the bike careened toward a giant tree. Bailen's bike shrank into the distance.

Time slowed to a crawl. Everything but the tree blurred into oblivion. My insides twisted. The tree loomed closer and closer. I tried to slam my eyes shut, but they were pinned open. They quickly grew dry and painful. *I'm going to die and there's nothing I can do about it. At least I'll be with Jake soon.*

If by some chance I live through this, I won't hold back.

My thoughts.

My feelings.

No regrets.

As my bike slammed into the trunk, pain exploded through my body like the sun incinerating me from the inside out.

Twenty-Two

Unknown faces leaned over me before my eyelids drooped closed again. Moments later, an awful vinegar smell assaulted my nose. I squinted under the bright lights. My body ached like I'd been used as a soccer ball. I lifted my heavy arm, but it stopped partway up with a snapping sound. A glistening chain connected a band around my wrist to the chair I was lying in.

"Ah, she's awake."

I flipped my head in the direction of the male voice, the room slowly spinning as I went. The small room had white walls devoid of any decorations. Scalpels, needles, and clamps filled the silver tray next my chair. The harsh light gleamed off the tools as if they were mocking me.

My feet were bare, and my jeans had been replaced by cream-colored scrubs complete with a matching top.

"Where am I?" I choked out, my mouth dry. "Let me go."

"I'm afraid I can't do that." A second, deeper voice laughed.

I gasped, immediately recognizing the man from pictures in my history briefs and on the news. Even though his khakis pants were wrinkled, his red sweater was faded, and his normal slicked back hair wildly stuck up in places, there was no mistaking who this man was, tired bags under his eyes and all. In the corner of the room stood Rufus Scurry, the inventor of Tracker220.

I swallowed hard. *Trouble* didn't even begin to describe my current situation. I was no longer walking the edge of the cliff. Things had spiraled so far out of control that I'd tumbled off, headed for a pit full of flaming, jagged rocks.

"You and your tracker have caused a lot of problems, young lady." He stared at me like he was trying to understand a calculus equation with no solution. "What do you say we run some tests?"

My mind raced. He was clearly smarter than his goonish agents. His mere presence meant he must not have trusted anyone else to fix my malfunctioning tracker. Lying was my only option, and I'd have to make it convincing.

The tracker network relied on unquestioning people who complied with the system and obeyed the rules. I hadn't done that.

Staring at my shackled hands, I thought of Jake, the one thing that would make me cry on the spot. I gave into the tears, knowing it might be the only thing that would save me. "I wanted to come home, but"—my bottom lip quivered—"the Ghosts—they held me prisoner. They killed my brother and told me if I didn't help them, they'd kill my parents too. I didn't have a choice." I let the tears well and my body shook, hoping he wouldn't see through the lie.

Mr. Scurry's face showed no emotion, but his eyes glimmered with a glint of something I couldn't quite place. Maybe it was triumph. He tilted his head to the side as if weighing the truthfulness of my words.

"I was scared. I didn't know what to do." I added hoping to tip the balance. At least that part was true. I was scared then and now.

His lips curled upward into an evil half grin as if to say, "*I'm onto your little secret. The ruse is up.*" "Your parents are here. They're in no real danger."

My insides coursed with dread. They might be alive, but in the hands of Rufus Scurry was way worse than anything I could imagine. With one expression, he'd taken me out of the fire and burned me from the inside out.

"Can I see my parents?" I put on my best hopeful, pleading face. "You can do whatever you need to with my tracker. Just let me see them first."

"You're right. We will adjust your tracker. But we don't need your permission." He nodded to the agents on either side of me, then strode from the room.

They wheeled over large machinery holding trays of needles and sharp objects that made the instruments to my left look like toys. Before I had time to struggle, they pressed my arms down and shoved needle after needle into them. The stab of each one made me scream louder and louder inside my head, but I bit down on the insides of my cheeks to keep the screams from becoming audible. I wouldn't give them the satisfaction.

Some of the liquids burned like a volcano while others cooled like an arctic blast. I broke into a sweat as I rapidly cycled between hot and cold. My body grew heavy. My eyelids drooped. The machines buzzed and whirled around me with increasing intensity. The crunching and grinding sounds were sickening. I fought to stay conscious, but with each substance they injected, more energy leaked from my body. My vision went white, like my tracker was hard-resetting.

After an eternity, my feet blurred into focus, followed by two men in green scrubs. They loosened the bands around my arms and hauled me from the chair. A blue light blinked in the corner of my sight, indicating some kind of health issue, but I didn't dare access the message. They dragged me out the door and down a hall, my dirty feet scraping across the pristine, white floors. I had trouble keeping track of the directions we went as we twisted through the nondescript hallways.

With a metallic whine, a door swung open, and they threw me to the floor by the far wall. The door slammed behind me with a second screech.

I groaned and struggled to sit upright. Shooting pains raged through my head, causing the room to spin.

"Easy. You've been through quite an ordeal."

The voice sounded familiar, but my head pounded too much to think clearly. I strained to focus on the figure helping me to a sitting position. Brown, shaggy hair, green eyes. "I've seen you before," I choked out in a hoarse whisper.

"Yes, we've met. I'm Myles, Bailen and Peyton's father."

I shook my head but instantly regretted it. Pain shot through every nerve in my brain. With it, came a sudden clarity. I knew where I'd seen him before, and it hadn't just been at the Hive. "No, you were on the news."

"Oh, they did a number on you, dear."

"No," I protested. "The crime, the murder, that was you." I knew his eyes were familiar when I met him, but I couldn't place it beyond that he, Bailen, and Peyton all had a striking resemblance. I struggled to process it then, with the emotions of Jake's death as fresh as a cut. But after everything I'd been through, things were clearer than ever.

"It's not something I'm proud of, but we needed supplies. You've seen the equipment we've been working with. It wasn't cutting it."

"But stealing? Killing." Everything was a blur. This didn't align with the Ghosts I knew.

"I tried to pay for the items, but he wouldn't sell the quantity we needed. That poor man came at me with a gun. I tried to stop him…" His gaze drifted to the floor, as if he were ashamed to face the truth. "But it went off. It was an accident. I never meant to hurt anyone. I grabbed the supplies and ran. I seem to be making a mess of things lately. Our current situation is no different."

With his resignation, the room slowly came into focus. We were in a cement cell with no windows, surrounded by hay on the floor. Light entered through a slit in the metal door, the only exit. The red message indicator on my tracker blinked.

"My tracker is active. I'm getting a message."

"It's a trap. Don't open it."

As much as I ached to see if the message was from my parents, I knew Myles was right. It would have to remain unread along with the two hundred unread messages Lydia had sent me since my tracker had reactivated. "How did you get here?"

He shook his head as if he was trying to clear away a fog. "I'm not sure. I was loading the semicopter with supplies and the next thing I knew I woke up here, in this cell."

"That's better than where I woke up," I muttered. I shut my eyes in an attempt to calm my pounding head, but when I opened them again, it wasn't any better.

"What about Bailen? Peyton?" Myles rubbed his temples. His head didn't seem to be in any better shape than mine.

"I don't know. The last thing I saw was Bailen speeding away from me on his bike."

Barry smiled as if he knew his son had escaped.

"What do we do?" I asked.

"We wait."

"We wait? There has to be a way out of here. We can't be trapped."

"I've spent years memorizing the maps of this facility. These cells are ironclad. No one is getting in or out unless they want us to."

"So we're stuck?"

"Even if we could break out of the cell—and that's a big if—there's no way we'd make it out of the facility alive. It's heavily monitored." He leaned against the wall as if he had given up.

"How do you know?"

"In all the map studying, if there was a way out, the Ghosts would have found it by now. They've excelled at cobbling together bits of intel and research over the years."

"The others know where we are? There's a chance of rescue?"

"We've only been able to steal schematics, but nothing indicates its location. It's well hidden. They make people disappear," he said. "But we've narrowed down the options considerably. It's only a matter of time before they find it."

"I'm guessing the authorities didn't leave much of a trail to follow."

"Probably not."

"We're on our own then."

"Like I said, we wait." He swallowed and lowered his voice. "They'll come for you, eventually."

"What about you?"

"Perhaps, but I have less time." He lowered his head as if he'd accepted a death sentence.

"Why me?" I asked, but I was pretty sure I already knew the answer. My head swarmed with painful thoughts, trying to keep up. I didn't know if I could withstand torture for days on end. I was already at my breaking point.

He leaned in and whispered into my ear. "They're listening," he said. "Besides, your father wouldn't want me to tell you."

I froze. Every part of me wanted to be angry at him for his vagueness, but the shock left me without words. After a while, I forced out the first ones that formed. "You know my father?" I whispered.

"Yes."

"How? He's not a traitor." I stopped. *That was harsh.* "I mean a Ghost."

Myles froze, as if his thoughts had taken him to a distant place. Somewhere long forgotten. Maybe he hadn't heard me slip up. I'd spent how much time with the Ghosts, and I still sometimes thought of them as the enemy? Maybe it was the current circumstances. The cell, the agents, Rufus Scurry, my parents; my brain was on overload. Despite what I'd said, I knew in my core I could trust the Ghosts, even if Myles had made a mistake. If it weren't for them, I'd have been locked up a lot sooner, or worse.

"Myles?" I touched his shoulder. He didn't jump, but he focused on me like he had finally woken up.

"You can't ever forget how important you are," he said in a

quiet but solemn tone that inherently told me he knew it to be true within his very soul. "You are the one thing that will allow us to overcome them."

The room started to spin again. I lowered to the ground and pressed my cheek to the cement. "I'm not sure anymore. They did something to my tracker. They may have even replaced it." I touched the back of my head, wincing when my fingers ran over a sore spot.

"They haven't replaced it. They tried to reset it, though." He lifted my head and twisted me so I could lean against his shoulder. I was grateful for the reprieve from the hard surface.

"How do you know?"

"Because they'll want to study you. They can't if they remove it. Besides, they would have to shave your head and perform surgery to remove it."

I shuddered at the thought. Brain surgery was not on my to-do list. "They wouldn't cut into my head just for the satisfaction of retrieving a faulty tracker chip?"

"Only as a last resort. It's a huge risk to remove the chip from its current environment. It may not function the same."

For the first time since I'd arrived, the tension inside me uncoiled a little.

Myles whispered into my ear again. "But if they knew what you were carrying on your tracker, they wouldn't hesitate to remove it."

I shot up, ignoring the shooting pain in my head. I inspected his serious expression, searching for meaning I couldn't find. A question formed on my lips, but the metal clang of the door opening prevented it from escaping.

Twenty-Three

Six armed agents in dark combat gear stormed into the room. Two wrenched me away from Myles. I flailed, but their vise-like grip numbed my arms and bruised my biceps.

A hot breath beat into my ear. "The more you fight, the worse it will be."

"You think I'm going to make it easy for you?" I yelled, slamming my head backward into the agent's nose. Pain shot through my head, turning my vision crimson.

The agent grunted but seemed otherwise unfazed by my attack. He whispered into my ear again. "Feisty little thing, aren't you? I like a challenge."

My skin crawled like I'd been infested with fleas. I continued to fight as one agent repeatedly kicked Myles in the stomach.

"*No!*" I screamed. Another agent punched Myles in the face

until his nose bled.

A third agent joined the two holding me down. He grabbed me by the throat, thrusting me against the wall of the cell. I coughed and gasped as his grip tightened around my neck. My throat burned. The two agents digging their fingers into my arms held me against the concrete. My flailing legs slowed until they tingled and I could no longer move them. They dangled, lifeless.

A low moan escaped Myles' lips. Two agents grabbed him under his arms and dragged him from the room, his knees scraping across the concrete.

As I struggled for air, I tried to cry out. All I could muster was a dull whine. My vision tunneled and grayed. My breaths became short gasps. The man's horrible, hot breath was on my cheek again. "Let this be a lesson to you."

My sight narrowed to pinpricks of white light. The three agents simultaneously released their hold. I crashed to the floor, gulping air and coughing violently. The three men exited the room, slamming the door shut with an echoing clang.

I lay on the ground in a crumpled heap. Every bone and muscle in my body felt like it'd been put through a meat grinder. Frustration and isolation flooded me with a strange mixture of fire and ice.

Despite my throbbing muscles, I pushed off the floor. My skin peeled away from the concrete, leaving hay and gravel stuck to the side of my face. I brushed the dirt from my cheek and huddled in the corner, alone.

My bottom lip quivered as the horrific things they might do to Myles and my parents surfaced. All because of me. I didn't care what they did to me. I deserved it, all of it. Everything I'd done, every decision I'd made, had hurt people—good, honest people who wanted their freedom back. And worst of all, there was nothing I could do to help from inside my cell. Maybe it was better that way. In here, I couldn't do anything that would get someone else killed.

I pulled my knees into my chest and tried to push the awful thoughts from my mind. With nothing to do in such a dark place, the nightmares soon overcame me. I'd lost the resolve to fight. I was broken. Even with the right glue, I knew the lines from the break would never disappear. Those scars would remain visible for the rest of my life.

I wanted so badly to give into the pain, but I refused to give them the satisfaction. I couldn't bring myself to access my tracker despite all the blinking lights in the corner of my vision. It made me twitch, but not enough to act. They were watching me and there was no way I'd give them a shred of intel.

I'd grown to enjoy the quiet. The moments without lights and messages popping up to distract me, to take my attention from what was truly important. With my tracker back online, they'd ripped away my freedom all over again. That Shabbat and Havdalah with Jake at the Hive had meant everything. But the loss of it all was too much to bear. I'd tasted what my life could be like, and I wanted it back again.

I finally understood Dad's pain—what had been ripped from us, the magnitude of the violation. It was everything I wanted to be and couldn't have because of the technology. I sat in silence, staring ahead. Letting my vision blur, I lost track of time altogether.

When the door crashed open, I jumped. My heart skipped a beat, hoping they'd brought Myles back, or even another familiar face. My veins coursed with acid when an agent in full gear and a helmet stepped into the room. The agent stopped right in front of me, tilting their head as if trying to see into my soul.

I pulled farther into the corner, wishing I could melt into it and never come out. I mentally prepared myself for another attack. Maybe against one agent I had a chance. I pushed into a crouching position, ready to launch when the agent got close.

The agent reached up. I flinched, unsure what came next. The gloved hands yanked off the helmet, allowing dark, brown waves to spill out.

"You look like shit!"

Instantly, my muscles uncoiled. I tried to laugh, but it came out as a half-choke, half-cough. I'd never been so happy to hear Peyton's sarcasm, even if it was at my expense.

"Give me your arm."

"Why?"

"Just do it."

I shoved my arm out, and she pulled a needle from her vest pocket. She yanked off the cap with her teeth and thrust the needle into my skin. My tracker functions faded away, taking the invisible chains with it.

"Ready to get out of this hellhole?"

Mouth dry, I nodded. Despite my aching body, I jumped to my feet. Instantly, I regretted it. Every part of me cried out in agony. My stiff joints responded slowly and popped painfully as I moved toward the door.

Peyton shoved me against the wall before I could peek around the doorframe. "We take it slow. Stay behind me. I'll lead you out." She checked the hall. "Can you run?"

I opened my mouth to speak, but a cough escaped instead.

"I'll take that as a *no*."

Despite every muscle in my body screaming, I wanted out of here more than anything. "Just go. I'll keep up." I didn't have another choice.

She dragged me into the hall by my arm. The deserted white corridor had a low ceiling. It was barely wide enough for two people to walk next to each other. Surprisingly, no alarm or warning light indicated any kind of intrusion. Not that there would be. The agents were all connected to the network. A luxury we didn't have and one I wasn't upset to abandon again. I hoped Peyton had a good plan for combating their technical advantage.

Around the next corner, an agent was slumped against the wall. I guessed kicking agent ass was her plan. Not the best idea. That would only work until the agents swarmed us. I swallowed hard.

We crept down the hall. She peeked around the corner. "There's a patrol coming. They'll never believe I'm escorting you alone," she whispered.

"Great. Which way?"

"We can't go back the way we came. It's a dead end."

"So we're trapped?"

She pointed upward to a small vent on the wall near the ceiling. "You've got to be kidding me."

She shook her head. "Come on. I'll boost you up. We don't have much time." Peyton waved me over and cupped her hands.

Without giving myself time to second-guess, I placed my right foot in her hands. She pushed me up to the ceiling.

I dug my aching fingers under the vent grate. "You wouldn't happen to have a screwdriver or a wedge in your back pocket, would ya?" I whispered.

"No, just pry it open," she said. "And hurry, they're coming."

I pulled with every ounce of strength I could muster. The grate pulled away from the wall, sending me toppling out of her grasp. Peyton caught the grate before it crashed to the floor. I fell past her and smacked into the floor with a groan. If I'd thought everything had hurt before, I was wrong. My head pounded. My knees twitched. I'd lost control over my muscles.

"Get up," she said through clenched teeth.

I pushed up on my hands, but my arms gave way. "I'm trying."

"Stop *trying*. Just do it!" She reached under my armpits and righted me.

"Here." She cupped her hands again. "Get up there."

The footfalls around the corner grew steadily louder.

Without hesitation, I stepped into her hands and she propelled me toward the vent. As she pushed upward, I shimmied through the hole. The metal clanged as my hands hit it. She waved me back and I slid farther into the vent, the stench of dust overwhelming. Her fingers gripped the edge of the opening, and seconds later, she was inside shoving me forward.

"Right," she hissed from behind me.

I slowed to catch my breath, but she smacked my thigh.

"Keep moving. It won't be long before they figure out we're in here, if they haven't already."

Unable to think of a good comeback, I huffed and inched through the tight space, allowing Peyton to call directions from behind. My hands and knees burned hotter with every move forward.

After what seemed like hours, I turned another corner. Hot air blew in my face.

"There's an opening ahead that leads to the laundry room."

I crawled to the source of the hot air and peered through the grate. Several washers and dryers hummed. I scanned the room for people. When I found none, I pushed out the grate. It fell into a laundry bin. I pulled myself through the hole and dropped into the bin next to the grate. Even though the towels stank of sweat, I let their soft cushion soothe my aching muscles. Peyton plopped down beside me. She reached for the edge of the bin, but approaching footfalls made her pause.

"Shh," she hissed into my ear as she threw a pile of towels on top of us.

A door creaked open. I held my breath. Peyton squeezed my arm in the darkness. My heart hammered in my chest. I said a silent prayer, hoping whoever it was wasn't coming for our bin of towels. If they noticed the missing grate, we'd be screwed.

The sound of dryer doors popping open made me tense. Moments later, there was a *slam*, followed by a second and a third. Squeaking noises filled the room. The towels above us rustled. An arm appeared between us. I froze.

Hurried footsteps approached. A female voice said, "Can I help you, gentlemen?"

The arm disappeared from the bin.

"You haven't seen anyone poking around the laundry room, have you?" asked a male voice.

"Besides you two?" asked the female.

There was a long pause in which I thought the sound of my pounding heart would give away our location.

"Let us know if you see anyone."

"Of course. I don't need anyone poking around my laundry room and messing things up. I have a job to do. Now out with you."

Scuffling feet faded into silence, followed by the same creak of the door. I let out a long breath in relief. Peyton shifted the towels and peeked out.

"It's clear," she said.

I stood in the bin, and she helped me out. Moving to the farthest dryer, she shoved it aside, revealing a small hole in the wall where the dryer vented to the outside.

She waved me over. "Time to leave this hellhole."

I couldn't have agreed more. But as I stepped toward our escape route, thoughts of Myles and my parents swarmed me. Halfway across the room, I stopped, unable to continue. I couldn't leave them. Not after everything we'd been through.

"Kaya, now! They could come back any minute."

"I can't."

"Why not?" Peyton propped her hand on her hip as if she were about to start tapping her foot at any moment.

"My parents, your dad." I choked. I couldn't go on. I lacked the words to say I was tired of leaving people behind.

"Now is not the time for heroics."

I stood my ground, refusing to move until she caved. "I can't lose anyone else." Her expression softened slightly, as if something I'd said had hit her deep down.

"I'm under strict orders to bring you out alive, regardless of what happens to anyone else."

"No, I won't leave them."

"You have to."

"Why?"

"Because if we lose you, this will all be for nothing. We won't be able to take down the tracker network."

I froze. Was everyone in on the plan but me? They all seemed to know something I didn't—aside from the fact that my tracker was the only one in existence to defy the system.

"They'll understand," she said quietly.

"They might, but if something happens to them, I won't be able to forgive myself."

"I'll carry you out of here kicking and screaming if I have to." She crossed her arms over her chest like she meant business. "If we don't get your chip out of their hands, then there's no hope for anyone."

As much as I didn't want to leave, she was right. More than right. It was time to go, parents or not. I limped toward the exit with a renewed sense of urgency.

Bending down to crawl through the opening, I inhaled my first breath of fresh air, but it smelt like burnt hair. I halted partway through the hole as my vision went white.

"Not now." I groaned.

"What?"

"My tracker's resetting."

"Shit. Are you kidding me?"

"I don't kid—" Before I could finish my sentence, she shoved me through the hole. "Hold on. I can't see a thing."

"We don't have time to hold on. They'll be on us any second. Keep moving. I'll guide you."

I plopped onto the ground. Wet grass brushed my cheek, and dampness seeped through the knees of the scrubs. The white slowly faded from my vision. I struggled to focus through the blur and blinking lights. Peyton hauled me to my feet and dragged me, the damp soil squishing between my toes. Ahead of us, I could make out the faint outline of trees. My breaths grew heavy. She ignored my discomfort and pulled me into a run.

"Keep going. Don't stop until we're deep into the woods."

My limbs fought every step as my bare feet slipped on the wet grass. My chest burned with each inhale, but I refused to give in. The treeline seemed like a mirage growing farther and farther away. Just when it appeared we would never reach it, we crossed over the threshold. The quiet rustle of the trees welcomed us, but the swooping blades of an approaching unicopter grew louder in the distance.

Twenty-Four

We ran, dodging trees and leaping over fallen limbs. My legs strained with each leaf crunching beneath my feet. I cringed as rocks stabbed into the souls of my feet. My mouth was so dry, I could hardly swallow. Every piece of me throbbed with a dull ache. My mind screamed to keep going, but my body slowly failed me.

I collapsed onto the forest floor, twigs and leaves digging into my hands and knees. "I... can't... run... any...more."

"It's okay. You don't have much farther to go."

"Bailen." I coughed, unable to say more. Thankfully, his name alone seemed to say everything I was thinking.

"I'm so sorry," he said.

It was such a short statement, but I knew he was sorry for more than just the capture. He was apologizing for everything that had gone wrong, including icing me out. With those three words, I knew we would be okay. Still trying to catch my breath, I shook my head, hoping he'd realize how sorry I was too.

He closed the gap between us and wrapped me in his arms. His lips met mine, stealing any remaining air I had left. I didn't care. The kiss took every awful thought and every pain from my body. His hands cupped the back of my head. I winced as his fingers grazed the sore spot. He started to pull away, but I leaned in closer. Our lips parted and the kiss increased in urgency. I wanted to stay in the moment forever where I was safe and nothing else mattered. Where everything that had gone wrong didn't seem to exist anymore.

A throat cleared behind us. Bailen drew away much too soon.

"I hate to break up the lovefest, but the authorities are breathing down our necks, and she has an active tracker."

Bailen removed some sensors from his pocket and tossed them to Peyton. "Put these on her." He disappeared behind a tree, returning with a bag. "We're going to have to take you offline. And we have to do it on the run."

He pulled his laptop from the bag.

"Is that what I think it is?"

"Yep."

"But I thought TROGS was lost."

"I rebuilt the portable version from my old code. Do you really think I'd not have a backup plan?"

My body relaxed while he booted up TROGS. There was something calming about seeing him so focused.

Peyton tossed me a pair of boots. "Put these on."

I shoved my feet into them as she stuck the sensors on me and ran the wires over to the laptop.

"Can you carry this *and* run?" Bailen's eyebrows furrowed.

I shook my head. "I don't know if I can run anymore."

"It's okay. I'll stay right by you." His attention flicked at

Peyton. "You better go ahead; let them know we're coming in hot."

She didn't waste more than a single nod before sprinting into the darkened trees.

Bailen helped me to my feet, slung his bag over his shoulder, and picked up TROGS.

On TROGS's giant clock, just over four minutes remained until I was offline. It would be the longest four minutes of my life. I wasn't sure if I could run for four seconds, let alone four minutes. The fear must have been written all over my face because Bailen kissed me on the forehead.

"You can do this. I'll carry you if I have to."

"I hope that won't be necessary." I forced a half-smile to hide the growing fear. If it went badly, I'd be back in that cell with needles shoved in my arms. Or even worse, they'd be prepping me for brain surgery.

"Whatever you do, don't stop moving," Bailen said.

We started at a bit of a jog. He quickly pulled me to the left.

"Didn't Peyton go the other way?" I asked.

"We have to keep the authorities away from the hideout. At least until you can disappear."

Keeping pace beside him, I stumbled over branches and underbrush. Bailen always caught me before I face-planted in the dirt. Somehow, he managed to hold TROGS in one hand and keep me upright with the other.

As the timer ticked down, lights penetrated the canopy of the forest, signaling the arrival of the unicopters. The swooshing of their blades generated a wind that whipped up stray leaves. The authorities were practically on top of us, a sure sign the ground team wasn't far behind. The countdown read a little more than two minutes. How had only half the time passed? We'd been running forever.

The distant sound of an engine tore me from my thoughts. Their ground vehicles were catching up to us. "We're never going to make it." I gasped. My wobbly legs were numb.

"We will. Follow me." He turned left sharply and backtracked the way we'd come.

I followed, but my calves burned. "Where are we going? We're running right at them."

"Not quite." He grabbed my arm and pulled me left again.

I caught a glimpse of a rocky overhang ahead.

With the shrubbery covering the mouth, I'd nearly missed it. If we weren't so close, I would have missed it completely. A renewed sense of energy coursed through me. I stumbled into the alcove and nestled against the far wall. Bailen dove in next to me and yanked a small kit from his bag.

"What's that?"

"A new toy." He opened the case and removed a small box.

I'd seen something like it before. I swallowed hard, memories from that night in the woods resurfacing. "Is that a radio wave generator?"

"Basically. Only I tweaked this so it has a much larger range." He flipped the switch, and the box hummed quietly.

But the roar of an engine drowned out the humming box.

I checked TROGS. Only thirty more seconds to go. While I was thankful for the reprieve from running, I was ready for the entire nightmare to end.

Brakes squealed. Three doors slammed. The sound of crunching leaves and snapping twigs grew louder.

"Find them. The signal cut out around here," said a male

voice.

"Yes, sir," said a second.

"Right away," said a female voice.

My heart hammered, matching the drumming rhythm of the blood pulsing through my ears.

Two black boots appeared in front of the alcove. I froze. Everything went silent.

Beep beep beep.

At first, I thought the alarm was some kind of authority equipment. But Bailen slammed the TROGS screen shut, muttering under his breath. I caught a glimpse of a flashing 0:00 on the screen as it closed.

"What was that?" asked the female.

"What was what?" said one of the male voices.

"I thought I heard something. Like an alarm," said the female.

We were so dead.

Bailen yanked the nodes from my temples and shoved TROGS into his bag. The radio wave generator followed close behind. He reached into his pocket, but I couldn't see what was concealed in his fist.

"Get ready to hold your breath and run," he whispered into my ear.

I nodded, afraid to speak and unsure if I could stand, let alone run, but I'd do what I had to.

"Now!" He lobbed the mysterious object into the air, and a cloud of smoke erupted.

I scrambled to my feet and ran from the alcove, slamming past an agent. Bailen had his hand on my back, guiding me in seemingly random directions until we were out of the smoke. My eyes burned as much as my legs, but I kept going.

We dodged around more trees until he stopped beside a large pile of underbrush. For the first time, I checked behind us, but there was no one.

"Did we lose them?" I asked.

"I don't know." He parted the brush, revealing his motorbike. "But I'm not sticking around to find out."

I collapsed against a tree, relieved we were almost out of this mess. He tossed me a helmet and climbed onto the bike. After securing my helmet, I joined him, wrapping my arms around his waist and resting my throbbing head on his shoulder.

He revved the engine but didn't engage the flying mechanism. We tore through the trees. After some time, we stopped in front of a cave. The mouth was not much bigger than a flying motorbike. Once we ducked inside, the cavern opened up much wider. Grayish-white rock climbed to the ceiling at least twenty feet high.

Bailen cut the engine and helped me off. He wheeled the bike around the mud puddles toward the back of what appeared to be a one-room cave.

"Limestone." He pointed to the walls. "GPS signals have a hard time penetrating it. Not that we need it with TROGS, but it's an extra precaution."

"That's a good thing. You know, in case my tracker decides to defy TROGS as well. I'd hate to be responsible for giving up two Ghost hideouts." I focused on the mud caking my boots, afraid the previous argument would resurface.

Bailen placed his fingers under my chin and raised my head. "Hey, don't talk like that. We've got you covered."

"Until it happens again."

"If it does, we'll figure it out. We always do."

"I betrayed the Ghosts." I braced myself for the second round of ice-out.

"It was an accident."

I blinked in silence. Accident? Maybe. I'd had no time to think. I'd felt trapped with no place left to go. I went back to the Hive because I'd had no other options.

"You're one of us. We all know how important you are. And we take care of our own. You have nothing to worry about." He wrapped me in a tight hug and kissed me. For the first time, it didn't melt away my guilt.

When he pulled away, he extended his hand, and I accepted. He grabbed his bike with his free hand and wheeled it deeper into the cave, taking me with him.

Tucked in the back, nearly out of sight, was a passage big enough for a person and the bike to fit through. Around two tight turns, Bailen parked his bike next to numerous others.

We continued through a series of narrow twists and turns, illuminated by the light on his watch. I lost track of the number of times we changed directions and squeezed through tight spaces. Even though I couldn't see well, several new scratches burned on my arms and legs. But it didn't matter. I was already so battered and bruised, what were a few more scratches?

Around another bend, Bailen flipped off his watch. Through a narrow passageway ahead, a light shined. After we scraped through, the cavern opened wider. We walked into a large room, almost as big as the first room in the cave. The soft glow of hundreds of computer monitors lit up the space.

Bailen reached for my hand. I ignored it. Throwing my arms around his neck, I collapsed against him, letting his body support my weight. I couldn't stand up straight anymore. He wrapped his arms around me and scooped up my legs. My body fell limp, glad to finally be somewhere safe. He leaned his head on my shoulder and whispered into my ear, "Welcome to the Quarry."

Twenty-Five

I awoke in a strange bed. When I tried to sit up, my head swam with throbbing pain. I took a few slow breaths and tried to sit up again, thankful for the soft mattress below me rather than a cold, cement floor. At the foot of the bed stood a figure I strained to see clearly.

"Bailen." His name came out as a hoarse whisper.

"Take it easy." Before I could say anything else, he sat on the bed next to me. "You've been through a lot."

I blinked, attempting to process everything that had happened. I'd woken up at the tracker facility. Peyton had rescued me. After that, things were fuzzy. "Where am I?"

"The Quarry. Makeshift Ghost Headquarters."

Now I remembered. I'd returned to the Ghosts and was exactly like them now. Well, not exactly. They'd switched my tracker over to TROGS, but it was still unique.

The full reality of the situation flooded back to me. Dread swarmed in my core. My parents and Myles were still in danger. I swung my legs over the side of the bed and pushed my feet to the floor.

"Whoa! Where do you think you're going?"

"To the control room. You guys need my help."

"That may be true, but you're no good to us in this condition. You need rest and food." He pointed to a bowl of soup on the table next to the bed.

"You think the authorities are going to sit around and wait for me to have a snack? We don't have time." My belly grumbled.

"Your stomach says otherwise."

Heat rose in my cheeks. "Fine." I picked up the bowl then scooted on the mattress so I could lean against the wall. I slurped a spoonful of soup. "Satisfied now?"

"About that, yes. But we need to talk."

"About what?" Sensing a long conversation, I gulped down a couple more spoonfuls. The steaming broth crawled down my chest into my stomach, warming me from the inside out.

Bailen swallowed, his expression serious. More serious that I'd ever seen him.

I set the bowl back on the table. "What now?" I asked, trying to break the intense silence.

He reached for my hand, entwining our fingers. He ran his thumb over my mine. The methodical motion of his soft skin soothed me. But concern over the mysterious impending conversation consumed me. It was big. The weight of the air proved it.

"You must know by now the strange behavior of your tracker is no accident."

"What do you mean? You think I did this on purpose?"

"No, I know you didn't."

"Then what? Just tell me." I shifted uncomfortably on the

mattress as a cloud of doubt formed around me.

"You know, your dad and mine aren't so different."

I scrunched my forehead. I wasn't sure what he was getting at. "How so? I mean, they both like technology, but my dad works for the government."

"Do you know what your dad does for the government?"

"Yeah, he monitors tracker diagnostics."

"He does that now. But that wasn't his original job."

"How do you know so much about my dad? Have you met him?"

"Only once."

"When?"

"When he brought Jake here."

"He brought Jake to the Ghosts? Why?" I couldn't believe Dad had never mentioned it, or Jake too, for that matter. Why did he act like Dad hadn't known where he was? Jake's list of secrets was growing out of control.

"To join the Ghosts. To be part of the small underground organization that would infiltrate Global Tracking Systems and take down the tracker network. We needed enough people to get the job done, but not so many that we'd get noticed. It's why we kept the individual cells small. We needed people we could trust. And if one was compromised, it wouldn't jeopardize the others."

A chill ran through my body. My mind raced to keep up. I couldn't find the words to ask the questions swirling in my head. Somehow, I managed one question. "How do you know all this?"

"My dad told me a lot. Your dad and mine were good friends."

"Friends?" My insides churned as Myles' confession in the cell came rushing back.

"They used to work together. But I also learned a lot about your dad from studying tracker technology. He's a legend," Bailen said. "Do you know what he did for the government before? Why they moved him into his current position?"

"I'm not sure I understand." As soon as the words spilled out of my mouth, everything started to make more sense. It couldn't be a coincidence that the daughter of the man who'd helped finalize the tracker technology had a malfunctioning tracker. In fact, it was contradictory.

It also made no sense that Dad had helped build the tech that violated his beliefs to his very core.

Outside of Rufus Scurry himself, my father knew more about tracker tech than anyone. I always thought he'd stepped down as Scurry's right-hand man so he could spend more time with us. But he was a danger to the system if he didn't cooperate. Moving him to a desk job like tracker diagnostics was some kind of punishment. But for what?

"My dad made my tracker malfunction?"

Bailen nodded once but studied the floor like he had something else to hide. "I think so," he muttered.

I cupped his chin and lifted his head so he had no choice but to see me.

"Why do you look so guilty?"

"Because..." He scooted away and brushed his shaggy hair out of his face. "You know, you're so stubborn."

"Yeah, what's your point?"

"I suspected all this time, but I didn't know what it would do to you. Not after..." The fragment hung in the air. He swallowed. "I wanted to tell you so many times, but I didn't know how."

"This isn't your fault." Assuming he was right, my dad was the one who'd been lying to me, not Bailen. "How long ago did my dad do this?"

Bailen's attention returned to the floor, more evidence he didn't want to tell me what came next.

"How long?" I repeated, more forcefully.

"I don't know for sure." He sighed, like he had no choice but to tell me. "Your dad found a loophole in the system. But it's not easy to smuggle information out of a tightly controlled development facility. He would have had to hide it somehow. The Ghosts knew he altered a chip and implanted it in someone he trusted. I'm guessing you got that chip as a baby."

"Since I was a baby? My dad's been lying to me my whole life?" I opened my mouth to speak but closed it again to collect my thoughts. "Why didn't he tell me?" But I knew the answer. If Dad lied, it was for a good reason, for the one thing that he held so closely to him—his family and his faith.

I sat in silence, digesting the new information. So that was why they were punishing my parents—for something Dad had done. What I now carried. Maybe I should have stayed in the tracker facility. If I had cooperated with the authorities, maybe they would have let us go. But then years of my dad's work would have gone to waste. The tracker network had taken everything. Of course he'd want to defy it. For the very same violation I felt now.

"How come Jake never told me?"

"I don't know if he ever knew for sure, but when your chip went offline, we all started to suspect. He also knew if you were ever captured, it would have ended the whole operation. Your dad was still undercover, and there were way too many people looking for leaks. Years of funneling secrets to the Ghosts would have been wasted. They'd know your tracker had been tampered with, and then they'd figure out what the Ghosts have been doing. They'd be able to close the loophole, stop us in a second." He let out a long breath. "And they wouldn't have hesitated to kill you."

"Why are you telling me this now?"

"Because things are changing quickly. We are running out of options, and there's not much time left. There's an upgrade in a couple of weeks that will lock us out of the system."

"So it's now or never?"

"Yes. And like it or not, your whole family is part of this. Your dad was a founding member of the Ghosts, like my father. After everything that happened, the authorities capturing you..." He took a deep breath, like he was preparing to unload the secrets of the entire tracker network. "When you told me about that message, I knew you needed to know the truth. But when you got back to the Hive, there wasn't time. Everyone was scrambling. Now that you're safe, I can't keep it a secret anymore."

"Wait a second. What message are you talking about?"

"The one you said your parents sent, right before the authorities showed up at your apartment. That wasn't just a trap; it was a trigger. A clue on how to unravel the whole tracker network. Your dad said he would get word to us when it was time. I'm certain that message was it."

I shook my head. "The authorities were just using my parents as bait. Besides, there was nothing in it resembling a clue." Hearing from my parents had been so wonderful, I'd not only saved it on my personal network, but I'd made sure to commit the message to memory. It could be the last thing I'd ever hear from them. Even if it was a trap, I'd take the memory with me forever.

"Well, to the naked eye, the message would appear normal. But think. Was there anything weird about it?"

I went over the message several times in my head. Was there something I'd missed? I thought about the words again.

"They mentioned more tests. I thought they were nuts. Dad tried to stop the authorities the first time they ran tests."

"Exactly. Anything else?"

I ran through the message a couple more times. "They called me 'honey.' They never call me that."

"Is that it?"

I shrugged. "I'm not sure."

"Hmm." He drummed his fingers on the table. "I wish I could see that message."

"You can." I popped up from the bed and searched the edges of the room.

"What are you doing?" Bailen eyed me as I moved around the room.

I picked up a small rock and etched the message onto the smoothest wall I could find.

Honey,
Are you okay? We miss you.
They hurt you Kaya. We are so sorry.
Let us help. Even if it means more tests, let's fix this.
Please come home. We're really worried about you.
Love you lots,
Mom and Dad

I stepped back and admired my work. "That's it."

Staring at the wall, Bailen rested his head in his hands. "Mind if I borrow that?" He pointed at the rock.

I passed it to him and watched as he wrote out some letters, but none of it seemed to make sense. He scratched them out then wrote some more. He stepped back and studied them for a couple of minutes. Shaking his head, he turned to me. "What was the time stamp on that message?"

"I'm not sure."

"Think. It's really important."

I tried to picture the message in my mind, focusing on the upper right-hand corner where the time stamp always appeared.

"1700." The number flew out of my mouth so fast, I knew it was the right one.

Bailen starred at the message again and tapped each letter with the rock like he was counting. He rubbed his temples. "Are you sure that's right?"

"Yep, 5:00 P.M.," I said. "Although that doesn't make sense because I was there well after five."

"Five," Bailen muttered. But then his eyes grew wide. "Kaya, you're a genius!"

"I am?"

But the only reply I got was the scratching sound of the rock on the wall. "It's a rail cipher."

"What's a rail cipher?"

"It's a way of sending a code embedded inside another message. The trick to decoding it is the timestamp."

"5:00 P.M.?"

"Yeah, count in five letters." He circled the Y in *honey*. "Then you continue down diagonally." He circled the next couple of letters O, U, H, and O.

I focused on the letters. "That's complete gibberish. How is that a message?"

"I'm not sure yet." He added two more letters to the list but stopped on the last line of the message.

The words *you* and *hold* stared back at me. Standing next to him, I could practically see the wheels turning in his mind. There was an intense fire burning inside him, like he was testing the latest tech. He was enjoying the puzzle.

His devilish grin appeared, as he circled more letters diagonally up from the last D in the word *Dad*. "I think I've got it." He scrawled all the letters off to the side and then stepped away from the wall, revealing the message.

YOU HOLD THE KEY.

Twenty-Six

"What does that even mean?" I asked with a mixture of awe and confusion.

"It tells us you are the key to unraveling the whole tracker network."

"Are you sure that's what my dad meant by *key*? We already know my tracker is important." I knew my dad and his cryptic ways. Nothing was ever as simple as it appeared. If the authorities were monitoring his messages, he would have been extra obscure, just in case they did decipher it. The message definitely had a deeper meaning. "Maybe I just have the knowledge to find the secret. It could be hidden anywhere. What makes you think he put the secret on my chip?"

"Where else would he have put it?"

"Good point. If that's the case, how do I access it?"

"That's what we're going to find out." He held out his hand. "Come on. Let's go to the control room and examine that chip again. Besides, the others will want to know you're awake."

248

I took his hand. He led me through a series of winding, dimly lit caverns. The narrow passageways grew wider the farther we went. Eventually, we entered a larger room filled with the familiar glow of computer equipment. Many of the Ghosts were there, but not nearly as many as at the Hive.

"Where is everyone?" I asked.

"This is it." Bailen spoke those words like this was the price we'd paid.

"What happened?"

"A lot of people disappeared when the authorities found the Hive."

The room felt smaller. I gasped for air as the walls closed around me. I scanned the computers. The group had easily been cut in half. I spotted Jeremy in the corner of the room. He nodded at me, a stiff short tilt of his head that said he was glad I was okay. I returned the gesture. He pointed at something on his monitor then turned to Peyton next to him. She said something, but I couldn't read her lips.

"What about Emily?"

Bailen's gaze fell to the floor, taking my heart with it. Yet another person lost to me. Because of me. I needed to fix it. Every single thing that had gone wrong, that I could still fix.

"I saw your dad."

Bailen's face softened as he gave me an expectant look.

I instantly regretted giving him hope. "They hauled him off before Peyton rescued me. I'm sorry. I don't know what happened to him."

His expression hardened again as he returned his focus to his monitors.

I turned toward the chair, the one that was quickly becoming a comfort despite all the mysteries that seemed to evolve from it. I lay back in it. "Hook me up."

Within minutes, wires dangled around me, and the computers *beeped* softly.

"Do you know what you're looking for?" I called over to the tower of monitors Bailen was hiding behind.

"No, but we're going to run some diagnostics and search for anomalies. If we compare it to your last set of scans when your tracker was offline but emitting that strange signal, maybe we can figure out what's different and uncover what's hidden on the chip."

Doubt consumed me. I wasn't sure of anything anymore. It was like chasing a target that didn't exist.

Something about the message bothered me. It spoke to me in a way that nothing ever had before. Intuition told me it was for me and me alone to unravel. But I couldn't tell Bailen. It would crush him to not be part of this.

He peered over the monitor at me. I couldn't see the bottom half of his face, but could tell the data was boosting his mood. I couldn't exclude him from the puzzle. He lived for that kind of stuff.

The sensors hummed to life. I closed my eyes and let the vibrations hypnotize me.

"We have all the data we need. Now we have to wait for the computer to run the comparison," Bailen said, bringing me back to full consciousness.

I peeled the sensors off and joined Bailen behind the glowing screens of data. The lines were meaningless, but the rhythmic up-and-down motions calmed me. Peyton and Jeremy joined us.

"How long will it take?" Peyton asked.

"At least a few hours," Bailen replied. "It's searching for tiny fluctuations. It could take a while to scan all the data at this level of detail."

"Good," Peyton said. "That gives us enough time for a recon mission."

"Recon? What kind of recon?" How much had I missed while I'd been captured?

"We need to scout out the authorities' main headquarters," Peyton said.

"We've been sitting around long enough. It's time to go on the offensive." Jeremy crossed his arms, making his muscles bulge.

What was with the sudden change in attitude? Was it the loss of numbers? Was it an act of desperation? "Are you sure that's a good idea? Maybe we should free your dad and my parents first. We can't just leave them with the authorities. Not to mention we could use their help."

Bailen shifted back and forth.

"You are such a chicken. Just tell her." Peyton was half a step from slugging him.

"Tell me what?"

We engaged in a three-way staring contest. I moved from Peyton to Bailen and back. Time slowed to a crawl as tension wrapped a web around us.

"Enough secrets," I said at last. "Just tell me!"

Bailen grabbed my arm and pulled me away from the group. "Our dad gave us explicit instructions not to rescue him or your parents. We're supposed to keep you safe and continue on with the mission, no matter the price."

"But how can you leave them there?" I chewed my bottom lip. With every passing moment, I got the sense they were going to let them die there if it came down to it.

"Kaya, this is a war. Freedom has a price."

I shook my head. It wasn't a price I was willing to pay. Losing loved ones for the sake of my freedom wasn't acceptable. I'd already lost my brother. That was far more than any person should have to endure—even if it did mean freedom for countless others. What was the point of freedom if you couldn't share it with your friends and family?

"A recon mission is too risky," I said. "I don't think you should go." After everyone I'd lost, I couldn't lose him too.

"Why not? We need to understand what we're up against."

"We already know the authorities have infinite resources. If we aren't holding on to every asset we have, then how can we expect to win?"

"Because a recon mission will give us something we need: information. Plus, we have your tracker now." Bailen glanced at Peyton, like there was still a secret between them. "We've been doing this a long time. We won't know what we're up against until we face it."

Peyton moved toward us and put her arm on my shoulder. I shot her a pleading expression.

"You're wasting that look on the wrong twin. I don't do puppy-dog guilt," she said. "Besides, Bailen is right. If this next upgrade is really going to lock us out, we need to fully understand it so we can use whatever information is buried on your tracker first. Beat the authorities at their own game for once."

I whirled around and headed for the exit. After a few steps, Bailen caught up to me. He spun me around and pulled me into a hug. "It'll be okay. We'll be back soon."

For the first time, I pushed him away and walked off without looking back.

252

Twenty-Seven

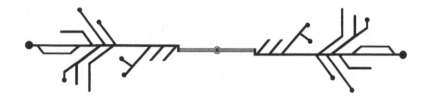

I trudged through the corridors in the direction of my room. When I reached the small cavern I'd awoken in, I yanked the curtain across the makeshift doorway and collapsed onto the bed. My body ached as waves of questions invaded my mind.

While getting a leg-up on the authorities' plans seemed like a good idea, it was likely to backfire. There was so much against us—time, resources, knowledge. And Bailen's energy would be much better spent here. I needed him. He was the puzzle king, not me.

No, what I really needed was Dad to explain everything. It was the only way I'd get answers. I couldn't believe he'd kept so much from me. Or maybe he hadn't.

Moments from my life whirled past me. Little things Dad had said and done stuck out in my mind. One night when I'd been in junior high, he'd caught me messaging Lydia on the network. He'd asked me why I hadn't gone over there. I'd told him why bother when I could message her? His response *"How would you talk to Lydia is you didn't have a tracker?"* I would shrug and say *"I'd go over there"* but secretly wonder why it mattered. Because I did have a tracker.

Then there was every Shabbat when he'd begged us to reduce our trackers to minimum function. He'd say the same thing every time. *"Just because you have the technology doesn't mean you should always use it. Don't become dependent. One day, it might not be there."*

It was a phrase he'd repeated often. It had always seemed like a parental nag, him forcing his beliefs on me. I'd never known why he'd kept saying it—until now.

In his own cryptic way, he'd already told me the truth. The message had been ingrained into my memory on purpose. He'd been preparing me my whole life, protecting me from the authorities when my tracker malfunctioned. He'd known what had been coming. As Bailen suspected, he must have arranged the whole thing.

He was giving me what he thought I always deserved, the kind of life he'd grown up with.

Understanding the situation didn't calm my nerves, though. Now that the moment had arrived, I was surrounded by confusion and uncertainty. I twisted the blanket around my fingers so tightly, they turned white. I wasn't prepared.

And all I had was a tiny sliver of a clue—a useless one at that.

What kind of message was *"You hold the key?"* That didn't tell me anything.

I needed to clear my head. I got up and searched the floor for a rock. I found one and ran my fingers over the smooth surface, stopping on the single rough edge. That would work perfectly. I pressed it against the cave wall and swung my arm out in a large arc, blocking out a space to draw in. My hand made short, abrupt movements, but with each stroke, the cloud in my mind thinned.

As the fog dissipated, I focused on the message. *You hold the key.* Nothing. I focused on each word separately. *You* obviously referred to me. That part was simple. *Hold* could be any number of things. I carried it. Literally or something else?

I supported it? No, that didn't seem right.

Maybe I had it? But where?

My thoughts blurred together.

I stepped away from the wall, focusing on the crazed art I'd produced. Lots of choppy lines. No pattern to them, just sharp, random lines. I moved closer and continued drawing, slowing my breaths and allowing the lines to take on a smoother, more fluid path.

I went back to analyzing the message. The word *hold* hadn't gotten me anywhere, but maybe *key* would. There was something about it that bothered me. Just like the message from Dad. That word was how to unravel it. I was sure of it.

K-E-Y. Those three letters meant nothing. They didn't stand for anything. Maybe the word was, well, the key.

Key, key, key. They turn, they unlock doors and secrets. But maybe I'd oversimplified things. It was Dad's message, after all. Was it something more abstract? Piano keys, or an old computer keyboard? Was it even a physical key? How many kinds of keys were there?

Dad had always liked metaphors and riddles. Did he mean I was the lynchpin to it all? Well, that much was obvious, but clearly, there was more to the puzzle.

What I'd give to get on the network right now and comb through some searches. Dad would be so disappointed, though. I could hear his reprimand in my head. *"Kaya, you're smart,"* he'd say. *"You don't need the network. People are too dependent on it. They should have built trackers with an* off *switch."*

I'd always thought he'd wanted it for Shabbat, but it hadn't just been that. It had been so much more, his beliefs, his life, and that of so many others. Deep down, I'd known he'd been right. There were times when all the tracker functions had more than overwhelmed me.

But I'd never wanted to fully shut off my tracker, even if it had been an option. It held a sense of security for me. What if it never came back on? But even though the idea of an *off* switch had once been a silly thought, I now understood why there wasn't one. Because the authorities wanted control over every minute of people's lives. The convenience of trackers just masked the truth; a tracker was a heavily monitored prison and the authorities were the bars.

Think, Kaya, think. Stop wasting time you don't have.

But there was something in Dad's words that kept nagging at me. He'd always said the same thing over and over again, as if he'd been trying to burn it into my skull. I went over the words in my head numerous times. In the repetition, something clicked. I knew what I needed to do, and Dad had given me the answer all along.

Twenty-Eight

dropped the rock and bolted to the computer room but found it empty. I plopped into Bailen's chair and studied TROGS. A small number of dots remained on the map. We were losing the fight. I wished I knew which one was Bailen's. Some sign to tell me he was okay. Not that it would tell me where he actually was.

In an attempt to distract myself, I focused on the data analysis, allowing the shifting graphs to hypnotize me. The lines blurred together, fuzzing and mixing into a strange blob.

A soft touch on my shoulder made me jump. I whipped around with my arms raised, ready for a fight.

Bailen grabbed both my wrists with one hand. "Whoa! Easy, killer. It's just me."

"Sorry," I said. "Can I have my hands back? I promise not to slug you." I put on my best innocent face.

"How do I know I can trust you?" A sly grin played on his lips, letting me know he was back to his usual self.

"I dunno, I am the key to this, after all. I could just leave if you preferred. You know, 'cause I'm not important or anything." I bit the inside of my cheek to keep from laughing.

"You think you're important, huh?" He gently pulled me from the chair and wrapped his free arm around my waist.

"Oh, I know I'm important. No question." I stepped closer to him, anxious to close the gap between us.

He dropped my wrists and ran his hand through my hair. He leaned in closer. Before our lips touched, I pulled away with a playful laugh. He gently coaxed me toward him.

Our lips met and shivers shot through me. I slid my arms up his chest and wrapped my hands around the back of his neck, pulling him closer. The kiss briefly took me to another place. But when it ended and the distance between us returned, my revelation did as well.

With a quick onceover, I committed the moment to memory because the minute I told him what I knew, things would change. I might have to go on the run again. Alone.

"What's wrong?" Bailen asked with a furrowed brow.

"Nothing. In fact, I think I've figured out the message," I said. "But first, how'd the recon mission go?" Changing the subject would only be a brief distraction, but I had to try. I needed a few more minutes of normalcy. Even if it was a sore topic of discussion.

His expression told me he knew I was up to something but couldn't figure out what. "It was fine. We got a lot of useful intel. However, this isn't going to be easy. The next upgrade is worse than we suspected." He hugged me and whispered in my ear, "But if you've deciphered the message, that will help."

I swallowed hard and concentrated on the stalactite

formations hanging from the ceiling. "You better sit down for this." I pulled back from our embrace and studied his expression.

His bright smile faded as he lowered into his chair, the magnitude of what I was about to say hitting him full on. I sat in his lap sideways but didn't face him. "I have to turn my tracker off."

"Wait, what? That's impossible."

"For you or anyone else, yes. That's why you have TROGS to trick the system. But for me, I don't think it is. I believe I can take it beyond the dormant state it was in before. Turning off my tracker is the key to taking down the tracker network. I'm sure of it."

"How do you know?"

Because Dad had given me the one gift he'd wanted since the inception of trackers. But how did I explain it to Bailen? "The message really bugged me. As I thought about it, I realized the message wasn't just a clue. It was meant to make me remember something my dad always said to me."

"What's that?"

"I shouldn't always rely on my tracker. One day it might not be there."

"Are you sure that means shutting off your tracker? What if he was talking about all the stuff that's happened up until now?"

"He wasn't. I'm sure of it."

Bailen remained silent for a minute as if trying to come up with something to combat my theory, then said, "If that's what you need to do, then I trust you."

"Thanks." I leaned my head against his shoulder, wishing I could stay here forever and knowing it wasn't possible.

"How are you going to shut it off?"

"I have an idea. Because I think I almost did it once before."

"So what are you waiting for? If you know what it takes, why didn't you shut if off already?" He cupped my chin and lifted my face to meet his. "It's because you don't know what will happen when you try to access what's on your tracker."

"I'm not willing to put the Ghosts at risk." I tried to swallow down the past. "Again. I did once before and look what happened." The absence of people in the room only drove home my point. "I have to go somewhere else."

"Where?"

"Far away from here."

"How will you get the information to us?" he asked. "Stay. I've got all this equipment. I can fix anything that happens. Let me help you. I'm willing to risk it."

His confidence melted into desperate pleas that tore me apart, one painful slash at a time.

"I'm not," I said. "It's not fair to everyone else."

"What if we voted? Or sent the others away temporarily? What if I figured out how to mask your signal? Or what if I came with you?" The suggestions came faster and faster, betraying his nerves. He was afraid to lose me. Everything he loved about being a Ghost was crumbling, one tiny piece at a time. As much as he wanted to, he couldn't help me. I had to do it on my own.

"I need you," he whispered, squeezing me so tightly, it told me more than what he had said.

The words tickled the edge of my ear, traveled inside, and moved down into my chest, where they strangled my heart.

"I'll protect you. I'll protect all of them." His words squeezed harder and crushed my heart.

I didn't even know where I'd go or what I'd do if something went wrong. Or how I'd get word to them if I uncovered the secret but couldn't turn my tracker back off. He was right. I needed him too, in so many ways.

I took a deep breath and kissed him, leaving so much meaning behind it. Words wouldn't suffice. We lost ourselves in the moment. With our lips locked together, I could sense the fear between us. When we parted things would change. But things already had changed.

My mind swirled. Could I really do it alone? Was it fair to put him in danger? He'd come if I asked, but I couldn't live with myself if I lost him, too. But there was no way to protect anyone anymore. Everything was a risk.

Tears threatened to fall, but I squeezed them between my lids. One slid down my cheek onto my lips. Together we tasted the salty sadness and frustration of the situation. Without warning, he pulled away.

"Something is still bothering you, isn't it?" he asked.

As he brushed my hair back, I realized I always bottled everything to avoid showing weakness. Even when Jake had died I'd tried to hide my tears from everyone. But not now. What was happening to me?

I swallowed the sadness. "There are too many questions. Too much uncertainty."

"Let me help you." He kissed my forehead and it comforted me, but only for a second.

"I can't ask you to do that."

"Then don't ask. Just say *yes* when I ask if I can come with."

"Where are you two going?" Peyton asked.

After nearly jumping out of Bailen's lap, I glared over his shoulder. She had the worst timing.

She crossed her arms over her chest and scowled at me. I

buried my head in Bailen's shoulder. I didn't want to have to explain everything again.

"Bailen, stop protecting her. You can't protect everyone. It's going to get you killed."

The chair spun, and he nudged me off his lap. A moment later, he was in Peyton's face. "Don't start with me. This is my job. If it gets me killed, so be it." He paused, breathing heavily. "Like it or not, this is a war and shit happens. At the end of the day, dead or alive, at least I know I was true to myself, which is more than I can say for you."

For the first time since I'd met her, Peyton avoided direct eye contact. She'd pulled her face so tight in some places and scrunched it in others that I hardly recognized her. Despite her reaction, she didn't move. I wasn't sure if she was stunned into silence or pain. Maybe some of both.

A fire ignited in her, and her expression hardened again. "That's not fair, and you know it!" she yelled.

"You were right there and you didn't even try." Bailen's hands balled into fists as he stepped closer to her. "You left him there. You know what they do to terrorists, what they'll do to him."

I pushed between them, holding each at arm's length. "Didn't try what? Left who?" But I didn't need answers to know it was about their father. That leaving him must have hurt Bailen more than he let on.

"I was following orders. It's what we do," Peyton fired back, ignoring me.

"Yeah, sure, Pey, be a good little soldier. When have you ever followed orders?"

Peyton shoved me to the side and moved inches from Bailen.

"Because they came from Dad."

They both froze in place, breathing hard. Watching them yell devastated me. I couldn't let their bond crumble. It sent a pang of regret through me. I missed Jake. I'd never fight with him again. Which seemed like a strange thing to miss, but it was a part of our sibling bond. I'd hated the fights Jake and I had had, but those had been nothing serious. We'd only fought because we'd loved each other. Now, I'd lost the chance to tell him how much I really did. But here were two siblings tearing each other apart when they should have been coming together. I had to do something.

Peyton's words tore me from my guilt-ridden stream of consciousness. "I hope your little girlfriend is worth it. 'Cause if she's not, this is the end. This fight is over." She shoved him away and stormed off.

Bailen leaned against his desk and stared straight ahead, not registering my presence.

Without any warning, he snapped into motion. He grabbed computer equipment and piled it into a large, black box. I put my hand on his shoulder. He stopped for a brief moment before continuing to pile more things into the box.

"Bailen, talk to me."

He whirled around and grabbed my arms. "There's nothing to talk about. I'm going with you."

He dropped his arms and brushed past me, making his way to the far corner of the room. After picking up another stack of equipment, he shoved it into his box and slammed the lid shut. With the kit under one arm, he offered his free hand and led me from the room without another word.

Twenty-Nine

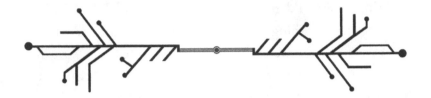

Minutes later, we were in the air. He still hadn't said a word to me. "Where are we going?" I asked, breaking the awkward silence. There was no hiding from the authorities. Not anymore. TROGS was a temporary fix. The ruse couldn't go on forever.

"Someplace no one will think to look for us."

Bailen pitched the bike into a wooded area. It seemed familiar, like it was from a dream or another life. When the collapsing barn came into view, I knew we were headed for what was left of the old hideout.

"Are you crazy? They could be monitoring the Hive."

No response. Between us was a silence so deep, I didn't dare pierce it with another question.

We landed in front of the barn, which seemed more like a lean-to. He rolled up beside it and cut the engine. Most of the windows were broken. Many of the splintered boards hung from the structure by a single nail. If I breathed too hard, it might blow over.

"Are you sure they won't find us here?"

Bailen huffed, as if that were a real response, then grabbed the kit off his bike and ducked inside. I followed at his heels.

The sight inside rendered me speechless. Unrecognizable tools and debris littered the barn. There wasn't more than an inch of unoccupied floor space. I couldn't locate the trap door, even though I knew its exact location. A giant hole in the roof let in what little moonlight penetrated the forest canopy, which lit up a massive pile of wood blocking the path across the barn. I coughed at the stench of rotting wood and mold.

Bailen set the box down and began clearing away the debris. As he moved toward the trap door, an icy chill crawled down my arms, leaving a pit in my stomach.

I'd done that.

Me.

I'd cost them their hideout, their home, and their technology. It had all been my fault, like everything else.

Smack.

Crack.

Smack.

Bailen snatched bits of wood and slammed them onto a pile of debris. He was like a machine, throwing rubble as if each piece removed would clear away some of the pain.

His chest heaved, his arms straining under the weight of a large crossbeam. He grunted and tried again before collapsing onto the heap. I wrapped my arms around his waist. He tried to shove me back, but I squeezed tighter.

"Shh," I whispered into his ear. "It'll be okay."

After much struggling, he collapsed into my arms, breathing

heavily.

"I just… I can't leave it like this."

"I know. I'm so sorry."

We huddled in the wreckage with no concept of how much time passed.

When his breathing slowed, I risked breaking the silence. "Are we safe here?"

He unburied his head from my shoulder, his eyes puffy and red. "Yeah."

"Are you sure?"

He opened his mouth but closed it as if trying to find the right words. "As long as it holds up. They stripped out everything of worth. They have no reason to think we'd ever return. It'd be suicide." He focused on the location of the trap door. "There's nothing left for them to destroy."

"Do I try it here or are we going into the Hive?"

He shook his head. "Here is good. At least we can run if the authorities show up."

I leaned against a stack of wood that appeared to have caved in from the roof. A breeze whipped through the small opening in the barn. I shivered, but not because of the cold. Because of what I was about to do. I didn't know if it would work. If it didn't, we could have the authorities breathing down our necks in a matter of minutes. There was no way I was going with them. They'd have to haul me out in a body bag.

There was no doubt they had a giant price tag on my head. Who knew if I was worth more dead or alive? Did they even care? I was sure they just wanted my tracker out of commission. Anything to stop me. To keep me from the information that would potentially end the tracker network. The information that would change everything.

Bailen placed his hand on my cheek and twisted my face toward him.

"You can do this."

I took a deep breath and dropped my head. I had to or the war was over. Whatever shred of freedom the world had left was mine to lose.

No pressure.

"What do you need me to do?" Bailen asked.

"Take my tracker off TROGS."

He reached for his kit, but I placed my hand on his as he grabbed the latch. "When I tell you to." I retracted my hand, allowing him open the box.

"I thought you said you didn't need me." Bailen winked as he fixed the sensors to my temples.

A smile played on my lips, but I did my best to hide it from him. I would have done it without him if I'd had to, but it was so much easier with him.

He pulled out his laptop and a series of wires, which he stuck to my temples. Then he inspected everything one last time before he returned to his computer.

"Do you want me to run an interference program? Give you some extra time?"

"No, no programs. It has to be me and my tracker."

"You sure?" He flashed me the saddest expression, like a puppy that had been left out in the cold.

"Positive. I have to do this."

"Well, the good news is, the barn has some lead shielding. The bad news is, it's hard to tell how much is still intact. Hopefully, it's enough to keep your tracker a secret until you can power it off." His voice sounded almost monotone, like he had lost his zest for technology.

I'd taken all the fun out of it for him.

"Okay. I'm ready," Bailen said, fingers on the keyboard.

I took a deep breath. "I'm not." And before I could overthink it, I launched myself at Bailen and kissed him. He squeezed me tightly. I lost myself. For that moment, we were just a guy and a girl kissing in a barn. Nothing else mattered.

Nothing.

Just him and me.

The desperation of the kiss said otherwise. Our lips pressed against each other, choppy and frantic, like we couldn't get enough of each other. Like it was the end.

Maybe it was.

His hands cradled the back of my head, urging me closer, as if there were still space to close. And somehow, we managed to reduce the nonexistent gap further. I gave him a final squeeze before pulling away. My heart lingered in the moment, but my head said it was time.

"Shut it off."

A cool chill enveloped me as he hit a single key on the laptop. Files and latent programs slowly brightened into existence in my line of sight. I thought back to when the authorities had shown up at the soccer game. When I'd fled from the bleachers, from Lydia, and from everything I'd thought I'd known about the world. When Peyton had rescued me—no, not *rescued*—changed my life, brought me to a world that had altered my entire mindset, brought me closer to understanding a world my parents had tried to give me but never could.

At the time, I'd been overwhelmed with a tornado of

emotions. Fear of the authorities, fear of what they might do to me, confusion about what was happening to my tracker, uncertain of my next step. I'd pushed it all onto the network, which had forced my tracker to a latent state.

Exactly what I needed to do now, only on a much larger scale. I had to overload my tracker with enough thought and emotion to shut it off completely. I didn't know what came after, though. I inhaled deeply and when I let it out, I made my decision.

I was all in.

Grabbing hold of every single emotion I'd harbored over the last couple of weeks, my thoughts clouded.

The confusion that surrounded me when my tracker had failed. The uncertainty of what it had meant. The sadness of leaving everything I'd known.

My head exploded in pain. I embraced more and more emotions and the events surrounding them.

Fear of what might happen if I got caught.

Anger at what the authorities had taken from me.

Each memory was more painful than the last. Until I found a time before the big mess. A time before I knew about the Ghosts.

Happiness. A thought of what could be.

Freedom. What sat right in front of me but just out of reach.

Support. What I stood to lose.

Love. Family. And what I'd lost...

"Jake!"

The name ripped from my mouth. The voice that had yelled it sounded foreign. I gasped for air as I shoved every emotion and thought onto the network. The windows changed so rapidly, I couldn't keep up with the images flying across my vision. I blinked faster and faster until the darkness blended with the blur of information swarming my sight.

My breaths grew short and stunted. My chest rose and fell as fast as I blinked. I felt a soft touch on my shoulder and collapsed in that general direction, everything going black.

I lay in his arms, my eyes squeezed shut, afraid to open them. Bailen weaved his fingers in my hair and removed the sensors. He massaged my temples, sending a wave of calming security through me. We sat in silence while my breaths receded into a normal rhythm. When I felt a soft kiss on my cheek, my eyes flew open. Everything was still black, except for a small, blinking white box in the upper left-hand corner of my vision.

"Did it work?" Bailen whispered into my ear.

I shot up, but the sudden jolt made my head swim. I leaned back into him as a single word appeared in my line of sight.

PASSWORD:

The blinking white box sat at the end of the word, taunting me.

Password? I'd done everything and now I needed a password? I exhaled loudly.

"What is it?" Bailen asked.

I stayed silent, letting his question hang in the air. Another task I'd have to figure out on my own. If Dad had hidden the message and the plans, he'd also come up with the password. It would have to be something he'd taught me. Possibly about technology. But my instinct told me that wasn't it. He'd spent more time teaching me to be independent. To not rely on technology. But even if I made a wrong turn, I was never alone. There was something I would always have with me.

As the answer became apparent, I thought of the single most important thing in my life. My safety net. My support system. My family.

I thought of the word and nothing else. The letters F A M I L Y appeared slowly, one after the next, in my field of vision.

The white box stopped blinking.

I exhaled.

The screen went black.

"What's happening, Kaya?" Bailen shook me gently.

"I'm not sure. It asked for a password, so I input one and then everything went…"

The sudden outpouring of images flying across my line of sight stopped me mid-sentence. The files settled into twenty-two rows of ten images and with it, my vision returned to normal.

I thought about the first image and blinked twice. The file enlarged. A series of swirling designs appeared. I collapsed that image and moved to the second. More of the same. I tried the third. It was similar too. So I skipped to the last image. More lines, but not curved. These were straight and jutted out at sharp angles.

"Interesting," I muttered under my breath.

"What is it? Do you have the plans?"

"I'm not sure what I have, but it seems familiar." I blinked twice, closing out the final file and minimizing the secret program.

"Is your tracker on?"

I gasped. In all the image deciphering and password uncovering, I'd totally forgotten about the tracking program. I blinked twice, pushing a simple search onto the tracker network. Nothing. I blinked twice again. Still nothing. "I think I'm disconnected. It seems like a separate program running in the background that's not linked to the tracker network."

Bailen checked his monitor and typed in a series of different things into TROGS. "There's no signal coming from your tracker. You're offline. But we'll keep an eye on it just in case."

I leaned my head against his shoulder, focused on what remained of the opposite wall. Some of my painted designs were still there, covered by debris. Others had giant holes in them. But they were partially intact. I traced the curving lines, going back to the time I'd started drawing them, shortly after Jake... I couldn't finish the thought. I concentrated on the remains of the designs, slowly moving over each line, following every twist and curve. Something about the design was familiar.

I shot up, ignoring my pounding head, and opened up the third file. Pushing to my feet, I moved closer to the image on the wall. I moved the picture of the third file to the edge of my vision and compared it to the wall. I blinked twice and rotated the image on its side then let out a gasp.

"Kaya, what is it?"

I enlarged the image and positioned it over the one I'd painted on the wall. I pointed at the wall, my mouth gaping. "That painting I did, it matches a portion of the file I have here."

"What? How is that possible?" Bailen moved next to me, studying my designs. He shoved some rubble out of the way, revealing more of the swirling lines. Stepping back, he said, "I can't believe I didn't see it before."

"See what?" I asked.

The same expression from when he'd solved the secret message appeared.

"Bailen, what's going on?"

He grabbed my arms, spinning me to face him. "Do all the files look like this?"

"Yes," I said. "Well, some of them have straight lines instead. Why?"

"How many are there?"

"Two hundred and twenty."

He shook me excitedly. "Do you know what this means?"

"No. Please explain what's going on."

"Do you think you can draw them?" he asked. He was like a kid whose parents had just told him he could have candy and ice cream for dinner.

"I think so," I said. "Bailen, what's going on?"

He pointed at the wall of the barn. "They're electronic schematics."

"Tracker schematics?"

"Yep."

It was everything we'd been searching for. Everything they'd hoped to find by analyzing my tracker. Everything we needed. The way to end trackers.

"If those files are all related like I think they are, then we should be able to see all the inner workings of the chips—what components go into them and how they connect and interact with the tracker network." He grabbed my cheeks and planted a kiss on my lips that made my knees go weak.

"Kaya, you did it. You gave us the key to our freedom."

Thirty

"**T**his is incredible! Your tracker was somehow interfacing with your subconscious on a level above normal tracker operation." Bailen cleared away more debris from the walls and admired what was left of my doodles. All along, those paintings had been something more. Something much more.

Somehow, I'd accessed the schematics in the Ghost program and not even known it. "What does this mean for my tracker?"

"Honestly, I'm not sure," he said. "You're safe now. I'm still not reading any signals from it. Not even the low-level one we picked up before." He dusted off more of the drawing. "We've got a lot of work to do. How quickly do you think you can draw these? We need a team to analyze them for weaknesses." The glint of excitement reappeared.

"I dunno. A week. Two at most." While I was happy for a path to the end, something felt off. The weight on me still remained. It was far from over. A lot of the plan, the future of the Ghosts, and the future of the world, depended on my ability to reproduce what was inside my head.

Bailen packed up his kit then stared at the wall as if trying to commit the design to memory. I flipped through more of the images, trying to gain a better understanding, but it seemed like a maze of lines with no clear path. Why did I have to be the one with the bum tracker holding the secrets to unraveling the network? I wished it were Bailen. He could actually do something with the images.

Bailen grabbed my hand and led me to his bike.

"Are you sure it's okay to go back?" I asked. "What if my tracker turns on again?"

"I don't think it will. But we'll keep an eye on it."

He climbed on the bike and I followed. Once we were in the air, he jabbered on about the possibilities the schematics held, about how the Ghosts finally had an advantage. After a while, his voice just became noise—a quiet droning in my helmet. I opened and closed the images on my tracker, searching for the one thing that nagged at me, but I couldn't quite grasp a hold of. As my brain struggled to pull the information from my subconscious and my tracker, my head swam, overwhelmed with data. Regardless of what was bothering me, I had a lot of work to do. At least I had an excuse to draw.

When we arrived at the Quarry, Bailen hunted down a giant roll of paper and some charcoal.

"Where did you get all this?" I asked as we stepped into my makeshift room.

"I was saving it for a rainy day."

I threw my arms around him then reached for the paper. It was ages since I'd last seen some. He playfully held the paper out of reach. I clutched his arm, but he flexed it. Bailen raised his arm, pulling me to my tiptoes. I laughed, surprised by his strength. Who would have guessed his lanky arms had that much muscle?

Releasing my hold before he raised me completely off the ground, I stepped back and crossed my arms over my chest. "You're wasting valuable time."

"Oh, you think that's going to work on me?"

I pushed my bottom lip out, trying hard not to laugh.

A giant smile erupted on his face. "You're right, it will." He lowered his arm and handed me the paper. I kissed him on the cheek then rolled the paper out on the rocky ground.

Grabbing a broken piece of charcoal, I blinked twice and opened the first image. It was far more detailed than it had originally appeared. Lines crossed and swirled every which way. Duplicating the image wouldn't be easy. And one wrong line or mistake could cost the Ghosts. It had to be exact.

I placed the tip of the charcoal on the paper and let myself loose. My hand trailed in smooth arcs. Every few lines, I stopped to check my accuracy. All time seemed to stand still around me as I worked.

At one point, I discovered I was alone but didn't pause long enough to see where Bailen had gone. I had a job to do, and he knew it.

When a sweet aroma filled my nostrils, I noticed the plate of food next to me. My stomach gurgled. I sighed and continued drawing. I couldn't stop. Not even for food.

A hand stroked my shoulder and I jumped.

"You didn't eat," Bailen said.

It wasn't a question.

I shook my head and added more swirling lines to the page,

which now appeared cluttered and complex. It was almost complete—almost.

"You have to eat. You can't ignore food just because you have important stuff on your tracker."

I shook my head, not taking my attention off the drawing. I was glad my tracker wasn't barking at me about low blood sugar.

"*Kaya*! Stop!"

The words rolled off as I drew more lines to the paper.

He grabbed my hand, forcing the charcoal from it. The stick, now a small stub, dropped onto the paper.

"Don't give me that look. You need a break. You've been at this for hours. It's nearly sunrise."

"Sunrise?" I'd stayed up all night with no concept of how much time had passed. My fingers weren't cramped, though, so it couldn't have been too long.

Bailen placed a hand on my cheek and gently nudged my face sideways so I could meet him. "I'm worried about you."

"Don't be. I'm fine."

"Girl fine, or really fine?"

"I'm fine!"

Pushing up from the floor, I grabbed the plate and moved over to the small table in the corner of the room. I picked up a piece of bread from the plate, tore off a chunk, and shoved it into my mouth.

I swallowed the cold, rock-like bread, wishing I hadn't let it sit so long. "See, I'm eating. Now can you let me finish?" I asked. "I'm almost done with this one."

"Sure."

He wasn't happy about it but seemed satisfied for now. I wished he had let me finish the drawing without all the nagging about eating.

I found a longer piece of charcoal and returned to the drawing. I added the last few lines, then sat back, admiring the picture. I put the image in the corner of my vision and compared, tracing over each line painstakingly slow to make sure I had gotten it right. Then, just to be certain, I moved the image in my line of sight over the one I'd drawn. Everything matched up perfectly. After checking the final line, I picked up the drawing and leaned it against the wall.

Backing away, I moved next to Bailen and laid my head on his shoulder. He brushed the damp hair from my forehead.

"I hope there's some good information in there," I muttered.

Bailen remained quiet for some time before he said, "I'm sure there is, but it's not entirely clear yet. It's one piece in a very complex puzzle."

I yawned and moved to roll out more paper, but Bailen grabbed my arm.

"Where do you think you're going?"

"To start another drawing."

"Oh, no, you don't." He scooped me up and laid me on the bed, dropping next to me. "Take a break."

I shook my head and opened my mouth to speak, but he put a finger to my lips.

"Less talking, more relaxing."

"But…"

"Shh." He leaned in to kiss me.

I didn't try to stop him. In fact, I welcomed the change of pace. His kisses were slow and soft, relaxing. He wrapped his arms around me and pulled me close, squeezing me as if he were a bubble protecting me from the world. My hand eased around his waist. I slid my fingers underneath his T-shirt, lightly brushing them across his skin. He shivered at my touch then slipped his hand under the hem of my shirt.

Bailen left a trail of kisses from my cheek downward. His hands made their way across my hips. My heart pounded. Each thud matched one of Bailen's kisses as they moved across the base of my neck. I tugged at his shirt and drew it over his head. He stretched out on his side next to me. My hand ran over his bare chest, warm and inviting.

I tilted my head so our lips could meet again and pulled him onto me, warming myself further with his body heat. I didn't want the moment to end.

Bailen slid next to me again and rolled on his back, placing his hands behind his head. I let out a long breath. Despite his warm body at my side, a cold emptiness chilled me from the inside out. "Is something wrong?" I whispered.

"No. Everything is perfect."

"Then why did you stop?"

He faced me. "Because you need to sleep. We can finish this later." He wrapped his arm around me and drew me into him, kissing my forehead. I rested my head on his chest, listening to the sound of his heartbeat, so unfamiliar.

I didn't get it. Most guys would have kept going. I wanted him to, but my eyes drooped as the rhythmic rise and fall of his chest soothed me. The gentle thumping of his heartbeat distracted me from the important job I had to do.

Thirty-One

I awoke to someone shuffling around the room. My head throbbed. *What day is it? Forget what day, what time is it?* The days were all blending together. As much as I loved drawing, it had worn me down. I rolled over, trying to focus on the giant blur.

"Bailen?" I asked in a hoarse whisper.

"No, try again. I know we're twins, but we don't look that much alike."

I groaned and flopped onto my back. Peyton. The last thing I needed was more smart comments from her. "What are you doing here?" I asked, blinking away my blurry vision.

"I brought dinner," she said in a sickeningly sweet, singsong voice.

"Dinner?" Had I really slept the whole day?

"Yes, dinner."

"Ugh," was all I could manage. I sat up and leaned against the wall. "What day is it?"

"Friday."

"*Friday*?" The days had all blurred together.

"Do I need to repeat myself?"

I shook my head, but the pain continued to swirl. "Night?"

"What part of *dinner* did you not get?"

I ignored her and focused on the word *dinner*. Shabbat. Oh, the irony of it all.

"You look like shit. You should get more sleep."

"I *was* sleeping until you marched your ass in here."

Peyton's stone face didn't crack.

"But seeing as I'm awake, I should work." Shabbat or not, I needed to draw. Surely, there was some kind of forgiveness clause for fighting evil tech overlords, especially ones that had kept Shabbat from so many for so long. Besides, we were running out of time. The upgrade was creeping up on us and the Ghosts still needed time to analyze all the drawings for weaknesses.

And yet Peyton wasn't budging.

"Where's Bailen?"

"He had work to do. He asked me to bring you food."

"Well, that was awful nice of you. What gives?"

"What? I can't get to know my brother's girlfriend?" She sounded innocent, but her grimace gave her away.

"Nope. Not buying it. He sent you to play nice, didn't he?" I asked. "What do you want, Peyton? I have a lot of stuff to do." I stumbled across the room and picked up half of a sandwich from the plate on the table, but my vision spun in protest. I squeezed my eyes shut for a moment of peace. When I opened them, I was met with Peyton's mock hurt expression. *Why is she acting so weird?*

"Come on. Cut me some slack. Clue me in," I said.

The expression remained, but she said nothing. "Out with it. I don't have time for your crap." I paused, hoping I'd pushed one of her buttons. Still nothing, so I let the next phrase spill out of my mouth before I had time to think about it. "Not to mention if you'd stop fighting with Bailen..." I stopped abruptly, not knowing where I was going with that statement. I'd heard them yelling through the halls for days, but the most I'd ever made out was comments about rescuing their dad.

Her lips pulled tight. She marched toward me with her finger pointed at my chest. "That fight with my brother is none of your business."

"Ah, now we're getting somewhere." I eyed her, attempting not to flinch as she closed the gap between us. "You and Bailen—"

"My relationship with my brother doesn't concern you." Our faces were inches apart.

"And my relationship with Bailen doesn't concern you. But that didn't stop you from sticking your nose where it doesn't belong!"

We glared at each other, neither of us wavering. I cocked my head to the side and crossed my arms.

Finally, she took a deep breath, backed away, and said, "I'm sorry." She shook her head and sat on the edge of the bed. "He's all I have left."

With one sentence, her hard edges crumbled. She drew her knees into her chest and wrapped her arms around her legs, her chin resting on top.

Why me? Why now? Peyton hadn't exactly made things easy on me, and I had drawings to finish. I didn't have time to deal with her breakdown. But a tiny voice inside told me to help her. Nagged me. She didn't have anyone. No family other than Bailen and her dad. No girl friends or females our age. Although Peyton wasn't very girly, I was guessing she needed some girl talk. I must have seemed like the best option.

She buried her head in her hands, her body quaking. *Is she crying? For fuck's sake!* If it were Lydia, I'd hug her and tell her everything would be okay. I'd let her cry until the whole problem came spilling out of her like an upturned carton of milk.

But it wasn't Lydia. Peyton was the opposite of Lydia—two different ends of the spectrum. If only Lydia were here now. She'd know what to do.

I plopped next to Peyton on the bed. I reached out but hesitated before I touched her shoulder. Dropping my hand, I asked, "What's wrong?"

She took a deep breath then muttered, "Nothing. I'm fine."

"Girl fine or actual fine?" I asked, hoping the stolen phrase might get a reaction from her.

She lifted her head. Her puffy red eyes met mine. Her normal sarcastic intensity masked the sorrow that previously filled her. "Jeez! You've been spending way too much time with my brother. I'm cutting you off."

"Ha! Then who would you make fun of?"

She snorted but didn't say anything. The awkward silence smothered us.

"Do you need to talk?" I asked in an attempt to move the conversation along.

"Maybe." She shook her head. "I don't know."

"Look, I know we aren't best friends, but you can talk to me. Whatever you say is between us."

She sucked in a deep breath, as if contemplating my trustworthiness.

"I always wanted a sister. And don't sisters tell each other everything?" I continued, hoping to push her into talking. The faster I got it out of her, the faster I could get to drawing.

"I don't know. I've always been stuck with Bailen." She paused. "Okay, *stuck* isn't the right word, but I didn't grow up around many women."

"Your mom?"

Without missing a beat, she said, "She died. Bailen and I were young. Dad doesn't talk about her much."

"I'm sorry." The words came out as a whisper. Another awkward silence persisted. Her words hung in the air like a thick cloud. I moved to the floor and pulled out my latest drawing. "Mind if I…" I pointed to the paper and Peyton shook her head.

I opened up the second-to-last image in the files. I was nearly there. I started to draw, letting my hand take over absentmindedly. The scratching of the charcoal on the paper filled the quiet.

Soon, I wondered if she was still there sitting behind me. "So what's really bothering you?"

The silence continued. I dropped the charcoal and spun around, expecting an empty bed. Peyton was still sitting there, staring blankly at my art, her legs drawn up, her chin resting on her knees.

I waved my hand in front of her a few times. She blinked then focused on me.

"It's Bailen. You're afraid of losing him."

"I think I already have. He spends hours inspecting your drawings. And whatever free time he has, he spends with you."

I didn't know how to respond. My first instinct was to apologize, but it wasn't really my fault. I wasn't sure she thought so, either. In the absence of words, I returned to my drawing. I could easily get lost in it.

"We used to be so close. We did everything together. Then he got into computers and spent all his time chasing this dream of freedom. I followed him, but I don't think I can anymore. It's going to get him killed," she said. "I'll either end up right next to him or have no one left."

"Your dad isn't gone, you know. We'll get him back. And my parents, too."

Peyton still seemed dazed, like her body was here, but her mind was in the tracker network. I wasn't even sure if she heard me, so I kept sketching.

"This goal of his... I'm not sure it's worth it anymore."

I slammed my piece of charcoal on the ground and it shattered. "That's enough! What happened to that strong, crazy rider who rescued me from the authorities? The girl who doesn't take any crap from anyone?" I whipped around. "What's wrong with you?"

Tears pooled in the corners of her eyes. "I didn't do that for you." She stood from the bed. "You know what? I can't pretend anymore." She stormed toward the door, but I beat her there and blocked the way.

"What's that supposed to mean?"

"You aren't the only one who lost someone they care about. I can't pretend it doesn't bother me anymore." She tried to shove past me, but I pushed back. "Kaya, let me go or this won't end well." The hard edge was back in her voice, but it lacked the usual sense of carefree sarcasm. There was so much pain behind it.

"Tell me what you're talking about, and I'll let you go."

I could have sworn the heat building in my face was coming

from the flames about to shoot out of her eye sockets. "You weren't the only one who loved Jake," she spat, "I'm done pretending he only cared about you," then she shouldered past me and was gone, leaving me frozen in place.

Her words ripped open the healing wound in my heart. How could I not have seen it? No wonder Peyton hated me so much. Jake had died protecting me. If it weren't for me, he'd still be here.

Images of him coughing up blood swarmed through my head. The massive bruise across his stomach. His last words. His pinky brushing against mine. My breaths waivered, and my vision blurred. I was back in the barn, Jake in my arms, glassy eyes fixed on me. My chest clenched, rock solid and unmoving, almost as if someone were standing on it.

My legs buckled, sending my knees hard to the ground. Red and white streaks crisscrossed in my vision. Pain shot through my kneecaps up into my stomach, where it settled, wrapping around my insides.

Thirty-Two

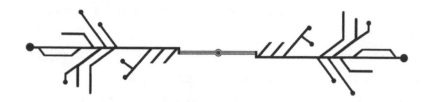

"**K**aya?" The voice sounded like it was coming from the opposite end of a tunnel. "Kaya!"

"Jake?" I choked out. My vision cleared. Not Jake. Jake had died in front of me weeks ago. And he hadn't told me about his feelings for Peyton. My body ached with the knowledge that he'd belonged to her too. Had I ever really known my brother?

Bailen pulled me into him and held me. He squeezed so tightly, as if his arms could remove all the upset energy coursing through my veins. Unfortunately, the pain couldn't be forced from my body like juice from fruit. Despite my fragile state, I was thankful for the pain. It let me know that everything was still real and not some awful nightmare. People were counting on me. The pain, the loss—it hadn't all been for nothing.

But Jake should have told me about Peyton. Hell, there were a lot of things Jake should have told me. About the Ghosts, about Dad, about so many other things. He used to tell me everything.

Now he'd never tell me anything again. What other secrets had he kept from me?

I didn't have time to worry about it. I had a job to do. I pushed away from Bailen and snatched the charcoal so I could draw. The lines were so sharp and heavy, as if they carried a portion of the burden, a fraction of everything I'd experienced and lost.

Sometime later, I felt a hand on my shoulder. I shrugged it off, continuing to etch lines into the paper. I slashed at the paper, hoping my abrupt movements would fling the sadness from my body. It didn't. My arm was the only part of me that still worked. Everything else had a dull, persistent tingle. The only thing telling me I wasn't dreaming or dead.

I swung my hand and the charcoal tore through the paper with a soft ripping noise. I cursed under my breath for being so careless. I wished it were my skin tearing instead. I wanted to feel something else besides frozen inside. I sliced at the paper again, imagining the charcoal as a knife. Again and again, I tore the paper until a hand grasped mine. The charcoal slipped between my fingers.

I spun around and buried my head in Bailen's soft shirt, letting the tears fall freely. Crying in his arms had become a habit. But I didn't care. I wanted so badly to be strong, but I couldn't keep that up forever. The stress, the exhaustion—it was all getting to me. I'd come a long way, but there was still so much left to do.

Although the Ghosts had opened me up to the world as it really was, a world that had challenged my *normal*, that had let me see things differently, nothing had prepared me for the realization that I'd known very little about my own family—my dad and now Jake. Did my mom have secrets too?

288

I just wanted it all to be over so I could move on, no longer stuck in these constant reminders, reminders of what I had and what was just out of reach. I couldn't go back. But I wasn't sure I wanted to. Although the end approached, it didn't seem close enough.

He pressed his lips softly against my scalp. "It's okay. Peyton told me."

"You think this is about Peyton?" I shook my head. "Why didn't you tell me?"

Bailen shook his head. "I never knew for sure, but I suspected. I never pushed her on it, though. She's always kept that stuff quiet. I just wanted her to be happy."

"Yeah, happy," I muttered as I wiped a tear from my cheek.

"Does it really matter if they hid their feelings?"

"I guess not. But I feel like I didn't know my brother."

Bailen opened his mouth then closed it again. The muscles straining in his forehead said it all. That he wasn't sure what words would calm me down. "You knew your brother better than anyone here," he said.

"Did he ever mention anything about struggling to remember things?"

"No. He had a great memory."

That wasn't exactly what I'd meant, but Bailen kept going. "He talked about you a lot. Shared tons of stories. Not being able to contact you killed him."

"I missed him, too," I said. "Miss him," I softly corrected.

"I'd never seen him happier than the day we picked you up. He was at your side moments after you collapsed. He sat outside your door for hours waiting for you to wake up."

"He was in the computer room at the Hive?"

Bailen cracked a smile. "I think you were a little too preoccupied blaming me for your tracker malfunctions to see anyone else in the room."

I choked down a laugh, remembering how pissed and confused I'd been. "I had good reason to think so." I stopped then added, "At the time."

Bailen picked up my sliced-up drawing. "And now?"

"Oh, don't tell me you're going to make me apologize."

"No, I was just hoping to hear I was right all along."

"Not going to happen." I grabbed the drawing and laid it on the floor. I sat back and admired it, hoping the rips hadn't ruined it completely. But if I had to start over again, I would. It was too important. It had to be perfect.

Bailen reached around me and smoothed out a section of the drawing. He rested his chin on his hand and pointed at the spot with a giant gash running through it. "I was afraid of this," he said under his breath.

"Of what?"

"Are you sure this group of lines here is right?" He pointed to the latest series of lines, which had turned the drawing into grated cheese.

Although I was certain, I did a quick comparison between the schematic on my tracker and my sketch. "Yes, it's a perfect match. Why?"

"I was afraid of this."

"You keep saying that. What's wrong?"

"Come with me."

Before I could protest, he grabbed my arm with one hand and the drawing in the other. He dragged me down the hall.

"Bailen, what's going on?"

Rather than respond, he picked up his pace. A minute later, we were in the computer room, where a very large schematic was projected onto the big screen hanging on the far wall. It was a giant computer simulation of my drawings. The only thing missing was a small cutout in the bottom right-hand corner of the screen—the placeholder for the final two drawings.

"You've been busy."

Bailen dropped my arm, leaving me alone in the center of the room. He picked up a roll of tape from his desk and held up my drawing to the edge of the computer-simulated one. He fixed the image to the screen with a piece of tape, leaving only a small corner of the image bare.

Jeremy came up next to me examining at the drawings. "Bailen, you were right."

"This was one thing I didn't want to be right about."

"Right about what?" I asked. "Would someone please explain what is going on?" I wanted to stomp my foot like a spoiled toddler, but I didn't think it was going to get me answers. "Seriously, what am I looking at? And don't tell me tracker schematics because I figured that much out."

"These are the tracker schematics, but this part"—Bailen circled his arm around a chunk of the schematic, including my taped-up drawing—"is the piece of the tracker chip that allows the authorities to impair movement."

"Yeah, so? We already know the authorities can stop anyone in their tracks. It keeps people from escaping them. This is nothing new."

Jeremy shifted, then moved his gaze from the drawing to me. "Well, every chip has a switch on it. Kind of like a deadbolt. In one position it's locked; in the other it's unlocked. In the case of the chip, in one position you keep your free will. In the other, the authorities have the ability to stop you. No more free will."

"So there's a switch. I still don't understand why this is a problem," I said, my gaze darting between Jeremy's and Bailen's grim expressions, hoping one of them would answer me. The weight hanging over me since I'd discovered the drawings on my tracker grew even heavier.

"Kaya, come here," Bailen said.

I walked toward him with the caution of a person walking on a rope bridge suspended over a lava river. With each step, my gut twisted further.

Bailen put his arm around me. With his free hand, he pointed to a small rectangular box that spanned between my taped-up sketch and the image projected on the screen. "This switch isn't like a normal on/off switch."

"What do you mean?"

"Our chips have a fatal flaw."

"What kind of flaw?"

"This is the part I was hoping to be wrong about."

"Would you just say it?"

"With the right activation code, a user could hack in and control someone. Not just stop them but bend them to their will. Turn the person into a mind-controlled minion."

Thirty-Three

"**W**ait, that flaw allows for complete mind control? How?" I asked.

"If someone hacks in, they can send signals to the parts of the brain that control movement," Bailen said.

Thoughts whirled around in a haze as I tried to form coherent questions. "Is that flaw in everyone's trackers?"

"I think so."

"If that's true, why aren't we all mind-controlled now? Why haven't we seen anyone acting weird?"

"My guess is whoever knows about it is waiting for the right moment to strike. But until we see the final drawing and do some research, we may not be able to uncover all the secrets."

With a renewed sense of purpose, I spun and ran from the room yelling, "I'm on it."

My heart pounded as I bolted through the corridors. My breaths and pulsing blood formed the rhythm of an ominous song. I collapsed in front of a fresh sheet of paper, accessing the

293

final drawing and putting the charcoal to the paper, letting my hand take over.

As the image took shape, I powered through the lines faster and faster. Adrenaline fueled me through the drawing. I owed everyone that much.

When I drew in the last line, I double, then triple-checked my work. It didn't mean anything to me, but it was a perfect match.

Dropping the charcoal on the ground, I peeled the sketch off the floor and bolted to the computer room. When I arrived, only Bailen, Jeremy, and Peyton remained.

"I've got it," I said as I tripped over my feet and quickly righted myself. Only then did I notice their foreboding expressions. "What's with the pity party? I finished. We should be celebrating."

Peyton flinched but said nothing. I moved from face to face, but no hint of an answer appeared. "Not this game again. This crap has to stop. What aren't you telling me?"

"There's no time," Jeremy said, shaking his head.

"No time for what?"

Bailen spun me around so I could face him. "After we saw the latest drawing, Jeremy hacked the network and..."

"And what?"

"The upgrade is tomorrow night. By Friday morning, they'll start mind controlling people. There's not enough time to stop it."

"The authorities aren't as dumb as they look. They know we've been scrambling, so this has to be a trap. They're trying to lure us in," Peyton said.

"A trap? So that's it? You're just giving up? After everything we've been through? You're going to let the authorities win?"

"Who said anything about giving up?" Bailen's lips curled up into a half-smile that said he was ready to get back into the fight.

"You just said..." I stopped as I watched his full excitement erupt.

"You know I love a challenge. Let's spring the trap."

Behind Bailen, Peyton winced. It was such a slight movement, barely detectable. The risk of losing Bailen was going to rip her apart. How was I going to balance the war and keep Bailen from getting himself killed? I'd failed Jake. Or rather, Jake had died protecting me. I didn't want to have to answer to Peyton if I let something awful happen to Bailen. I'd never forgive myself. Everything was going to work, or I'd die trying to save everyone I loved—what was left of them.

Bailen held out his hand. "Let me see that drawing."

I passed it to him, and he tacked it to the empty space next to the now computer-generated image of my previous sketches. The schematic resembled an aerial view of a giant hedge maze, and its meaning was equally confusing.

Bailen studied the image before returning to his terminal. He typed in a few commands. "According to the computer analysis, these areas"—circles appeared around sections of the schematic projected on the wall—"are the possible weaknesses in the tracking chips."

"So what can we do with that information?" I asked, searching the four circles on the image, one of which encompassed the final addition to the schematic.

"If we can figure out a way to interrupt the signal to any one of these pieces before the upgrade, it should disconnect every person from the tracker network," Jeremy said.

"That doesn't sound too bad." Even though the words made it sound easy, I knew it wouldn't be. Nothing was ever that easy.

"In theory, yes. In reality…" The normal fire in Peyton was replaced by a deep sadness, as if someone had opened the blinds to her soul.

"These two sections require direct access to the chip," Bailen said as two of the circles flashed on the screen. "There is no way to physically access every living person's chip and certainly not in less than two days. So, those loopholes are out."

"And those other two?" I asked with a hint of hope that it wasn't impossible.

"Although altering how this one receives data would permanently cripple the chips, it would require a program that will take weeks, maybe months to write," Jeremy said.

"So that leaves the final one," I said, pointing to the section circling the newest piece of the schematic.

"Yes." Bailen propped his elbows on his desk and rested his chin in his hands, peering between the computer equipment at my sketch. "That one will be tricky, but I think it's our only shot."

Peyton walked up behind Bailen and whacked him on the back of the head. "Are you crazy? I'm no computer expert, but even I know what that does, and it's a suicide mission."

"It's not suicide." Bailen rubbed the back of his head. "But it is nearly impossible."

"Let me guess. Corrupting that piece of the chip requires access to tracker labs?" I said half-sarcastically.

"Worse," Jeremy said. "We have to break into tracker headquarters."

"Not just headquarters. We need access to the brain of the

building—the main server room inside Rufus Scurry's private office. A place only mentioned in rumors," Bailen said.

"How in the hell are we going to get in there? That place is more tightly controlled than a pair of authority binders."

Peyton opened her mouth, then paused as if contemplating her next words very carefully. She took a deep breath and focused directly on me. "If we are going in there, we'll have to look the part. We're going to need a prisoner."

Thirty-Four

"**M**e, a prisoner? They'll never buy it." The fact that they were using me as bait didn't faze me. The plan was so insane, it was bound to fail from the moment we arrived at Global Tracking Systems.

I quickly ran over every possible scenario in my head. Imprisoned, injured, lab rat, death, mind-controlled zombie. It wouldn't end well. It couldn't.

"I've still got the authority uniform. We could steal a few more," Peyton said.

"Sounds like we need to assemble a mission," Bailen added.

"I'll grab my gear. We can leave in a half hour." Jeremy headed toward the back caverns.

"I'll change my clothes," I said, pulling at my grungy T-shirt and sweat pants I'd been wearing for the last three days. The whole process had put me in survival mode. I'd completely forgotten to do the day-to-day things, like showering. I turned on my heel, but before I could take a step, someone had the collar of my shirt.

"And where do you think you're going?" Peyton asked.

I whirled around, ripping the shirt from Peyton's grasp. "To shower and change for the mission. You're going to need bait, right?"

"That's cute, Kaya. You really think we're taking you with us to go steal authority uniforms? There's a bounty on your head. You aren't going anywhere."

"Seriously?" I scoffed. She might as well have been channeling Jake. I was seven years old again, and he was ditching me for his friends. They really were perfect for each other. I couldn't believe I hadn't seen it before. I searched her for an indication she was enjoying this, but it wasn't there. She actually seemed a bit sad. Maybe we had bonded a little.

Bailen grabbed my hand. "I'm sorry. We have to protect you. Now more than ever. Without you, we will never make it into Rufus Scurry's office. We won't even make it into the building."

I contemplated my next statement, trying to choose my words carefully. But then I thought better of it and clamped my mouth shut. He was right, but I wasn't going to give him the satisfaction.

Before any regretful words spilled from my mouth, I shook my head and yanked my hand free of Bailen's. I darted from the room in an attempt to distance myself from their pathetic expressions. I didn't want their pity.

I collapsed onto my bed exhausted, but sleep didn't come. Rage welled inside me. I wanted everything to be over. I wanted my life back, my family, my friends. I buried my face in the pillow and screamed. I kept screaming, hoping the rage would leave, but it only fueled the anger.

I knew I should shower and change my clothes. That it would make me feel better, but my whole body ached. I didn't want to feel better; I wanted to feel normal. But I wasn't even sure what normal was anymore.

The rage was something I had control over, even if it was stupid. I had every intention of holding on to control for as long as possible. I fought the waves of exhaustion with every last ounce of energy, but eventually, fatigue formed as my anger slipped away.

***

"It's time to go," Bailen said.

"Go where?" I asked groggily.

"Global Tracking Systems."

It was time to end it. "Now? Why didn't anyone wake me?"

"We thought you could use the sleep."

"Sleep? No, I needed to help you guys plan." I threw the tangle of blankets off and swung my legs over the edge of the bed.

"Don't worry. We'll walk you through it as we go. Honestly, the less you know, the better. If for some reason you're captured." He paused to kiss me, but it didn't reassure me. "Then you can't tell them anything."

"Okay, let me shower."

"Kaya, there's no time."

"No time? I look like a crazy person." I pulled the neck of my T-shirt over my nose. I smelled pretty bad, too. How could Bailen stand that close to me? I was disgusting.

"Actually, that's a good thing. It'll make it seem like you've been on the run. It'll be more believable. But we have to go now.

The upgrade is in three hours."

"Three hours?"

"Yeah. We had to wait until the night shift. It'll be easier to get inside."

How had I slept so long? Three hours and it was all over. I couldn't wrap my head around the number. Three. It was so small, such a short amount of time.

A part of me realized the time frame was comforting. Whether we won or lost, I wouldn't have to worry anymore. But the other part of me shook from the inside out. Pulling the plan off would be nothing short of a miracle. Even worse, they were taking me in blind, as a hostage. We were doomed. No, *they* were doomed. I was as good as dead. I wasn't sure if I was okay with that or not, but I didn't have time to decide.

Ten minutes later, we were in the makeshift motorbike garage with Jeremy and Peyton dressed in full authority gear. Bailen pulled on the authority jacket that matched the pants he wore. Their attire made my stomach churn, as if I were guilty of something. That same feeling I'd gotten in the woods, like I'd done something wrong, even when I hadn't.

"How many guys did you have to take out to get the gear?" I asked.

They stared at me like it was a stupid question.

"Never mind. I don't want to know." A subtle reminder of how much longer they'd been fighting.

Jeremy and Peyton climbed onto their bikes. I approached Bailen's, but he pulled me toward him. "Nope, you're coming with me. We have other transportation." He gave me a quick kiss on the cheek, then led me out of the Quarry.

"You stole a unicopter? Are you nuts? Do you even know how

to fly it?"

"I flew it here, didn't I?" he said. "Once is plenty of pract—"

"Nope. Stop right there. I don't even—" Before I could finish, his lips were on mine. The kiss sent sparks past my lips, down my throat, and into my chest. He ran his hands through my hair and cradled the back of my head. My knees buckled, and I fell into him. He caught me around the waist and lifted me upright. Rather than putting my feet on the ground, I wrapped my legs around him and let him hold me up. He ran his hand up my side as the kiss quickened.

An alarm went off inside my head, a little voice telling me, *Three hours, three hours, three hours.* I unwrapped my legs and dropped them to the ground. After one final deep, passionate kiss, I pulled away. For a moment, I studied his face, committing it to memory—his brilliant green eyes, his ruffled, brown hair, and his perfectly imperfect smile that always held more meaning behind it.

"You ready?" he asked softly.

I nodded, too afraid to speak. He pulled a pair of metal bands from the kit on the unicopter and slipped them on my wrists without locking them. He snuck a quick peck on the tip of my nose before helping me into the rear-facing seat and strapping me in. I watched over my shoulder as he climbed into the pilot's seat. With a soft hum, the vehicle purred to life.

The others emerged from the cave on their bikes.

"We're going to use the roof landing pad. But you guys should ditch your bikes a block or two out." Bailen tossed them each a small object. "Put those tracking chips in your helmets. They should give you access to the building through the front door." After they both obeyed, he asked, "Do you guys know your part of the plan?"

"Yes," Peyton said. "We've been over it a billion times. Relax, Bailen."

"Good. Whatever you do, don't take those helmets off. Otherwise, the building will be able to detect your real tracker chips."

Without a word, they put on their helmets and sped away.

"Where did you find those chips?" I stopped and shook my head, spinning around to face out the rear of the unicopter. "Never mind. I don't think I want to know the answer to that, either."

Deep down, I knew. Bailen was a tech nerd at heart, but his life had forced him to become a thief and a fighter. There was a lot of gray area. Myles proved that. I swallowed hard and reminded myself it was war. But that justification didn't make me feel any better. Who were we to make important decisions for the world? If we did, were we no better than the authorities? The line was so blurry it was hard to know which side of it we were on.

The swooshing of the unicopter blades rumbling to life drew me from my thoughts. The vehicle rocked as it lifted off the ground, almost as if groaning and struggling under our weight. From a few feet up, the unicopter gave in and slammed to the ground. The engine cut out instantly and the blades slowed. I choked down stomach acid.

"Are you sure you know what you're doing?" I asked.

"Yeah, I've got it. Just give me a sec," Bailen said over the loudspeaker.

A tracking chip would have been nice, or at least a helmet. Not just for safety, but so I wasn't so alienated from him. I felt like the prisoner I was impersonating. No rights, no freedom, no communication.

The engine whined to life a second time with a subtle whooshing sound. The blades spun, whipping my hair in all directions and sending wind pounding into my ears. The trees slowly sank below us as we climbed and flew toward the city.

On the outskirts of town, Bailen's voice came over the speaker. "When we get close, I need you to put up a fight. You don't have a functioning tracker, so there's no way to subdue you."

"Sure," I yelled. It was all I could get out. My heart was pumping blood so fast that my veins started to throb. A giant lump welled in my throat. The spire of Global Tracking Systems stood out on the skyline against the standard rectangular skyrises. Its steel exterior reflected the city lights. The closer we came, the more I struggled to breathe. Maybe I wouldn't have to resist. I'd be lucky if I didn't pass out before we reached the landing pad.

The unicopter lowered onto the roof of Global Tracking Systems. Bailen cut the engine and the blades slowed. Showtime. I screamed and thrashed in my seat, flailing my cuffed arms in random directions.

Two uniformed agents approached as Bailen jumped from his seat and came around the side to unstrap me. I clocked him in the cheek and silently apologized.

"If you don't stop thrashing, I'm going to knock you out," Bailen said, his voice dripping with hate. The voice was so convincing, it shocked me into a frozen state.

"That's better." He pulled me down from the seat and pushed me toward the two agents.

"Hold it right there," said the first agent. "Your landing code is expired."

"Sorry. I was told considering what I'm bringing, it wouldn't be a problem." Bailen nodded toward me.

"What do we have here?" asked the first agent.

"Isn't she a pretty thing?" said the second, eying me like a buffet.

"Get away from me!" I shrieked and kicked at them with both legs, but Bailen managed to pull me down to the ground. I collapsed to my knees.

"Careful, boys. She's feisty." Bailen laughed sarcastically. "A priority one fugitive."

The first agent laughed as well. "Oh, we can handle her."

"Yeah, no problem. We'll have some fun with this one," said the second.

"Sorry, but I'm under strict orders from Scurry to personally escort her. You understand?" Bailen said, his voice wavering ever-so-slightly. I'd never heard him sound unsure.

The two agents' faces drew tight in disbelief.

"Who authorized this? No uniformed authority has that kind of clearance," said one agent.

"And with an expired landing code?" asked the second agent. "You're going to have to visit personnel and get everything sorted out. Leave the girl with me."

"Well, this is way above your pay grade," Bailen said.

The second agent eyed me, then Bailen, as if trying to peer through his blackened visor. "I'm going to have to call it in."

My heart jumped into my throat.

"That won't be necessary…"

The first agent stared directly at Bailen's visor, as if he could see right through his helmet. "No, I insist."

Thirty-Five

ailen jumped over me and knocked the bands from my wrists. They hit the ground with a *clang*. He launched himself at the agent on the left.

The one on the right charged me. I kicked and my foot slammed into the agent's kneecap. His leg buckled, and he crumpled to the ground, screaming in pain. Bailen pulled a knife from his belt and slit the first agent's throat then turned and did the same to the second.

I turned from the sight, breathing heavily. My stomach churned as bile crawled up my throat.

A hand squeezed my shoulder. "You okay?"

I shook my head, still trying to catch my breath.

He reached for me, but I stepped away.

"I didn't have a choice. You understand?"

I heard his words, but they weren't making sense, like he was speaking gibberish. I'd known that other part of him had existed, but I'd never wanted to see it, to acknowledge it. Now that it was right in front of me, I didn't have a choice.

"They already alerted the others. We have to go," he said.

Despite his words, I couldn't move. He picked up the cuffs and held them out. "Sorry, but I have to put these back on."

Without saying a word, I thrust out my shaking hands. He fastened them on loosely and grabbed my arm, leading me toward the roof access door.

"Nice kick, by the way." His voice dripped with concern.

"Thanks," was the only word I could manage.

Bailen raced to the stairwell door, which clicked as he reached for the handle. The chip inside his helmet must have had access to the building. I hung close to Bailen as we crept down numerous flights of stairs. If it weren't for the large, black numbers marking the floor levels, I would have lost count a long time ago. When we hit the thirty-third floor, Bailen stopped.

"What do you mean you can't get in?" he whispered. After a slight pause, he said, "Do what you can and hurry! We need you guys."

He pulled me down the next thirteen flights of stairs so quickly, I tripped and would have toppled down the stairs if Bailen hadn't caught me.

"What's going on?" I asked after catching my breath.

"Peyton and the others have restricted access chips. I can't do anything to help them from here. They're going to have to sneak in, which means we need to hurry in case we have to help them."

"Great, more complications."

"You have no idea." He pushed open the door to the twentieth floor and peered into the hallway. I peeked over his shoulder. A single light from the security camera at the end of the hall illuminated the shadows dancing across the walls of the otherwise silent floor. We stepped into the hall, then ducked into a utility closet one room over. An authority guard rounded the corner as I closed the door with a soft click.

"Now what?"

Bailen pulled off his helmet. "This is the fun part." A slight hesitation betrayed the amount of fun it would actually be. "You won't be needing these anymore." He pulled the cuffs off and tossed them aside. He pointed to a small grate in the ceiling.

"You and your sister have a thing for tight spaces. I'm glad I'm not claustrophobic."

"The tight space will be the least of your worries when you see what we have to do."

"Care to clue me in?"

"Yeah, as soon as you get that grate off." He held out his cupped hands.

I stepped into them, and he hoisted me up. I pried the grate free. It came loose a lot easier than the one from my rescue.

"Push me up," I called down to Bailen, but he lowered me instead. He removed several items from his belt and shoved them into his jacket pockets. Other items he tossed aside. His gear hugged him a lot tighter now. "What are you doing?"

"That duct is laser tracked, in a rotating sequence." He pulled a slip of paper from his jacket and unfolded it. "Memorize that pattern. We'll have to time our movements to match it."

I gulped. Things were getting worse by the minute. I wished I'd known what I was walking into. "What happens if one of us trips one of those lasers?"

"You don't want to know." His face pulled tight as if he were trying to hide his fear.

"I know, but I'm asking anyway." Even though I was pretty

sure the answer involved some kind of unpleasant death or maiming.

"Those lasers trigger a silent ten-second countdown that explodes the entire duct."

I trembled. It was an impossible mission. Finding my voice, I said, "Okay, avoid the lasers. Got it." I swallowed hard. I could do it. Just take it nice and slow. "How long between laser settings on the pattern?"

"Five seconds."

"You can't be serious!"

"I know you can do it," he said, but his voice shook, betraying him.

It was insane—no, worse than insane; it was suicide. I reviewed the sequence again, making sure I committed it to memory. If I forgot one thing in the ten-step sequence... *Kaboom.*

"You want to go first, or should I?" Bailen asked.

"I'll go first," I said without hesitation. The faster I entered that duct, the faster I exited.

Bailen hoisted me up. I grabbed the edges and noticed the sequencing lasers dancing through the duct. Every five seconds, the laser pattern blinked out briefly. When the lines flicked back on, they had shifted down to the next section of the duct. A new pattern appeared in front of me with each shift. My stomach knotted. One wrong move and we would be splattered all over the place like a piece of abstract art.

"I'll count you through it," he called up to me.

I nodded, even though he couldn't see my head, and dragged myself inside.

"What pattern is it on?" he asked from below.

"Five... now six." As soon as I finished, he quietly counted out the seconds.

"When it gets to one, I want you to move through the sequence. Every five seconds, move forward with the blank space."

"Okay," was all I could manage to choke out. The sequence was back around at four. I counted the seconds between shifts. Sure enough, every five seconds.

When the tenth sequence appeared, Bailen counted to four then said, "Go."

I froze. Sweat beaded on my forehead and dripped down the bridge of my nose. I wiped it away with a shaky hand, then watched the dancing lasers. The sequence had passed by the first pattern. I'd missed my window.

"Kaya, you can't hesitate. Once you go, you have to keep moving. Got it?"

"Yeah, I just..." But I couldn't finish the sentence. It didn't matter if I could or couldn't do it, I *had* to.

The sequence cycled through a couple more times. At pattern eight, I closed my eyes, took a deep breath, and opened them again. Pattern nine flashed out of existence briefly then made way for pattern ten. I counted to five then pulled myself forward into the pocket between the laser patterns. I counted to five again. When the lasers blinked, I moved. I continued at that pace, only focused on counting and moving.

"You're doing great. You're almost there." Bailen's voice nearly distracted me from my next move.

When did he get in here? But it didn't matter. *Move, Kaya,* I told myself then continued counting. *Move.* A five-count. *Move.* Another five-count. *Move.* I kept pushing forward until I saw the grate ahead. That must have been it, but I didn't dare stop to ask. As I moved closer to the grate, I watched the lasers dance over it.

"Bailen," I called, using his name as the first number in my five count.

"Yeah?"

"That grate"—*three, four, five, move!*—"must be open in five"—*MOVE!*—"seconds?" *Two, three, four, five, move!*

"Yep, you got this."

Two more moves and I was on the grate. *One, two, three, four, five. MOVE! One, two, three, four, five.* At the grate, I shoved the heel of my hand into it, but it didn't budge. I did it a second and third time and then the lasers were on me. Blood froze in my veins. My head throbbed. Time stopped.

"Bailen, *the alarm.*"

I kicked the grate with all my strength, and it gave way. I hit the ground so hard, all the air rushed from my lungs. Pain shot through my midsection. I gasped and whipped around to face the empty hole in the ceiling. *Please make it. Please.*

I had no idea how many seconds had passed. It felt like an eternity.

A long rumble tore through the metal ventilation. But still no Bailen. A brief silence persisted before a deafening roar.

"Bailen!"

A cloud of smoke billowed from the vent.

Thirty-Six

A dark body fell from the opening, followed by chunks of drywall, metal, and flames. He landed on the floor next to me. A second, louder explosion boomed. I rolled on top of Bailen as more debris flew around us. Not again. In my mind, I was back in that stockroom with Jake.

When my ears stopped ringing, I shoved Bailen aside and inspected him. His left pant leg was on fire. I rolled him over and used the bottom of my shirt to smother the flames.

He wasn't moving.

Please be okay. Please, please, please. Oh gosh, what have I done? Finally, he let out a soft groan, and his eyes fluttered. His curious expression said he'd be okay, but the scratches on his cheek, neck, and arms stood out more. Every injury. Every mark.

"Are you okay?" he choked out.

"Shouldn't I be asking you that?"

"I'm fine. Just some cuts, scrapes, and minor burns. Nothing serious."

"Are you sure?" I searched him up and down for additional wounds. Spun him around and checked his back, too. I ran my hands over his stomach. I couldn't lose him, not the same way I lost Jake. Thankfully, Bailen didn't flinch.

"Yeah," he said, grabbing my hands and kissing them. "We have to go. I'm sure they will be on us any minute."

I inspected him up and down again to make sure he really was okay. He grabbed my cheeks and forced me to lock eyes with him. "I'm fine. I promise."

Those words said far more than their meaning on the surface. It was his quiet way of reassuring me it wasn't going to end like last time. A quick peck on the lips told me he meant it.

Standing up, Bailen offered me a hand and pulled me from the floor. I winced as a pain shot through my side.

"What is it?" He stepped toward me with his brow furrowed.

"I'm fine." I shooed him forward. When he turned away, I slid my hand under my T-shirt and winced as my fingers grazed a sore spot. My hand returned streaked with red. I shoved my hand into my pocket in an effort to wipe the blood off. I couldn't let Bailen see. If he knew I was hurt, he'd never let me help him.

I stumbled behind him before I found my footing. We rounded a corner and stopped in front of solid wood door adorned by a gold plaque with the initials *R. S.* etched into it. I ran my fingers over the letters. A shudder ran down my spine as the door clicked open. Bailen's devilish grin returned. Once a tech nerd, always a tech nerd. I shook my head and stepped inside.

Rufus Scurry's private office.

A single lamp lit a giant L-shaped desk that filled only a small portion of the enormous room. Large glass cases packed with awards and trophies lined two of the walls. A third wall contained images of Rufus Scurry at various ceremonies and exotic places. The final wall was a giant window that ran the entire length of the room.

The city outside seemed so quiet. Not a single car or unicopter. I leaned against it, expecting to feel cool glass against my skin, but it wasn't glass at all, merely some kind of elaborate projection that made the view seem like a glass window. Of course Scurry's office didn't peer onto the real city. Just like the tracker, only see what one has chosen to see.

The sheer beauty of the office and its fake view wasn't fooling anyone. If only the sun could leak through those photos and brighten our haunted souls.

"This way. We don't have much time."

Bailen pulled me over to one of the glass cases. He stopped to remove a flat, metallic device from one of his vest pockets then affixed it to the case. After stringing wires to the device, he hooked them to a small box. Green numbers flashed across the screen until each one locked into place. 82021920.

The case hissed before it slid forward and swung open. A dark hallway extended out in front of us.

"Okay, now that's pretty cool. But how did you know this was here?"

"We had an inside man, remember?"

"My dad?"

"Yep."

How long had it taken him to amass that much information? The schematics, the intimate knowledge of Scurry's office, the loophole in my tracker? And all the while evading the authorities and Scurry himself.

Bailen laced his fingers through mine and led me through the opening. The case closed behind us with a quiet click.

A soft hum surrounded us as we entered a dimly lit room filled with rows of floor-to-ceiling machines. The blinking red and green lights formed a signal warning us away.

"Welcome to the brain of Tracker220," Bailen said.

"If this is the brain, where are Peyton and Jeremy headed to?"

"The heart and the lungs."

"So, we're going to take away its breath, give it a heart attack, and a stroke all at once?"

"Exactly. And you're the stroke. But we need to move. That explosion alerted Scurry's private guard. They'll be here soon." Bailen moved to the nearest panel.

We were inches from taking down Tracker220, and yet we had such a long way to go. The functionality of every chip in the world came down to these machines. The whole world had to be taken offline simultaneously in order for it to work.

The machine's blinking lights and the vibrating floor sent me into a hypnotic state. A part of me felt like I was about to invade the privacy of every person on the planet. I was about to destroy the very nature of society that everyone was accustomed to. It would free everyone. But it could also create chaos.

By taking away the trackers, were we removing peoples' right to choose technology? I was sure that was how the public would see it, but they didn't have the full story. I couldn't let Rufus Scurry turn the world into mind-controlled minions.

Bailen pried open one of the cases on the machines illuminating the room. He leaned the metal cover against the wall and scanned the inside contents. "Nope, not this one." He slid down the aisle to the next case and repeated his search then shook his head.

I could only watch him as he worked, useless to do anything else. I stepped to one of the panels connected to the giant casings and tapped it. It came to life with a photo of an unknown woman. After a handful of seconds, the image changed to another photo. Then another. And another. Beneath each, the word TRACKERU followed by a dash and a number displayed. I didn't recognize any of the people as they flashed by, but I kept watching.

After a dozen faces, I pivoted from the monitor, but the newest face that flashed onto the screen caught my attention. Even though the image was grayed out with the word TERMINATED across it, I knew that smile and those eyes. It was Jake. Underneath his image, the sequence, TRACKERU-70285, showed like a product number. What did it mean?

In an attempt to pause the flashing images, I tapped the screen. But the next image appeared in place of Jake's face. I searched the edges of the monitor, waved over it, and tapped various places on the screen, but nothing stopped the scrolling images. It didn't matter, though. I knew what I'd seen. If Jake and those others were on that screen in the brains of the tracker network, Scurry surely had plans for them. I shuddered then resigned myself to the fact that Jake would never come back on the screen. I turned to Bailen and the more important task at hand.

"Anything I can do to help?"

"Yeah, check those casings." He pointed to the row of machines on the opposite side of the aisle. "We're looking for a box containing a satellite server."

"What's that?"

"A component about the size of a shoe box. It'll probably be blue but might be gray with hundreds of blinking lights on it."

I pulled the panel from the first casing and it came loose easily. I scanned inside and found a series of blinking lights but nothing resembling the satellite server. At the next box, I did the same check. Nothing. Another. Still nothing. After searching a dozen or so, I noted the long row of computer casings.

"We could be at this a while," I said.

"I know. Just keep going. We don't ..."

I sensed he was about to say we were out of time. Instead, he turned to me with wide eyes and an expression of sheer horror. "They have Peyton and Jeremy. They're on their way up here. That was the last thing I heard before her communication cut out."

My blood pulsed ice cold. *This is it.* Either we stopped the tracker network here and now, or we were dead. The world would never be free again. I wanted to run to Bailen and hug him until the end, but we still had a job to do. I whirled around and winced as a stabbing pain shot through my side. Hoping Bailen hadn't noticed, I moved to the next casing and searched for the server box. Nothing.

I pulled off the front panels with renewed vigor until I reached one that wouldn't budge. I took several deep breaths, ignored the raging pain in my ribs, and yelled as I tore the panel from the front of the metal box. Inside, I found a blue rectangular box with rows of blinking lights. A shiver crawled up my spine.

"Bailen," I choked out in a hoarse whisper. No answer. "Bailen!" I nearly yelled it.

"What?"

"I think I found it."

317

"That's it." Bailen pulled the series five thousand chip from his vest pocket.

"That thing has certainly proved useful," I said.

"You have no idea. I've rigged it to match the signal on your tracker. With your help, and the relays the others set up, we'll create a virus in the network that will destroy the link between the tracker chips and the satellite signals connecting everything together."

"When did you have time to do all that?"

"I had to keep busy while you were doing all that drawing. Once the schematic started coming together, it became clear the signal on your tracker was linked to it. So I rigged this up, figuring it would be useful. When I saw the final drawings, I was glad I had. The low-level frequency from your tracker is like a password for the server box. It'll give us access to the network."

All the tech talk made my head swim. "Let's finish this."

He reached into the casing and pushed aside a wire bundle, clearing a path to the server box. "Can you help me with this?"

Behind us, the unmistakable sound of a charging authority weapon buzzed.

Thirty-Seven

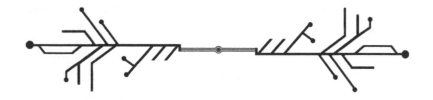

"**S**top what you're doing. Slowly raise your hands and turn around," said a deep voice.

A pit formed in my stomach. Bailen dipped his head ever-so-slightly, telling me to follow instructions. I lifted my arms, and Bailen did the same. Together, we turned to face whoever had bested us.

A set of familiar dark brown eyes starred back. Rufus Scurry, in full authority gear, pointed a standard-issue authority gun at us. His tousled, graying brown hair made it seem like he'd just fallen out of bed. But the bags under his eyes and tired evil grin said he'd been waiting for us for a very long time. Scurry had outmaneuvered us again and was quite proud of himself.

"Hand me the chip," he said, holding out his hand. "Easy now. No sudden movements."

Bailen lowered his hand and inched toward Scurry. He dropped the chip into Scurry's gloved hand then stepped next to me. As the chip fell into the enemy's hand, my hope plummeted off a cliff. The end wasn't here yet, but it was fast approaching with increasing velocity.

Scurry slipped the chip into his vest's top pocket without taking his gun off us. "You two think you're really clever, don't you?"

Neither of us spoke. I stared over his shoulder to avoid direct eye contact.

"Let's go," Scurry spat.

As he finished his sentence, a shadow darted behind a row of machines a couple aisles behind Scurry. Out of the corner of my eye, I checked to see if Bailen had noticed it too. If he had, his expression gave nothing away. Over Scurry's shoulder, I hoped to catch another glimpse of the mysterious shadow but saw nothing. Maybe I was hallucinating.

"I said *move*." Scurry stepped sideways and motioned his gun in the direction of the door.

Bailen nodded to me, indicating I should go first. I crept toward the door, but Scurry shoved his gun into my injured side, and I winced. Before I could fight back, Bailen stepped between me and Scurry.

I thought about running, but it wouldn't do any good. Either Bailen or I would end up shot. Or worse, both of us.

With each step, my side burned more and more. Maybe if I feigned collapsing, we'd have the element of surprise. It was only Scurry. How much combat training could he have? We could take him.

A horrific pain shot through my ribs. I cried out. Maybe I wouldn't have to fake it. If it continued, I really would collapse.

I swayed and Bailen caught me around the waist. I wailed as his touch stabbed into my side.

"No! Put her down," said Scurry. "I won't tolerate any tricks."

Bailen lowered me to the ground. My head lay in his lap. He pulled his hands from my sides, and his glove returned wet with my blood. He inhaled sharply as he no doubt realized how hurt I really was.

"Step away from her."

"But she's injured." Bailen held out his gloved hand so Scurry could see the blood.

"I don't care. Move away."

Bailen shook his head. "You're going to have to kill me."

I zeroed in on Bailen, catching his gaze. Nothing else mattered in that moment but him. But out of the corner of my eye, I saw a shadow dart by again. And now I was certain I was seeing full-blown hallucinations.

The end was here.

"Last chance before I shoot you both."

"You're going to kill us anyway, so what difference does it make if it's now or later?" Bailen spat.

"No, I'll shoot her instead." Scurry blinked and angled his head at the row of casings to his left. A girl with brown hair in her face crept into the aisle next to Scurry. Behind her, Harlow pointed an authority weapon at her head. Even though we fought the last time we saw each other there was no way he was helping Scurry. I inspected Harlow with a mixture of shock and horror. His complexion was paler than usual, and his hair looked like it hadn't been washed in a week. An emotionless expression masked what he was thinking which normally would have been so easy to read.

"What are you doing, Harlow?" But his lifeless eyes stared

back at me. His body was frozen, not responding to my words. "Harlow, stop it!" But he didn't even blink. It was no use. He was a zombie.

"Kaya?" The girl lifted her head, and her stringy hair fell out of her face. Her puffy red eyes pleaded with me.

A sinking sensation filled my core. "Emily." I reached out for her.

She launched for me, but Scurry blinked twice in quick succession. Harlow snapped to action, grabbing her by the arm and yanking her back before she took another step.

"Let her go, or you'll pay for every ounce of pain you've caused," I said through gritted teeth.

"*Tsk tsk*, Kaya. I thought you of all people would recognize the severity of your situation." Scurry's evil expression indicated he knew he'd won.

"You've taken everything from me! I have nothing left to lose."

"Your brother was an unfortunate casualty, but there will be others like him. Many more."

"Don't you dare talk about my brother!"

"Fine, then let's talk about the other men in your life. Starting with this one." He pointed his weapon at Bailen. I refused to flinch. I wouldn't give Scurry the satisfaction.

Bailen pulled me up to give me a painful hug. I didn't care that it hurt to have additional pressure on my wound. If I was going to die, at least I'd go out fighting until the very end.

A high-pitched whine emanated from Scurry's weapon as a shadow loomed behind him. Scurry's finger closed on the trigger.

With a horrific cracking sound, Scurry crumpled to the floor. An instant later, Harlow collapsed next to him. Emily nudged

Harlow with his shoe to confirm he was out then ran to me and threw her arms around my back, sandwiching me between her and Bailen. A low groan escaped from between my lips.

"I've been waiting a long time to do that," said a familiar voice.

"Dad?" I coughed out. The shadowy figure staggered from the darkness into the fluorescent glow of the lights. His normally clean-cut hair was overgrown and tousled. His clothes resembled shredded rags around his pale thin frame, but he appeared otherwise unharmed.

"What?" Bailen asked me.

"Bailen, it's my dad." I tapped his shoulder. Bailen's iron grasp released me, and Emily's hands slipped away as I fell to the floor and winced. A sharp pain shot through my midsection.

"Mr. Weiss? What are you doing here?"

I pushed into a sitting position. Dad searched Scurry and pulled the chip from his top vest pocket. He tossed it to Bailen. "No time for questions. Just do whatever you came here to do."

Bailen caught the chip and moved to the panel with the satellite server. He shoved the chip inside the casing and activated the screen attached.

I pushed to my feet and stumbled into Dad's arms. "I love you," he said into my ear. "Now help him." He winked then spun me around to face Bailen and the computer casing.

I wobbled forward but stopped in front of Emily. I hugged her and said, "Stay with my dad."

"Sure," she said, backing away from the computer casing.

I inched next to Bailen, my chest heaving. He pulled a series of wires and discs from his vest. After everything I'd been through, I knew exactly what to do with them. I pulled the backs from the discs and stuck them to my temples and the base of my neck while Bailen ran the wires directly through the chip.

Once they were connected, he said, "Do your thing."

I didn't have to ask him what he meant. I just knew. It was a primal instinct inside me, a quiet voice telling me exactly how to end it. Almost as if the satellite, the server, and the entire population whispered into my ear simultaneously, telling me to disconnect them. The signals hummed inside my head, and yet it was far from overwhelming. Because a single voice cried out to me. A piece that felt new and familiar at the same time. Something in the code that that was meant just for me. A message that urged me to follow it.

So I did.

I closed my eyes and began overloading the signals along the path like I'd done in the past. I didn't need to come up with the motivation. It enveloped me. Every pain, every loss, every horrible thing sat front and center as ammo in the final assault. Once I loaded it all in my mind, I released it like a barrage of weapons fire on the network.

The satellites screeched in my mind with a high-pitched whine. I shoved back, trying to push a mountain of thoughts and feelings through a garden hose. My head ached as the network of satellites jammed the information back into my mind. I put up a wall in my mind. Each data packet slammed against it pounding in my brain like sledgehammer. Resisting, I propelled everything back down the frail connection, flooding the link between my tracker and the network. The pathway swelled like a water balloon and overflowed into the billions of connections on the network. The satellites screamed with an almost human-like pain before blinking into silence.

My mind emptied like a slashed tire. The Ghost program went dead. My normal tracker functions disappeared with it. Everything was completely silent. When I opened my eyes, nothing clouded my vision.

Just the world in front of me.

Alone.

Uncluttered.

I finally understood.

Silence.

Inside the giant casing, the satellite server lights had gone dark.

"You did it, Kaya!" Bailen pulled me into a hug.

"Are you sure?" I coughed. My side burned under the pressure.

"Yes! My tracker fell silent. It's not sending or receiving signals anymore. You really did it!"

I peered over my shoulder at Dad. He didn't have to say anything for me to know it really was over.

At Dad's feet, Harlow groaned, sat up, and rubbed his head. "What a nightmare." His gaze darted around the room before he mumbled a quiet, "Or maybe not."

Dad put his hand on Harlow's shoulder. "Easy there, bud, you've been through quite an ordeal."

"You're telling me," Harlow said. He searched the room for understanding but stopped on me. His body quaked as his head lowered, almost too heavy for him to hold up.

Dad crouched in front of Harlow and checked him over.

"How did I get here?" Harlow asked. "My head is pounding."

"What do you remember?" my dad asked.

"I was headed home and then, I woke up here."

"I can't believe Rufus went through with it."

"Went through with what, Dad?" I asked.

"The mind control. He said if he could control them, he could protect them. He took things too far," Dad said.

"I thought it wasn't possible until the upgrade. Didn't we stop it?" I asked.

"Pilot program. But it's all over now." Dad helped Harlow to his feet. "Take it easy. Things will be fuzzy for a while."

Harlow grabbed the sides of his head and leaned against a server for support.

I rested my chin on Bailen's shoulder, too tired to move, and stared into the server casing in search of answers to questions I couldn't find the words to say.

Darkness.

I'd never thought a dark computer casing could be so freeing and confusing all at once.

A signal light flashed on inside the box. I blinked and focused on the spot the light emanated from, hoping I was just seeing things from staring into blackness too long. I pushed onto my tiptoes to see over Bailen's shoulder better, but the box remained dark. My legs shook beneath me, but I didn't care. I'd never felt so free. My head so quiet, so calm. No network, just me and my thoughts.

As my knees buckled, Bailen scooped me into his arms and carried me toward the door.

"What's wrong?" Dad asked.

"I think I got nicked by a piece of debris. I'll be f—" A fierce pain shot up my side and stabbed continuously. I screamed out and tears streaked down my face.

"Oh, Kai." Before I could protest, Dad peeled up my shirt

and checked my wound. "We've got to get you out of here now, and no protesting."

"What about him?" Harlow asked, indicating the crumple heap on the floor that was once a conscious Rufus Scurry.

"You mind dragging his sorry ass out of here?" Dad asked.

"With pleasure." Harlow grabbed Scurry under the arms and pulled him toward the door.

"I've got one thing left to do. You got her?" Dad asked Bailen.

"Sure." He put me down but let me lean on him as we left the server room.

Dad darted into the hall. Bailen reached out and took Emily's hand, guiding her toward Scurry's office.

When we reached the hallway, I rested my head on his shoulder and gave into the exhaustion seeping into my body.

Thirty-Eight

After the tracker network crashed, I spent days in bed with no shortage of visitors. Mom and Dad, Bailen, Lydia, and even Peyton came from time to time. They all had to make sure I was on the mend.

Once we got off the twentieth floor, it hadn't been too hard to slip past the authorities at Global Tracking Systems. They were too busy scrambling to figure out what had happened to the tracker network to notice our group. It hadn't taken Peyton and Jeremy long to figure out the authorities were preoccupied. They slipped their binders with a piece of code Jeremy embedded into the stolen tracker chips and blended into the chaos.

The Ghosts had started to rebuild the Hive almost immediately. It wasn't finished yet, but it was coming along. With Scurry in a secret prison and his plans revealed to the world, we didn't need to hide anymore. But the Ghosts made sure that Scurry would never be found. Everyone thought it too risky to leave his punishment to whatever new system popped up so they leaked to the news that he'd gone missing after the technology malfunctioned. The news ran with it crafting all kinds of stories of sabotage and not wanting to answer for his mistakes.

I flipped on the radio on the table next to me. With the satellites down, the world scrambled to find some form of communication to stay connected. The reports sounded much like the past week. Looting. Crime. Thousands of missing people. Mass hysteria. It was like people forgot how to function without a tracker. Maybe taking down the tracker network hadn't been the right decision. I didn't know anymore.

A knock at the door drew me away from the radio. I turned it off.

"Come in."

The door swung slowly and Harlow's head peeked around it. I blinked. It was the first time I'd seen him since Scurry's office. His torn jeans were in better shape than the dark circles under his eyes.

"Visiting hours haven't started yet." It sounded stupid. I didn't have visiting hours, but I didn't know what else to say. It was the most I'd said to him since he'd chased me down on the bike.

He shut the door behind him and stepped up to the bed. "I think we should talk."

"About what?" I knew exactly what, but the words failed me.

Harlow sat in the chair next to my bed but said nothing. He stared at the floor like he'd lost the state championship five times in a row.

I waited for him to speak, but after the silence persisted for a long while, I asked, "Are you okay?"

"Those things Scurry made me do." He shook his head, like

he was trying to get things straight in his mind. "I keep replaying it in my head. At least the bits I can remember. Some of it feels so foggy and blank. Other parts I saw as it was happening, but no matter how hard I fought, I couldn't control myself. He made me into a robotic monster, forced me to do all these horrific things. Things I can't even make sense of."

It wasn't what I'd expected when I'd asked the question. "It's not your fault." I reached for his hand but pulled back. I didn't know where our line was anymore, but for the first time, I confirmed I'd made the right decision about the tracker network. Harlow's expression told me everything I needed.

"He was going to make me kill that girl." He lifted his head and finally looked me in the face. "And after that girl, he would have made me kill you, too. I never could have forgiven myself."

"It's not your fault," I repeated. I didn't know what else to say. "Bailen told me—"

"Yeah, that guy. You ditched me for him?"

There was the conversation I'd been expecting but was still so unprepared for. "It just kind of happened. I tried to wait..." I shook my head. "Everything was a mess. I just..." I didn't know how to explain it.

"You didn't give me a chance."

I nodded. I'd run from everything I'd known before anyone could do anything. But as much as I knew he meant well, he couldn't have helped me. "You didn't exactly wait around, either."

"Would you believe me if I blamed it on Scurry and the tracker hack?"

"Not a chance."

"Didn't think so." He frowned, like he was disappointed his

weak lie hadn't worked.

"You and I…" I paused to collect my thoughts. "We're headed in different directions. We want different things."

He let the silence hang in the air like dead weight.

"I'm not sure we were ever on the same path," I said.

"That's harsh."

"But you know it's true."

"I guess you're right."

My choices had hurt him. But I hadn't known the right path for me until I'd found myself already on it. And despite all the mistakes, most things felt right, even if the world was a messy place.

Without another word, Harlow rose from the chair, went out through the door, and was gone without saying goodbye.

A small hole formed inside me. I didn't know if I would see him again, and that was a strange feeling. But it was for the best. And with time, I'd stop thinking about him, worrying about what he might think. But I'd never forget him.

Less than a minute later, Lydia glided past the open door in a cute top and jeans and plopped onto the foot of my bed, her long ponytail bouncing. "What'd Harlow want?"

"He just wanted to talk."

"Oh?" Her eyebrow arched.

"Not like that. We're…" I sighed. "It's complicated."

"I see," she said, instinctively knowing I didn't want to talk about it.

"What about Troy?"

"I ditched him when he started making nasty comments about you being too chicken to deal with consequences. I knew if you ran off, it was for a good reason. But don't ever scare me like that again by not answering me! Let me know what's going on."

"I tried, but there aren't exactly any carrier pigeons around here." The memory of the same conversation with Jake warmed my heart.

"So when can I spring you from this dreadful place?"

"Thursday, I think."

"Perfect!"

I eyed her with caution. She had that devious glean. The one she got when she wanted to drag me somewhere with some sort of ulterior motive. The kind that almost never ended well. The last that time she'd done, I'd ended up in my current mess. Although it wasn't really her fault. It just seemed like the radio wave generator and my tracker malfunction had been linked at the time.

"Oh no you don't. Doc told me to take it easy," I said.

"But there's a Ghost celebration at the club. You have to come."

I shook my head. "Even if the doc said *yes*, I doubt my parents would let me."

"Would let you do what?" Dad asked, standing next to the partially cracked door. His appearance had returned to his usual—clean-shaven and dad-like.

Lydia whipped around and tried her puppy-dog face on him. "Mr. Weiss, you have to let Kaya come to the Ghost party. They're going to honor all the big players in the tracker takedown, and seeing as Kaya was the—"

Dad held up his hand, silencing Lydia.

"Lydia." He shook his head as she continued the pleading expressions with a slight sniff every few seconds for added affect. His serious appearance faded into one of complete helplessness.

"You girls will be the death of me," he said. "Fine. Kaya can make an appearance. But only for an hour."

Before I could protest, Lydia squealed and launched herself at Dad. "Thanks, Mr. Weiss. You won't regret it."

"Oh, I'm sure I will. Especially when her mother finds out. But if I could have a word with Kaya…"

"Sure thing." Lydia wiggled her eyebrows at me then scurried from the room, giggling to herself.

"Thanks, Dad," I said sarcastically.

"You're welcome."

"I was being…" I blew out a breath in exhaustion. "Never mind. You still have some serious explaining to do. Big time!"

Dad sank into the chair next to my bed. He'd been avoiding the conversation until I was well enough. At least he'd been nice enough to confirm that Peyton had sent a side mission to rescue my parents, Myles, and some of the other captured Ghosts while everyone else was gearing up for the final mission. But that story only held me over for a short time. I was sure Dad knew I wasn't going to let it slide forever. But where did I even start?

Before I could think of the right question, he said, "It took me sixteen years to steal secrets and funnel them onto your chip. If I accessed too much data at once or searched it too close together, they would have been on to me. I had to work tasks that allowed me to access each piece of the puzzle.

"With each upgrade to the tracker network, I loaded small packets of data onto your tracker through the loophole I implanted on your chip as a baby. There was no other way to sneak things out of Global Tracking Systems without getting caught. Any large downloads would have alerted the authorities."

"And in sixteen years, you couldn't have told me once?"

"I'm sorry I never told you. You have to know if I had, it could have risked everything and put you in grave danger. The authorities watched everything. They even listened in on conversations." He sighed as if collecting his thoughts. "I regret the position I had to put you in but there was no other way. Your mother begged me not to get involved, not to put anyone in the family at risk. But we all already were at risk. And once she saw what was happening with the technology and the dangerous decisions being made, she reluctantly agreed."

He was right, of course, but it didn't make it any easier.

"I know I have a lot to answer for. When your tracker malfunctioned ahead of schedule, I panicked. The code that had been implanted on it was a rush job. There must have been some errors. When the authorities showed up the night your tracker went offline, it was clear I had to act. Even though I still had information to steal, I got word to Jake so the Ghosts could pull you out. Hardly any of them knew I was the mole inside Global Tracking Systems. No one could know I was involved. Least of all you. If the authorities ever caught you, the whole plan would have come crashing down. I'm sure I'll spend the rest of my life apologizing for what I put you through. And I'm sorry. You should have never had to carry that burden alone."

"It's okay." If losing Jake had taught me anything, you couldn't waste time hating people for making mistakes when they had good intentions in mind. Even though Jake had lied to me about Dad knowing where he was. I'd never know why for sure, but it seemed like he had been trying to protect everyone's secrets. While I had the faulty tracker, he was carrying more burdens then I would ever know.

"I did the best I could to prepare you without drawing

attention from the authorities. I hope you understand why I was so hard on you growing up. I wanted you to understand the life you should have always had. The traditions I grew up with."

It wasn't so much that he was hard on me; he was just my dad. "I get it. You were trying to protect me."

"I was trying to train you." His lips pulled upward. "Looks like I did a pretty good job."

"It wasn't easy, but I felt like you were with me every step of the way."

He rose from the chair and wrapped me in a bear hug. "You did well, Kai. I always knew you could. And I knew Jake would be there to help you."

Tears welled. He hadn't been there for long. I'd had to do it alone. Well, not completely alone, but with people who were strangers when it had all started. Now the Ghosts were so much more. They were family.

I couldn't say any of that to him, though. He'd put Jake and me in danger and knew the risks. It couldn't have been easy for him to hear he'd lost his son as a result of the great sacrifice he'd asked of him. Just as it hadn't been easy for me to witness it.

I studied him, searching for some sign of emotion, but his face remained blank. Maybe he was numb to it. It probably hadn't fully processed yet. It had only been a couple days since he'd found out. I'd been dealing with it for much longer.

"Dad, can I ask you something?"

"Sure, anything."

I swallowed and shoved the image of Jake's face with the number out of my head—right next to the words Harlow had used about foggy memories. "Did you ever send Jake to work for Scurry or the authorities? Maybe undercover?"

He furrowed his eyebrows, but he stayed quiet for some time like he was running scenarios through his head. Finally, he said, "No. Why do you ask?"

I was afraid of that response. With that single word, Dad confirmed everything I'd feared. If Dad hadn't sent him to the authorities, no one else would have either. Which meant his picture on the screen at Global Tracker Systems was no coincidence. His scattered journal notes suddenly made sense. The authorities had gotten to Jake. Somehow.

It explained how Scurry had known about Jake's death. They'd been watching him. Using him. Watching through him.

And if Jake would have been able to say something about it, he would have. Which could only mean one thing, like Harlow, Scurry had found a way to control Jake. And if Scurry had been controlling Jake, he must have been the one who'd given up the information, the mole Myles had been searching for. But how could Jake live with himself knowing what information he'd given up?

I remembered Harlow's face when he'd told me he had witnessed it all but had had no control. How awful that must have been for Jake. Or maybe as time had gone on, he hadn't known he'd done it. Maybe Scurry had made him forget. It explained the final note in his journal. I'd never know for sure what horrors he saw and did. But one thing was certain. I could blame Scurry for Jake's death. And I'd find a way to make him pay.

Icy fingers of dread wrapped around me. And what about the others like Jake? What horrible things had they been forced to do? How many others had Scurry engaged in that pilot program? I shook it off. We'd deactivated the tracker chips, and no one would ever be forced to do things against their will again. That hack was no longer a threat.

"Kai? Is everything okay?"

"Yeah, fine." I forced a smile to convince Dad to let it go. I couldn't bear to tell him the very thing we opposed, the thing that had taken so much, had turned his son, my brother, into a weapon. Scurry abused his power to nearly end the Ghost movement and in the process caused my brother's death. Dad couldn't know what happened. It was a burden I'd have to carry alone, and it weighed heavily inside me.

"Are you sure?"

Dad's words shook me from my thoughts. "I'm just worried about the memorial." He was, too, but he'd never admit it.

"You ready?"

"No." But I swung my legs over the side of the bed and Dad pushed a wheelchair next to me so I could slide into it. I winced as my stomach muscles clenched, still healing from the injury.

Dad wheeled me through new tunnel leading us outside the new wing they were adding to the Hive. He pushed me a short ways into the woods then parked me next to a tree with a bare patch of dirt stretched underneath it. Plush green grass surrounded the dirt plot. I hadn't known where'd they'd buried Jake until now. But with those he'd fought for nearby, it seemed like a fitting resting place.

Mom stood next to Dad and squeezed my shoulder. I pushed up from the chair, refusing to let the pain get to me. I was standing. Nothing, not even my injury, would stop me. I'd only let one form of hurt pass through me today: sorrow.

Dad started the Mourner's Kaddish. I could barely whisper the words through my tears. And long after we all fell silent, the words echoed in my head on repeat.

Dad held a small white bag of dirt in front of me. I grabbed it. A little piece of Israel. Dad clutched my arm as I stepped forward and flipped the bag of dirt over the empty space in the grass. Jake was finally free.

We all were.

Mom placed a rock on the edge of the patch of dirt and Dad followed. He wrapped his arm around Mom as she quaked, wracked in sobs. She buried her head in his chest. Dad mouthed "I love you" then escorted Mom away. He knew I needed more time. I wasn't ready to say goodbye, even though I kind of already had.

I attempted to squat next to the patch of dirt but ended up sitting on the ground instead.

"I miss you." It came out more as a cough. After a few ragged breaths, I tried again. The result wasn't any better, but I was sure Jake was there. He'd heard me.

I pulled out a crumpled piece of paper from my pocket. I whispered through the lines of his poem, the one he'd painted on the wall of the high school. Each line grew louder and more confident as I progressed through. Until I finished with one strong ending phrase, "Family defies blood."

"I always loved that poem."

The voice made me jump. Peyton knelt next to me and placed a rock next to the others.

"I heard you're supposed to do that." She indicated her rock then turned away from me and sniffed back her tears.

I wrapped my arm around her and pulled her toward me in an awkward side hug. "May his memory be a blessing," I whispered in her ear.

"It will."

And his memory would. Despite not having my tracker to pull up images of Jake in the blink of an eye, I'd never need them again. Jake's memory was all around me. Present in Mom and Dad, in Peyton, and within me.

His legacy was now mine.

Thirty-Nine

everal days later, I stood on the balcony above the party at Neon Nectar. I smoothed the shiny tank top over the jeans I'd borrowed from Lydia. Miraculously, after everything the Ghosts had been through, the small club remained unharmed.

"Stop fidgeting with your outfit. You look hot." Lydia slid her arm around mine and led me down the steps and across the floor, her dress swooshing with each stride.

I wasn't worried about how hot I looked. I wanted out of whatever situation Lydia was dragging me into. I quickly reminded myself to be a good friend. Not to mention, I owed it to the Ghosts to make an appearance. I'd become an unintentional hero for them.

Across the room, Bailen donned a blue polo and jeans. He smiled then headed toward us. He slung his arm around my shoulder and kissed me on the cheek. "Bailen, this is my best friend, Lydia. Lydia, this is Bailen, my…" I didn't know what to call him.

"Your boyfriend," Lydia said. "And we've met. In fact, we've talked. Quite a bit." Lydia patted Bailen on the arm. "Right, Bay?" She winked at him liked they'd shared an entire universe worth of secrets already.

"Oh, yeah, Lydia and I are great friends. We had lots of time to chat while you were recovering." If he was trying to pay me back for the fast ones I'd pulled on him, his inability to stop grinning ear to ear gave him away immediately.

Regardless, knowing Lydia she'd used her magic to get all the finer details from him. The thought of them already meeting and chatting set my nerves on edge.

Lydia must have picked up on my discomfort because she pulled her arm from mine. "I'll let you two talk." She wiggled her eyebrows and disappeared.

As much as she dragged me into things, I loved Lydia for her ability to take subtle hints. She may have embarrassed me, but never too much. She definitely knew when to drop something and back away.

"Your *boyfriend*, huh? Why wasn't I made aware of this?" Bailen whispered in my ear.

"It's news to me too. Lydia likes to make assumptions."

Bailen lightly slung his arms around my waist and coaxed me closer. "Well, I like Lydia and her assumptions."

"Oh, do you now?"

He nodded with his usual charming grin. "You look"—he sucked in a breath like he was trying to breathe me in all at once—"amazing."

"Thanks." The temperature in my cheeks rose ten degrees.

"Remember the last time I brought you here?"

I did.

He was so close, his warm breath beat on my ear. His words sent shivers through me.

I was back in that moment. The neon drinks that had made my head spin. The music thudding through my body. A stolen moment. Our first kiss. It was a shame thoughts of Harlow had marred it. Regardless, I leaned in. "I think I need a reminder."

He kissed me, lightly at first, then our lips crushed together, sending sparks into my chest. When he finally pulled away, I checked the room to see who was watching. Everyone seemed preoccupied. In one corner, Lydia was already working her charms on Jeremy. I'd have to remember to ask her about that later. Peyton danced with a group of people I didn't recognize. It was good to see her almost smiling. And Mom chatted with Lydia's parents and Myles by the bar. But where was Dad?

I stepped back and turned right into him. My cheeks flushed. How much had he seen? But then I noticed his glazed-over eyes staring into space.

"Dad?" I waved my hand in front of his face, but he appeared frozen. If I didn't know better… I shook my head. He must have been lost in thought. He'd been through a lot. We all had.

"Dad?" I touched him lightly on the arm.

He jumped then focused on me. "Yes, sweetheart?"

"Are you okay?"

"Yeah, I'm fine." He held up the glass of neon liquid. "You guys didn't drink any of this, did you?"

I stifled a laugh and shook my head.

He shot Bailen a look I'd often seen on Jake's face when he'd been trying to decide if he'd wanted to pummel someone or not.

"No, sir," Bailen said, straightening his posture.

"Good. It's vile stuff. It'll mess with your head."

"Trackers will mess with your head too." Bailen turned his back on my dad and stared straight at me with a devious grin. "But I prefer the drink," he said in a hushed tone.

I leaned in and whispered into his ear, "Maybe later."

Acknowledgements

When they say it takes a village to make a book happen they are *not* kidding. It takes a literal army of Jedi Knights to make a book. There were so many people that had a hand in making TRACKER220 come to life. And I'm so thankful for every single one of them.

Shawntelle Madison and Heather Reid, thank you for being my Jedi Masters on my indie publishing journey. I'd be completely lost without you.

Tom Torre, we've been through the good, the bad, and the ugly on this journey and I for sure would not still be here without you. Thank you for reading. Thank you for believing in me. Thank you for talking me off the ledge… more than once.

Mandy Pietruszewski Self, my evil twin, I never expected to meet a fellow rocket scientist who also writes similar stuff to me, but I'm so glad I reached out when I saw your CP match post. It's been an adventure online—and in real life. I'm a better writer and person because I know you! Thank you for being you and for nerding out with me!

Bert Beattie, you believed in me before anyone else. I was looking for an excuse to quit writing and you were right behind me cheering me on from the very beginning. None of this would have been possible without your initial enthusiasm.

Stella Luciano, you haven't read this one, but thank you for reading my other book that might never see the light of day. Your enthusiasm as someone in the target audience (at the time) was infectious. I still think about your excitement often when I'm writing. You inspired me to be a better writer.

Kira Watson, thank you for believing in this book enough to take it on. Thank you for your wise notes and pulling things out of me I never thought possible.

Gwen Hayes, you made this book shine. Thank you for taking my words and teaching me how to make each one count.

Amy McNulty, you gave this book the polish it needed. Thanks for fixing all the verb tenses, grammar, homonyms, misplaced commas, and various other punctuation. You're a lifesaver!

Jennifer Stolzer, thank you again for my GORGEOUS cover. You took my incoherent babbling and turned it into a masterpiece.

Sam Tilson, thank you for the AMAZING book trailer. I always wanted one and you made it happen. You have incredible vision, and I appreciate you letting me steal some of your time for this book.

Meredith Tate, Jennifer Stolzer, Michelle Mason, Debra Spiegel, Paula Stokes, Lydia Kang, Christina Kim Ahn Hickey, and Julie Sharp, you all read various versions of this book and it would not be where it is today without each and every one of you.

To the storycrafters, John Sullivan, Ruth Donnelly, Donna J. Essner & Christy Burkley, you helped nurture my craft early on, cheered for this story, and helped shape it into something magical.

To the CSS, Sarah Johnson, Nicole Lanahan, Shawntelle Madison, Heather Reid, Emily Hall Schroen, Linda Stevens, and Cori Bair. Thanks for the laughs, the tears, the coffee (even though I don't drink it), and more importantly the wine. You're the best sounding board a girl could ever have.

To all of Snowy Wings Publishing. You've been a light in a very dark tunnel. Thank you for all the guidance and support. You lifted a huge weight off my shoulders and made all this possible.

To the whole Middle Grade Minded team (old and new), I

feel like I found my people in you. This may be a YA, but MG still has my heart. You gave me hope that MG is awesome and should have its day.

To the Write Pack/SLWG clan, Jessica Mathews, Jennifer Stolzer, Amy Zlatic, David Lucas, Lauren Miller, Brad Cook, Teresa Fendley, and Cherie Postill. Thank you for the writing foundation, all the write ins, and the hours of sci fi and nerdy talk. And thank you letting me babble endlessly about ideas until I finally worked through all the plot bunnies.

To anyone who ever gave me feedback in a contest or during write on con or whoever liked, retweeted, or shared my pitches for TRACKER on Twitter: Thank you!

And last but not least, thank you to my family. Thanks, Mom and Erin, for the enthusiasm around my writing. Thank you, Andrew, for giving me the time and space to write. And to "little man," thanks for being you. Keep smiling and laughing. I love you all.

About the Author

Growing up with a fascination for space and things that fly, Jamie turned that love into a career as an Aerospace Engineer. Combining her natural enthusiasm for Science Fiction and her love of reading, she now spends a lot of her time writing Middle Grade and Young Adult Science Fiction and Fantasy.

Jamie lives in St. Louis, Missouri with her husband, Andrew, their son, and their dog, Rogue (named after the X-men not Star Wars although she loves both). When she isn't being a Rocket Scientist by day and a writer by night, she can be found catching up on the latest sci fi TV, books, and movies as well as spending time on Twitter (maybe a little too much time :-P). And no, the rocket science jokes never get old!

Through Snowy Wings Publishing, Jamie is the author of Tracker220 (October 2020). She also has two female in STEM short stories published in the Brave New Girls anthologies and two engineering-centered nonfiction pieces that published in Writer's Digest's Putting the Science in Fiction.

Social Media Links
Blog – http://jamiekrakover.blogspot.com/
Twitter – https://twitter.com/Rockets2Writing
Instagram – https://www.instagram.com/jamiekrakover/
Goodreads –
https://www.goodreads.com/author/show/16483406.Jamie_Krakover?from_search=true

Printed in the USA
CPSIA information can be obtained
at www.ICGtesting.com
LVHW040209210823
755790LV00019B/65